The Common Lot and Other Stories

The Common Lot

and Other Stories

The Published Short Fiction, 1908–1921

EMMA BELL MILES

EDITED BY GRACE TONEY EDWARDS

Swallow Press   Ohio University Press   Athens

Swallow Press
An imprint of Ohio University Press, Athens, Ohio 45701
ohioswallow.com

Printed in the United States of America
Swallow Press / Ohio University Press books are printed on acid-free paper ∞ ™

26 25 24 23 22 21 20 19 18 17 16 5 4 3 2 1

Library of Congress Cataloging-in-Publication Data

Names: Miles, Emma Bell, 1879–1919, author. | Edwards, Grace Toney, editor.
Title: The common lot and other stories : the published short fiction, 1908–1921 / Emma Bell Miles ; edited by Grace Toney Edwards.
Other titles: Short stories
Description: Athens, Ohio : Swallow Press, Ohio University Press, [2016] | Includes bibliographical references.
Identifiers: LCCN 2015044695| ISBN 9780804011730 (hardback) | ISBN 9780804011747 (pb) | ISBN 9780804040747 (pdf)
Subjects: | BISAC: LITERARY COLLECTIONS / American / General. | LITERARY COLLECTIONS / General. | FICTION / General.
Classification: LCC PS3525 .I482 2016 | DDC 813/.52—dc23
LC record available at http://lccn.loc.gov/2015044695

This book is dedicated to the memory of the Miles children,
Judith, Jean, Joe, Kitty, and Mark,
and to their living descendants.

contents

illustrations

Following page 18

preface

I first came to know Emma Bell Miles and her work almost four decades ago. Shortly after the 1975 launch of the facsimile edition of *The Spirit of the Mountains*, a friend gave me a copy of the book just as I was heading to the University of Virginia to begin work on a doctorate in English language, literature, and pedagogy. With no time for extra reading, I shelved it along with many others and plunged into a rigorous load of literature and folklore courses. Scarcely a month later, my folklore professor, Dr. Charles Perdue, carried in a copy of *The Spirit of the Mountains* to ask if I knew the book. When I confessed that I owned a copy but had not read it, his admonition was, "Read it!" Always the dutiful student, I went straight home and started in. From that moment on, I've been hooked on Emma Bell Miles!

When the time came to propose a dissertation topic, I knew Emma was my girl—provided I could convince my advisors that she was worthy of study. By then I had learned that she wrote not only the fictionalized ethnography about Walden's Ridge, Tennessee, but she also wrote poetry, short fiction, a book on birds, newspaper columns, and more. I had also learned through the help of Chuck Perdue and Dr. David Whisnant, then at the University of Maryland in Baltimore, that four of Miles's children were alive and well in various parts of the country. I set out to interview her children and people who had known her in Chattanooga and on Walden's Ridge (now Signal Mountain and Walden). I intended to find everything she wrote that was "out there," to synthesize and analyze, and ultimately to put it all together in a literary biography.

My research moved from phone calls and letters to scheduled visits—first to Miami, Florida, where daughter Jean Miles Catino lived. With family in tow, including a rambunctious two-year-old son, I spent a couple of days talking, listening, taking notes, sifting through photographs, admiring art work—both Emma's and Jean's—and enjoying Jean's beautiful orchids. Like her mother, she had developed a talent for painting and a love of nature, which manifested itself through the cultivation of dozens of varieties of orchids. Upon our departure, Jean presented me with a lovely hand-crocheted pink afghan in anticipation of the arrival of my second baby, who she predicted would be a girl. Months later I wrapped my bouncing baby boy in the pink afghan simply because it came from the hand of the daughter that touched the hand of the author and artist I so admired! To this day I still cherish the gift and am apt to carry it along to show it off whenever I have opportunity to lecture about Emma Bell Miles.

My second major visit was to the home of the other twin daughter, Judith Miles Ford, in Aline, Oklahoma. Because she lived, as she put it, "out here in the middle of the prairie," she insisted that I stay in her home. (I went sans family this time.) For three days and nights, I lived, breathed, ate, and slept Emma Bell Miles! Judith was such an avid advocate for her mother's work that she plied me with abundant material: her own memories and stories; letters and newspaper articles, both by and about her mother; magazine articles; pieces of artwork; and most important of all, her mother's original journals. At that time she had in her possession four volumes of handwritten journals, kept in what looked to be worn account ledgers. A fifth volume was a typescript of the original that had somehow made its way into the Chattanooga public library. These journals covered the years from 1908 to 1918. Believing them to be of great value, Judith was eager to share the journals with me, but only in her home under her watchful eye! Needless to say, I was ecstatic to see these original documents and willing to use them under any restrictions she imposed. She allowed me to take copious notes and to read some segments into a tape recorder so that I could include direct quotations in my writing. Later, after I returned home, she sent me photocopied segments of the journals that I especially wanted to access. She also gave me multiple pictures of her mother and other family members with permission to use them in the dissertation I was writing. I am eternally grateful to Judith for the generosity and hospitality she showed me on that visit and in the communications we had thereafter.

Initially I had planned to fly to California to visit the two younger Miles children, Joe and Kitty, who lived in San Diego and Ventura, respectively. But after phone calls with all four, we mutually agreed that this expensive trip was unnecessary. Joe and Kitty anticipated being of minimal help in light of the deeper knowledge of their older sisters. In retrospect, I wish I had gone, for as I have learned more through the years, I know both would have had fascinating life stories to tell.

Nevertheless, my research travels were by no means over. Kay Gaston, then of Signal Mountain, Tennessee, had been studying and collecting Miles memorabilia for years. She was a tremendous help in sharing her knowledge and collection and in taking me to meet various other people in the area who had known Emma personally or who had collections of her artwork. In the many years since then, Kay has continued to be an inspiration through her own writing and lecturing about Miles. Kay's home on Signal Mountain was but a twisty mountain road away from Chattanooga, where I found a treasure trove of forty-four letters written by Emma Bell Miles to her friend Anna Ricketson in New Bedford, Massachusetts. These were housed in the Chattanooga-Hamilton County Bicentennial Public Library and provided a wonderful record of Miles's life as she portrayed it to a long-distance friend between 1907 and 1917.

Other research stops were the Tennessee State Archives in Nashville, where a few Miles poems resided, and finally the Library of Congress in Washington. My goal in our national library was to discover and make copies of everything Miles had ever published—a task much easier said than done! I could find the stories, poems, and articles in major magazines such as *Harper's*, *Lippincott's*, and *Century*, but the smaller unindexed publications were another matter altogether. Because I had only approximate titles and dates gleaned from journal entries and occasionally letters, I gained permission to go into the stacks of the Library to search through multiple volumes of publications such as *Nautilus* and *Mother's Magazine*. I have fond memories of sitting flat on the floor in the Library of Congress between tall shelves of musty periodicals, leafing through bound tomes, searching for the name of one almost unknown writer from the mountains of East Tennessee. When I found something, my inclination was to jump up and shout in those hallowed basement recesses, but I restrained myself out of respect for another scholar who might have been laboring in some secluded corner.

At long last in 1981 a dissertation emerged, and one might have thought my Emma Bell Miles immersion had ended. But that was by no means true. In the thirty years that followed, I introduced hundreds of students to Miles's work in various courses I taught at Radford University. I wrote and published several articles about her over the years and had the pleasure of guest-editing the Fall 2005 edition of *Appalachian Heritage* devoted to the centennial celebration of the publication of *The Spirit of the Mountains.* I have delivered innumerable lectures and slide presentations about Emma in venues far and wide and continue to do so today.

Multiple other scholars have also maintained interest in this remarkable Appalachian mountain woman whose lifespan was far too short. (She died at age thirty-nine.) In recent years notable efforts include the work of Czech scholar Dr. Katerina Prajznerova of Masaryk University in Brno, who has written extensively about Miles, particularly her interest in nature and the environment. Steven Cox, Director of Special Collections at the University of Tennessee at Chattanooga, has worked for years to amass a wonderful collection of Miles materials and in 2014 published excerpts from her journals through Ohio University Press. George Brosi, former editor of *Appalachian Heritage,* and wife Connie have long been advocates for Miles and have written articles about her. Lincoln Memorial University sponsors a biennial Emma Bell Miles lecture and an annual Emma Bell Miles essay contest at its Mountain Heritage Literary Festival. The University of Tennessee at Chattanooga and Signal Mountain friends periodically put on symposia and other events to honor their renowned author and artist. The list could go on, for her appeal does not wane.

My own ambition for many years has been to make Miles's fiction available to the public. Other works have been reprinted, including *The Spirit of the Mountains, Our Southern Birds,* and *Strains from a Dulcimore,* but her stories have remained virtually hidden in musty magazines and scarcely accessible library stacks. In this collection all seventeen of her known stories have been brought together in chronological order of their publication, ranging from 1908 to 1921. I have transcribed the stories primarily as they were published in the original periodicals, maintaining Miles's spelling and punctuation. The one concession made for modern readers has been to close up spaces in contractions to eliminate inconsistencies in the original publications, sometimes even in the same story. For each story I have identified the source and date and have written a brief editor's note as a guide to readers who may desire such.

Though writing styles and subject matter have changed significantly over the hundred years since most of the fiction came to print, there is a wealth of cultural and biographical context to be gleaned from these stories. This book achieves what feels like a lifelong quest for me and fulfills a promise made long ago to the spirit of the artist who created the fiction. I am greatly pleased to bring Emma Bell Miles and her work into the twenty-first century.

Grace Toney Edwards
Christiansburg, Virginia
October 2015

acknowledgments

My first debt of gratitude must go to Emma Bell Miles herself for providing such rich material to work with, then to her children, all deceased now, for their generous willingness to help in my endeavors that started long ago. I am grateful to the late Dr. Charles Perdue and Dr. Harold Kolb of the University of Virginia who encouraged me to follow my heart in my desire to make this little-known author the subject of my academic study. To my students, colleagues, and friends over the past decades, I offer thanks for their ongoing interest in Miles and my work with her. Scholar and Miles aficionado Kay Gaston proved to be an invaluable resource in those early days and has continued in that role in more recent times. Dr. Katerina Prajznerova, because of her passion for Miles's work, inspired me to refresh my study of Miles and to pursue publication of this book. Steven Cox has been a stalwart supporter for many years, helping me access materials from the Miles collections on my various research trips to Lupton Library at the University of Tennessee at Chattanooga. Most recently he has scanned numerous photographs and artworks from the originals for use in this volume. To all of these I am grateful for their help and encouragement. To editors Rick Huard and Gillian Berchowitz of Ohio University Press, along with their conscientious staff members, I extend my warm thanks for their assistance in bringing this book to print. And I am forever indebted to my immediate and extended family, whose unflagging support I can always count on. Finally to my husband, John Nemeth, my most ardent and always helpful enthusiast, I will simply say, "Thank you for being."

G.T.E.

introduction

The Published Short Stories of Emma Bell Miles, 1908–21

GRACE TONEY EDWARDS

> They are all romance, these luxuries of the mountaineer,—music, whiskey, firelight, religion, and fighting: they are efforts to reach a finer, larger life,—part of the blue dream of the wild land. Who knows him? . . . Who has tracked him to that wild, remote spot, echo-haunted, beautiful, terrible, wherein he dwells? (Emma Bell Miles, Journal, I, November 13, 1908)[1]

So asked Emma Bell Miles as she reflected on the mountaineer's love of a roaring fire to warm his cabin when winter's storms pushed him indoors. In her fiction she took up the trail leading to that "wild, remote spot . . . wherein he dwells." She explored his romantic luxuries: the music, strong drink, fighting, home fires, and religion. But the references to "him" and "his" are not neutered pronouns; the romantic luxuries are clearly those of the mountain male. As she says in her fictionalized ethnography, *The Spirit of the Mountains,* "He is part of the young nation." The woman, on the other hand, "belongs to the race, to the old people." "Her lot is inevitably one of service and of suffering, and refines only as it is meekly and sweetly borne."[2]

Miles spoke from years of observation and participation in the lifestyle of the people she grew up with and chose to live among on Walden's Ridge, one of the bare-rock bluffs that rise above the city of Chattanooga, Tennessee. Emma Bell was not born in those Tennessee highlands but moved there with her schoolteacher parents from Rabbit Hash, Kentucky, when she was eleven years old. An only child of Ben and Martha Mirick Bell, she was primarily home-schooled on the classics of great American literature and, as she put it, a steady diet of *Harper's Monthly Magazines*. She loved the outdoors and was given free rein to roam the woods and learn the flora and fauna of her environment firsthand. In her teen years, she developed an interest in art, and eventually, through the efforts and influence of Chattanooga art patrons, she enrolled in the St. Louis School of Design, where she studied for two terms. Amid talk of sending her to Paris for further study, she made a decision to return to her "blue mountains" and a young mountain man who had won her heart. In October 1901 Emma Bell married Frank Miles.

And so began her life as a mountain wife and mother. In September 1902 she gave birth to twins Judith and Jean. During the next seven years she bore three other children, Joe, Katherine (Kitty), and Mirick (Mark). She also began to write seriously and succeeded in placing several poems and several short stories in popular magazines. In 1905 James Pott & Company published her book *The Spirit of the Mountains.* From time to time she traveled down to Chattanooga to paint portraits, landscapes, and murals on art lovers' walls. Though her life appeared to be very full, it was also very hard. She and Frank struggled to provide food and shelter for their brood; they made numerous lateral moves from one rental house to another; and Emma's earnings, paltry as they were, often had to carry them through.

By the start of her second decade of marriage, Emma's health had begun to fail. Somewhat frail even as a child, she suffered in adulthood from years of frequent childbearing and miscarriages, hard work, and inadequate housing and food. She also suffered the emotionally debilitating loss of her youngest child, Mark, who died of complications of scarlet fever shortly before his fourth birthday. Blaming their desperate poverty and striving to provide better for her other children, Emma landed a job at the *Chattanooga News* in 1914 and for several months wrote a column called "Fountain Square Conversations." She lived in the Frances Willard Home for Working Girls and for a time enjoyed a bit of freedom from the daily toil of housekeeping and motherhood. That respite was not to last, "sacrificed," as she put it, "to a man's pleasure" (Journal, July 24, 1914).[3] Pregnant again and ill, she had to resign from the *News*, only to lose the baby a few weeks later. Ultimately she was diagnosed with tuberculosis and confined for periods of varying duration in Pine Breeze Sanitarium in Chattanooga. Ill health and wracking poverty notwithstanding, Emma Bell Miles managed to publish or sell during her lifetime more than one hundred poems, including those in a self-published booklet called *Chords from a Dulcimore*; seventeen short stories; a series of newspaper columns; and two books. The second book, entitled *Our Southern Birds*, was completed during her last stay at Pine Breeze and was launched just two weeks before her death on March 19, 1919. She was thirty-nine years old.[4]

The seventeen short stories in this collection constitute all of Miles's known fictional output. There were most likely other stories drafted, as indicated by her journal entries and letters. In his introduction to *Once I Too Had Wings: The Journals of Emma Bell Miles, 1908–1918*, Steven Cox lists titles of works that Miles says she has written and in some cases submitted for publication, but these have not come to light. However, I suspect that at least two of those in Cox's list may have been published under titles other than the ones given in her journals and are in fact present in this collection.[5] All of the major magazines of her era, such as *Harper's*, *Lippincott's*, *Putnam's*, *Century*, *Craftsman*, and *Red Book*, have been thoroughly searched, as have the smaller, more obscure publications that she wrote for, including *Mother's Magazine*, *Youth's Companion*, *Nautilus*, and *The Lookout*. These seventeen stories are the result of those searches.

Some scholars have theorized that she may have allowed other writers to publish her work under their own names. Possibly that happened, for we know from her journals and letters that she collaborated extensively with Caroline Wood Morrison in 1908; she also wrote that she worked closely in 1908–10 with the sisters Alice McGowan and Grace McGowan Cooke, drawing illustrations and providing ideas for their books. All three of these collaborators, writers of some renown in Chattanooga, were publishing novels and stories set in Miles's own home territory during the period from 1908 to 1910. A study of their work shows that they clearly benefited from Miles's knowledge of the mountain people and her wordsmithing talents; what she gained from them is less clear. However, she may have allowed them to borrow her ideas, her drawings, and even her actual writing because they were better established than she and perhaps promised help in getting her work published.

Whatever the case, in the seventeen stories that we know were written by Emma Bell Miles (including one in collaboration with Caroline Wood Morrison), as well as in many of her poems and essays, her perceptions of men's and women's opposite realms of existence infuse the corpus of her work. Feminist that she is, her writings belong generally to the local color school, though literary historians usually claim that the local color movement was in decline by the time Miles began to publish.[6] In the decade following her death, a new regionalism reached fruition, its proponents sharing a strong sense of place with the local colorists but imbuing their fiction even more overtly than most of their predecessors with social motives. According to critics Harry Warfel and Harrison Orians, "Authors wrote to support theses rather than to photograph a group of people against a setting."[7] Emma Bell Miles's fiction and nonfiction stand between these two closely related impulses, her form and style taking their pattern largely from the nineteenth-century local colorists—that is, "photograph[ing] a group of people against a setting"; her purpose, however, with its intense seriousness, providing a bridge to the twentieth-century regionalists.

Miles's stories can be profitably examined by these standards, for her whole body of fiction is a crusade for the liberation of women, coupled in her mind with the oppression of poverty. Yet Miles was well aware that poverty alone does not fetter women; in her Appalachian Mountain culture, as in most others throughout America, the traditions of the patriarchal society determined woman's place.

Miles approached her subject matter at a time when the organized suffrage movement was still relatively new in the South, and virtually unknown in the mountain South. In her stories her vision of women and their utter dependence on marriage localizes itself to the Southern mountains, in reality her own Walden's Ridge, Tennessee. Others were also writing about the Appalachian Mountains during this same period. "Somewhere on [her] blue horizon"[8] reigned the queen of mountain fiction, Mary Murfree, whose view of the mountaineer fixed itself in the minds of Americans and to some extent remains there today. John Fox replicated Murfree's picture to become one of the most popular authors in the country soon after the turn of the century. Dozens of other writers flocked to the Appalachians to view the scenery, to poke and prod the natives—if they dared—in their research for their next "piece." Constance Fenimore Woolson put in her time on the Blue Ridge near Asheville; Joel Chandler Harris paid some visits to folks he knew up in North Georgia; Lucy Furman set up shop at Hindman Settlement School in Knott County, Kentucky. But Emma Bell Miles did not have to go anywhere: she looked out her door; she listened to Frank, to Grandma Miles, to sister-in-law Laura Hatfield, to Aunt Lucy, to her babies. She wrote about the Appalachian mountaineer from home, and the view looked different from there. In 1914, after she had already composed most of her fiction that came to print, she remarked to an unidentified correspondent, "To one who has lived the life, the ordinary novel of moonshine & rifles seems merely newspaper twaddle."[9]

It is hardly a wonder that Miles should ignore, if not reject, the "otherness" of Appalachia that critic Henry Shapiro claims was not initiated by, but solidly established in, Murfree's fiction.[10] The perception of otherness actuated an opposition between Appalachia and the rest of America, a strange incongruity, for the mountain region had once been the frontier of America. Its settlers, both those who stayed and those who passed through, were America's settlers. But somewhere along the way, partially because of the region's insularity, the ordinary changes of civilization were arrested. Appalachia retained into the twentieth century folkways attributed to ages and places as diverse as Chaucer's England and eighteenth-century America. In the fervid search for local color by those who lived beyond the mountains, the differences, the otherness, spotted among the mountaineers became a rich vein to be mined. In fiction the contrast, and ultimately the opposition, between the familiar and the unfamiliar has been emblemized by the conflict between insider and outsider, represented most often by moonshiners and revenuers, feudists and lawmen, mountain girls and city boys.

But little of that touched Emma Bell Miles. She "lived the life"; she did not need to create dramatic tension through conflict between insider and outsider. She saw it daily between insider and insider, between woman's dream and her reality. She verbalized her own concept of the normalcy of Appalachian culture when she wrote in 1907 to Anna Ricketson, a friend by correspondence in New Bedford, Massachusetts: "It is often hard for me to notice points of difference between our way of life and civilization, I am so used to the backwoods."[11] Her fiction does not build from without, then, as does that of other writers about Appalachia in her time. It grows from within, showing respect for the traditional folkways that have sustained the mountain people, but at the same time crying out against the cultural bonds that restrict, limit, and dehumanize the women. Her characters are mountaineers, but they are not peculiar or different from common people anywhere.

Three years elapsed between the publication of Miles's fictionalized ethnography, *The Spirit of the Mountains,* and the first of what I am calling her "quasi-fictional" stories, a term not meant to diminish her work but rather to explain it as a type of discourse that draws from both literary and expository writing with a definite aim to convince and persuade. In a bit of prepublication criticism, she showed that she knew the qualities of her own writing, qualities that she seemed to consider detriments to her success. To Anna Ricketson she wrote in 1907 of her stories: "Mine generally lack the keen interest of action and plot which 'The Circle' [prize competition] makes a first consideration." A few days later she continued, "I think my stories will never be popular; they are too serious. . . . Perhaps I shall acquire a lighter touch as the children grow older and the daily stress is somewhat relieved."[12]

Two striking points emerge from this self-assessment. First, Miles is aware that her writing does something different from standard fiction; it lacks the "keen interest of action and plot." At this stage in her life she could not recognize that the chronological mode of fiction with its past-tense narrative of "what happened" was not sufficient for her purposes, which tended toward a more generalized present-tense analysis of "what happens."[13] She wanted to write fiction, but her worldview demanded exposition. What emerged was a hybrid product that combined fabricated plots and characters based on her own experiences and observations, heavily laden with social commentary. Thus, she dubbed her stories "too serious." Of course they were serious, because they carried her message to the world about the status of her gender; they were loaded with her moral conviction of wrong, which she could not express openly, even to herself, and so must camouflage in fiction. The second point to emerge from Miles's statement is that in her own person she offered a perfect example of the cause she crusaded for. "Perhaps I shall acquire a lighter touch as the children grow older and the daily stress is somewhat relieved."

Miles placed her first story, "The Common Lot," in *Harper's Monthly Magazine* in December 1908, where it appeared with three full-page illustrations drawn by Lucius Wolcott Hitchcock. It was the first of five stories by Miles that *Harper's* would publish between December 1908 and November 1910. During this same period, notable authors such as William Dean Howells, Mark Twain, Rudyard Kipling, and Willa Cather were writing for *Harper's*—thus putting Miles among heady company.

"The Common Lot" serves in many ways as her signature piece by probing the dilemma of the mountain woman's lot in life: marriage versus spinsterhood. Sixteen-year-old Easter Vanderwelt examines the life of her married sister as she helps with the unceasing toil to meet the needs of the babies, the husband, the women themselves, the little house they live in. From tending the garden patch to milking the cows to nursing the ailing baby, sister Cordy confronts a new pregnancy and begins to mend the clothes that her last baby has barely outgrown. Death precedes birth, however, and Easter hears Cordy's fatalistic declaration over her baby's grave, "I've got no idy the next'll thrive any better."[14] In a foreshadowing of her own plight years later, Miles has Cordy deliver the only prayer offered for her baby before its burial. Frequent pregnancies, the rigors of childbirth, and the specter of infant death define Cordy Hallet's view of married life—and that of most mountain women.

With such a vision before her, Easter understandably fears marriage. Practicing the restraint that her times required, Miles can only imply that Easter's fear is rooted in part in the sexual and biological demands of wifehood. Easter occupies the curious position, as many a rural child does, of having witnessed and assisted at births and deaths; she knows much of the elemental aspects of life. Yet the sex act and the workings of her own body represent mysteries that she is not sure she wants to fathom. Although she never verbalizes the cause of her worries, she shares her concern with Cordy. The sister replies, "You don't need to be afeared. . . . You'd be better off with him [Allison, Easter's suitor] than ye would at home, wouldn't ye? Life's mighty hard for women anywhars." From this discussion and her own long consideration Easter comes to see that her choice is "slavery in her father's house or slavery in a husband's." Harsh as such an assessment may seem, it depicts a woman's view, unhampered by illusion, of what her culture has to offer. She ultimately chooses a husband and her own home, realizing that to refuse them means refusing "the invitation of life" and "the only development possible to her."[15] In so doing she has acknowledged the common lot of mountain women, and perhaps of rural women everywhere.

Miles softens her picture of woman's toil and constriction with the promise of romantic love and spiritual fulfillment of sorts. Yet she persists in pushing the hardships to the forefront. Like other local colorists, she straddled a splintery fence between realism and romanticism. On the one side grew the rose and on the other the brier; their commitment to fidelity obliged local colorists to include both. Readers of the popular magazines, and consequently editors, seemed to prefer roses in their endings. Disturbing resolutions or indeterminate endings are rare exceptions in local color writing. Melodrama, defined as "an affirmation of a benevolent moral order in the universe,"[16] is much more common.

In her presentation of the mountain woman's experience, then, Miles runs the risk of uncovering the ugly, the lewd, the tragic. To ameliorate those revelations, she steps into most of her stories and works the details into a seemingly happy resolution. The reasons for her manipulation are more complicated than the mere satisfaction of reader expectation. We must remember that she was a crusader with an ideal worldview; in her personal life she summoned an eternally rebounding hope to help her cope with problems far greater than any she ever depicted in fiction. The stories become her wish-fulfillment of situations working out satisfactorily within the mountain culture. In her fictional sorties she spotlights the privation, subservience, and limitations of mountain women; but in her retreats she withdraws to the safety of compensations. The divisiveness in herself and her fiction probably swells from two factors. First, the mountain culture truly does offer rewards to women through the giving and nurturing of life, as Miles allows Easter Vanderwelt and her sister protagonists to see. And second, as spokesperson for her culture, Miles must bear in mind her personal relationship to the people about whom she writes; they are a proud and fiercely independent lot who look with suspicion at her work because it is alien to their largely oral culture. Her mother-in-law, Cynthia Jane Winchester Miles, allegedly remarked, "These here writers and type-writers will do to watch." Is there any wonder that her daughter-in-law alternates her attacks with rewards?

As indicated earlier, "The Common Lot" in both title and subject matter can stand as Miles's battle cry in her crusade. Almost all of the other stories are variations on its theme. In fact, the first seven published stories feature a girl or young woman as protagonist—one who faces the prospect of marriage or deals with the consequences of it. "The Broken Urn," published in *Putnam's Magazine* in February 1909, opens with two small girls already wearing the yoke of their gender, as shown in the play they engage in. They cook and clean in their rock playhouse; they piece quilt patterns from scraps of cloth cast off by grannies and cousins; and they talk of being married someday. But their paths are to diverge and their burdens to differ as they grow into womanhood. One stays on the mountain and marries her childhood sweetheart; the other weds the hotel proprietor's son and leaves the highlands behind. Sarepta Kinsale's battle with poverty, toil, and infant death is set against her childhood playmate's wealth, idleness, and thriving baby. Yet Nigarie Stetson, the playmate who migrated from the mountain and formed a new life in a totally different culture, is the restless one, the malcontent. Sarepta is the character who grows into an "understanding of the quiet, unassailable dignity of her own position, and [learns] the intrinsic worth of usefulness as contrasted with the false value of unearned riches."[17]

The story's title comes from a quilt pattern that Nigarie and Sarepta as little girls had altered to make a whole vessel they called "the Friendship's Urn." Miles's choice of "The Broken Urn" rather than "The Friendship's Urn" as title suggests Nigarie's incapacity to have a life filled to the brim as Sarepta can. Nigarie is the incomplete vessel that has no room for the pain and suffering Sarepta experiences, and also no room for the sublime happiness that is Sarepta's as she fills her whole urn of life day after day with a mixture of the bitter and the sweet. Nigarie's broken urn contains only fleeting moments of gaiety, only brief occasions of real usefulness, but she does offer the gift of life to Sarepta's baby when she lifts him impulsively to her breast. "Why, he's starved most to death. . . . I reckon you ain't been able to nurse him. I wish I could—why couldn't I?" It is her richest moment, this season in her friend's humble home, where she coaxes a tiny life to blossom through the nourishment of her own body and receives in return nourishment for her soul. But it is not to last. Nigarie is the displaced mountaineer, one who longs to come home, but who cannot stay there when she arrives. In a moment of candor she confesses to Sarepta and her husband: "'We've been everywhere, Sam and me. . . . I've lived at the sea-shore, in the West, and we had a winter in New York; but I always wanted, I think, to come back here—on a visit,' she added the concluding words hastily, for she knew that no place on earth could hold her long."[18]

As the restless Nigarie flits back to her adopted culture, and Sarepta realizes the value of her own simple life in comparison, Miles meticulously controls her story's close. She describes the mountain girl's new awareness in language that Sarepta would never use and in concepts that Sarepta would never formulate. Miles leads the reader carefully by the hand as she editorializes: "Later, she [Sarepta] might lose sight of the vision somewhat, for we are all as incapable of holding constantly to great thoughts as of putting such definitely into words; but when the trailing glories paled, here was a child, gloriously alive, to remind her that she had once been inspired with the profoundly rational courage of seeing things as they are."[19]

The author's over-control in the ending may grate on the sensibility of the reader who wants a more subtle resolution for her fiction. However, if she can accept Miles's aim as an expository one, she will understand how the author is operating. Exposition is designed to inform, to instruct, to persuade—all purposes that fiction may also fulfill. But much fiction employs a chronological scheme to accommodate the narrative; and elements of plot, setting, character, and conflict convey the writer's meaning. In exposition, analogical and tautological schemes carry the argument on a theoretical or general level, though specific illustrations and narrative anecdotes often exemplify points. When story and exposition converge, as in Miles's quasi fiction, the structure has a narrative organization with an expository intent. "The Broken Urn" looks like, and is, a story, but Miles is first and last a teacher. As such, she must reiterate her point and moralize: "for we are all as incapable of holding constantly to great thoughts as of putting such definitely into words." The narrative itself is her exemplum; the authorial commentary her sermon.[20]

As Miles parades her fictional women before us, we note the slight variations in their common lot. Two young women are matched with preachers, and in both cases, the outcome of the match is problematic. Averilla Sargent, the village flirt in "A Dark Rose" (*Harper's,* February 1909), at first refuses Luther Estill's proposal, but after a bit, she accepts him and vows to go with him as he preaches, to lead the singing, to show that she can be "good" for him. But the conversion comes too easily for Averilla and makes one suspect her sincerity. This manipulated ending raises other questions: Does Miles deliberately choose not to convince us of Averilla's conversion? Does she see Averilla as a type for those women who have employed a ruse and lived it because they think they must in a male-centered world?

"Mallard Plumage" (*Red Book,* August 1909) gives us a young wife who has the audacity to rebel against her May-December marriage to old Preacher Guthrie, who has locked her into a staid, restrictive existence. She flees with her young love from her premarriage days, only to bear the child of the husband she runs away from. In a predictable turn at the end, old Guthrie is taken in by the young people and nursed until his death, which comes as a result of a fall suffered while pursuing the runaways. True to the local color formula, Roma and Atlas display "hearts of gold" in their final actions toward Guthrie, and he does the same when, on his deathbed, he gives them his blessing to marry.

"The Dulcimore" (*Harper's*, November 1909) hands us a twist in the form of a mother-daughter conflict over an impending marriage, one that sounds much like Emma Bell's experience with her own mother. Selina Carden has groomed her daughter, Georgia, for a life outside the mountains. She wants Georgia to study music, to find a mate different from those offered by the circumscribed mountain culture. But Selina's ambitions for Georgia are to be thwarted by the same implacable fate that had thwarted her own twenty years earlier. The girl has, "while awaiting the Prince, unwittingly become bound to Return," the mountain blacksmith who secretly whittles her a dulcimore because he knows she likes music.[21] None of Selina's pleas can change Georgia's mind.

> The mother felt as though striving in a nightmare with bending, splintering weapons. . . . Had she not fought this same losing fight once before? She had never forgotten the days and weeks before her own marriage; the struggling, resisting, calling to her aid all habit and tradition, all maidenly reserve and family pride—in vain. She had suffered in withstanding; she had suffered in yielding; and her suffering had not mattered in the least, would not matter now.[22]

In desperation she spills her own story, her own struggle, her own sacrifice. "One baby after another. Yet the babies were all that kept me alive. . . . It would be easy enough to die for a man; it's hard to live for him—to give him all your life just when you want it most yourself." The mother's story wrenches the girl's emotions, but it effects an opposite reaction from the intended one. Georgia recognizes why her mother has stayed in this hard life when she whispers, "Mother! Don't you see, now— . . . Now you *have* showed me—what love is, what it means to us women."[23]

Miles's crusade becomes the more plaintive when one realizes that Selina Carden perhaps takes her words from Emma's own mother, Martha Bell, when she warns her talented daughter, "You're blinded. . . . You can't see now; but when you wake up and find yourself dragged down to the level of his people, it will break your heart."[24] Emma may well have been recalling the parental struggle she faced in her determination to marry Frank Miles some eight years earlier, coupled with the truth she knows now about married life. Creativity frustrated, ambition suppressed, body and spirit worn thin—these are the costs of womanhood. In 1909 the author can only arraign "the great laws of the universe" for this biological and spiritual demand that pits woman against herself, giving her fulfillment on the one hand and privation on the other.

Miles shifts her focus somewhat in "Three Roads and a River" (*Harper's*, November 1910), possibly her best-crafted story and certainly one of the most powerful. The marriage theme is still present, but it takes a backseat to dire poverty. Shell Hutson becomes a criminal out of bitter need. In debasing himself to commit theft, assault, and robbery to supply food for his starving family, he forfeits two of the mountaineer's strongest characteristics: his pride and his independence. Sociologists have noted the mountain man's reluctance to ask for help; he would prefer to suffer, starve, and even die rather than take charity. But Shell is responsible for children, women, and an aging parent. In Dreiser-like fashion Miles drags Shell and the whole family lower and lower—from the once proud and prosperous keepers of the toll road and ferry to shamed, destitute starvelings. Caught in a deterministic trap, old Zion, Shell's father, the patriarch, believes himself morally responsible for the family. Reaffirming the mountaineer's choice of death over such a life, he asks for—and thinks he receives—a sign from God, making him the implement to carry his family from misery to peace "jist over, jist over Jordan." The poison added to the poke-stalk pickles is taken by old Zion almost like a sacrament and passed with the same reverence to his unwitting family. Only his daughter Nettie refuses to eat, fearing her nursing baby will take colic from the sour.

Appropriately Nettie is spared her father's salvation by death because she is the only member of the family who has maintained hope for betterment in life. But Miles, with her usual penchant for inveigling a happy ending, is not content with letting Nettie and the baby live. She must bring in at the moment of Nettie's greatest horror a rescuer in the form of the husband who had deserted her, pregnant and penniless, months before. Now just as Nettie discovers the deaths of all her family, Steve appears with sheltering arms, money, and a promise of a new start in a new town. Miles's compassionate view of human nature and her fervent wish for a benevolent universal order explain why she invents a turn-around ending, but they do not justify it for the fiction.

Nettie's words summing up her commitment to life provide transition into another of Miles's topics: "We seed a awful hard time . . . but look like where the' was little 'uns—nobody would aim to die."[25]

"Little 'uns" populate much of Miles's writing—their begetting, birthing, nurturing. They are an important part of her affirmation of life. In only one story, though, does a child serve as the central character, and she is a catalyst who effects positive changes in the adults she encounters. Scarcely a plotted story at all, "Flyaway Flittermouse" (*Harper's*, July 1910) is an enthusiastic, if somewhat sentimentalized, celebration of primal innocence and goodness as vested in a toddler.

As a sidenote, this story, like several others by Miles, took its genesis from an actual happening. In July 1909, Emma's two-year-old daughter Kitty wandered away from the other children on a quest for huckleberries. When her mother discovered her missing, an all-out search began. Eventually a young man who had been on his way to see his girl in the valley "appeared with the dirty, berry-stained, scratched & tangled little maid, very wide-eyed, in his arms. He had heard her crying, in a sand-flat towards Middle Creek."[26] And so Kitty's escapade provided the outline for "Flyaway Flittermouse."

Although the quality of Miles's fiction varies, her crusade for women's causes never tires. It marches through stories where the women are mere stereotypes, as in "The Home-Coming of Evelina" and "At the Top of Sourwood." It entertains a skirmish in "The White Marauder" when the young wife shows more spirit than usual and even enjoys a momentary, though tainted, victory over the powerful men in her life. It pauses to reveal a relative equality between the elderly husband and wife in "Turkey Luck," a parable that erases Miles's usual life struggle and substitutes the local colorist heart-of-gold formula in the ending, in which husband and wife, unbeknownst to each other, give away both turkeys they had meant to have for their Christmas dinner. Without berating one another, however, they contentedly settle for "possum and sweet taters" and are happy in their knowledge that other families on the ridge will have good turkey dinners for Christmas!

While Miles's women characters most often seem to be victims as a result of their cultural bonds, one woman manages to shake off those shackles in "Flower of Noon" (*Craftsman*, January 1912). The story is set during the wake and funeral of Harmon Ridge, a relatively prosperous landowner who is believed to have no direct heir. Miles highlights the interrelationships of the pious family members who crowd in to share the spoils. She pits a grasping, hypocritical pair of brothers and their wives against young Fan Walton, Harmon Ridge's housekeeper and supposed confidante. Though Fan must face alone the suspicions and inquisition about Brother Harmon's money, she is not without allies in the dead man's widowed sister and his young hired hand. Had Fan Walton been what she appeared, a housekeeper, she might have merely paid her respects to her former employer and walked away. But she was clearly more than that, and much of the story's tension grows out of just what her relationship with Harmon Ridge was. The reader's first hasty conclusion is that they were lovers, or maybe husband and wife; but young Byron Standifer's obvious romantic devotion to Fan complicates that notion. Finally, in a confrontation where the family members demand to know her rights to their brother's property, she yields her secret: "'God's my judge!' she cried in a clear ringing voice. 'Can't you all see?' And in her strong features, her firm neck and square-set shoulders so like those on which they had looked their last an hour ago through the glass of a coffin, they read the answer."[27] Playing on understatement to strengthen her story, the author gives only vague hints about the girl's background before coming to her father; but the discomfited relatives are well aware that they have lost a farm and gained a niece.

Miles revels in Fan's victory but restrains the impulse to flaunt her woman triumphant. In fact, the ending of this story demonstrates greater fictional art than do several of the others. Fan is clearly a woman in control, a propertied woman, generous and caring, as illustrated by her invitation to her widowed aunt to move her family into Fan's home. She is confident and comfortable in her relationship with Byron. She is the one woman in all of Miles's fiction whose promise of fulfillment in love is not compromised by self-effacement. As such, the story does not rely on the oft-used expository techniques of authorial comment and reader control. In woman's victory, in her emerging personhood, Miles can afford to loose her grip and allow her crusade to find its own momentum.

The circuitous paths of Emma Bell Miles's writing, then, always lead back to one center: woman. Perhaps Miles set out to portray the larger scheme of Southern mountain folk culture, but as she molded her material, one aspect of it continually pushed to the forefront. A teacher by inclination, a crusader by moral necessity, she devoted the bulk of her life's work to demonstrating how mountain woman's inevitable lot of "service and of suffering . . . refines only as it is meekly and sweetly borne." Rejecting the "moonshine and rifles" that sent Murfree's and Fox's popularity soaring, she elected to deal with the serious, to advance a social criticism, though she felt compelled to camouflage her campaign beneath her stories of romantic love. The social criticism's dominance so controlled her form that she evolved something more than or different from fiction. I have chosen to call it *quasi fiction* because of its definite aim to convince and persuade. With this kind of motivation and with her subject matter at her doorstep, Emma Bell Miles could follow only one course with her corpus of work: a record of the life of mountain woman, as she knew and lived it.

Notes

1. Four volumes of Emma Bell Miles's original journals are housed in the Jean Miles Catino Collection of Special Collections, Lupton Library, University of Tennessee at Chattanooga. A copy of a fifth volume is also there; the original of that volume is in the Chattanooga Public Library in Chattanooga, Tennessee. Thanks to the work of editor Steven Cox, Special Collections Librarian at UTC, an edited print edition of the journals was published in March 2014. Steven Cox, ed., *Once I Too Had Wings: The Journals of Emma Bell Miles, 1908–1918* (Athens: University of Ohio Press, 2014), 22.

2. Emma Bell Miles, *The Spirit of the Mountains*, A Facsimile Edition (Knoxville: University of Tennessee Press, 1975), 69, 66. This is Miles's best-known work, first published in 1905 by James Pott & Company, and republished in 1975 in the facsimile edition cited above.

3. Cox, 192.

4. A collection of Miles's poetry, *Strains from a Dulcimore*, edited by Abby Crawford Milton, was published by Bozart Press in 1930, eleven years after Miles's death. The collection contained all of the poems previously published in *Chords from a Dulcimore*, as well as others that had appeared in magazines and newspapers.

5. Cox, introduction to *Once I Too Had Wings*, xlvi–xlvii. The $25 Miles says she received for "a Madonna story" may have been a reference to "A Dream of the Dust," published in *The Lookout*, although the date of that publication does not coincide with the journal date; the story, however, could certainly be described as "a Madonna story." When she writes in September 1916 that she sold "A Mess of Greens"

to *Mother's Magazine,* that is likely the story that appeared under the title "The White Marauder" in August 1917; a mess of greens figures prominently in the plot.

6. See, for example, Harry R. Warfel and G. Harrison Orians, introduction to *American Local-Color Stories* (New York: American Book Company, 1941); Claude M. Simpson, introduction to *The Local Colorists* (New York: Harper & Brothers, 1960); Robert E. Spiller et al., "Delineation of Life and Character," in *Literary History of the United States: History,* 4th ed. rev. (New York: Macmillan, 1974).

7. Warfel and Orians, xxiii.

8. Emma Bell Miles, letter to Anna Ricketson, March 4, 1907, Chattanooga Public Library, Chattanooga, Tennessee. Ricketson lived in New Bedford, Massachusetts, and had become a friend to Miles following the publication of Miles's poem, "After Reading Thoreau." The two corresponded until near the end of Miles's life, though they never met in person. Emma's letters to Ricketson have been preserved; forty-four originals are in the Chattanooga Public Library.

9. Emma Bell Miles, letter to an unnamed correspondent, dated January 15, 1913 [1914], Hindman Settlement School Archive, Hindman, Kentucky. Facts within the letter and contextual evidence indicate the date should be 1914. I am grateful to Professor David Whisnant, retired from the University of North Carolina at Chapel Hill, for unearthing the Hindman letter and sharing it with me.

10. Henry D. Shapiro, *Appalachia on Our Mind* (Chapel Hill: University of North Carolina Press, 1978), 18–31. The following sketch of Appalachia's people is partially based on Shapiro's study. It is necessarily simplistic because of the brief space I have allotted to it.

11. Miles, letter to Anna Ricketson, April 5, 1907.

12. Miles, letters to Anna Ricketson, March 31, 1907; April 5, 1907.

13. I have adopted James Moffett's terms from "Kinds and Orders of Discourse," in *Teaching the Universe of Discourse* (Boston: Houghton Mifflin, 1968).

14. Emma Bell Miles, "The Common Lot," *Harper's Monthly Magazine* 118 (December 1908): 149.

15. Ibid., 151, 152, 154.

16. John G. Cawelti, *Adventure, Mystery, and Romance* (Chicago: University of Chicago Press, 1976), 262.

17. Emma Bell Miles, "The Broken Urn," *Putnam's Magazine* 5 (February 1909): 580.

18. Ibid., 578, 579.

19. Ibid., 580.

20. Miles most likely used her sister-in-law Laura Miles Hatfield as model for the young mother who could not adequately breastfeed her baby. Laura and her husband suffered the loss of several infants, all of whom are buried in a row in Fairmount Cemetery in Signal Mountain, Tennessee. One of these was named for Emma.

21. Emma Bell Miles, "The Dulcimore," *Harper's Monthly Magazine* 119 (November 1909): 952.

22. Ibid., 954.

23. Ibid., 954, 956.

24. Ibid., 953.

25. Emma Bell Miles, "Three Roads and a River," *Harper's Monthly Magazine* 121 (November 1910): 889.

26. Emma Bell Miles, Journal, I, July 1909. Cox, 39.

27. Emma Bell Miles, "Flower of Noon," *The Craftsman* 21 (January 1912): 394.

Emma Bell, age twenty-one, shortly before her marriage (photograph in editor's collection; also in Jean Miles Catino Collection, Special Collections, University of Tennessee at Chattanooga)

Frank Miles, age twenty-three, about the time of his marriage (Jean Miles Catino Collection, Special Collections, University of Tennessee at Chattanooga)

Emma Bell Miles with husband Frank and twin daughters, Judith and Jean, in front of their tent home, summer 1903 (photograph in editor's collection; also in Jean Miles Catino Collection, Special Collections, University of Tennessee at Chattanooga)

Emma with children, Judith, Kitty, Joe, and Jean, outside the home Frank built, summer 1908 (photograph in editor's collection; also in Jean Miles Catino Collection, Special Collections, University of Tennessee at Chattanooga)

Emma, the twins, and friends from Chattanooga who had come to visit on Walden's Ridge, about 1910 (Jean Miles Catino Collection, Special Collections, University of Tennessee at Chattanooga)

Emma and her youngest children, Mirick (Mark) and Kitty, summer 1911
(Jean Miles Catino Collection, Special Collections,
University of Tennessee at Chattanooga)

Emma and the twins, Judith and Jean, summer 1913 (photograph in editor's collection; also in Jean Miles Catino Collection, Special Collections, University of Tennessee at Chattanooga)

MRS. EMMA BELLE MILES

...Mrs. Miles will lecture tonight in the Normal Park School on "The Bird of Walden Ridge."

Emma, probably 1914, age thirty-five—newspaper advertisement for a lecture author was giving (photograph in editor's collection; also in Jean Miles Catino Collection, Special Collections, University of Tennessee at Chattanooga)

Pen-and-ink sketch of the bluff on Walden's Ridge by Emma Bell Miles (Jean Miles Catino Collection, Special Collections, University of Tennessee at Chattanooga)

Pen-and-ink postcard sketch of a cabin on Walden's Ridge by Emma Bell Miles (Jean Miles Catino Collection, Special Collections, University of Tennessee at Chattanooga)

Watercolor of a cabin and attached fence on Walden's Ridge by Emma Bell Miles
(Jean Miles Catino Collection, Special Collections,
University of Tennessee at Chattanooga)

Pen-and-ink postcard sketch of an open fireplace with cooking pot on Walden's Ridge by Emma Bell Miles (Jean Miles Catino Collection, Special Collections, University of Tennessee at Chattanooga)

Watercolor of a girl cooking over an open fireplace by Emma Bell Miles. Daughter Judith posed for this painting, which was used in the individually illustrated copies of *Chords from a Dulcimore.* (Jean Miles Catino Collection, Special Collections, University of Tennessee at Chattanooga)

Pen-and-ink postcard sketch of a cabin under the hillside by Emma Bell Miles (Jean Miles Catino Collection, Special Collections, University of Tennessee at Chattanooga)

Watercolor of a fern and a pink lady's slipper by Emma Bell Miles (Jean Miles Catino Collection, Special Collections, University of Tennessee at Chattanooga)

Handmade greeting card in watercolor by Emma Bell Miles (Jean Miles Catino Collection, Special Collections, University of Tennessee at Chattanooga)

Illustration by Lucius Wolcott Hitchcock for Emma Bell Miles's first published short story, "The Common Lot," in *Harper's Monthly Magazine,* December 1908: "On the Mossy Roots of a Great Beech She Awaited His Return" —Easter sitting by the tree waiting for Alison (Special Collections, University of Tennessee at Chattanooga)

Illustration by W. Herbert Dunton for "The Dulcimore," published in *Harper's Monthly Magazine,* November 1909: "He Fired the Mass, Pulling Regularly on the Bellows"—Georgia and Return in the blacksmith shop (Special Collections, University of Tennessee at Chattanooga)

Illustration by W. Herbert Dunton for "Flyaway Flittermouse," published in *Harper's Monthly Magazine,* July 1910: "D'You Reckon She's Lost, Jeff?"—Flittermouse with two of the adults she meets in her travels (Special Collections, University of Tennessee at Chattanooga)

Illustration by Howard E. Smith for "Three Roads and a River," published in *Harper's Monthly Magazine,* November 1910: "Secretly Adding the Contents of the Bottle"—Old Zion acting on what he thinks is his sign from God (Special Collections, University of Tennessee at Chattanooga)

one

The Common Lot

From *Harper's Monthly Magazine* 118 (December 1908): 145–54; illustrated by Lucius Wolcott Hitchcock

"The Common Lot" serves in many ways as the signature piece for most of Miles's fiction. It is her battle cry for the crusade she is waging for the liberation of mountain women from the patriarchal culture they are forced to live in. The story probes the mountain woman's dilemma: to take on the burdens of marriage and the cares of a household or remain a spinster and be condemned to much the same drudgery in the homes of others. Sixteen-year-old Easter Vanderwelt confronts the dilemma as she helps her married sister with the endless toil of caring for her babies, her husband, and the household, with little time to care for herself. Ultimately Easter must make her own choice between "slavery in her father's house or slavery in a husband's," a decision that will determine the course of the rest of her life.

The big boy in the doorway was hot and dusty, but not tired. It was impossible to be really tired with running free on a morning when all the

earth was awake and trembling with the eager restlessness of young summer. His head was carried high, with a deerlike poise; the dark young profile with its promise of early manhood flung up a challenge to greet the world. His gait all morning had been the wolflike pace by which the mountaineer swings the roughest miles behind him.

The woman—she was hardly the mistress—of the big log house was tired, however; she could scarcely remember a time when she had not been so. Life had resolved itself, for her, into conditions of greater or less weariness, and she had learned to be thankful if the weariness were not complicated by rheumatism or other pain. Her day was always long, her night was short; she had no time to think of the sunshine and roses in her own dooryard.

"I come apast Mis' Hallet's," he explained his presence, "and she stopped me to send word that she wants Easter to come and stay with her a spell. I've got a note in my pocket, if I can find it."

Mrs. Vanderwelt read the pencilled scrawl from Cordy Hallet, her married daughter. "Allison," she began, a distressed frown puckering her lined forehead, "if you're goin' by the spring, would you just as soon stop and tell Easter? She's churnin' down thar. Ye might as well carry her a pokeful of cookies."

She filled the boy's hands with freshly baked saucer-wide cookies, scarcely more than sweetened soda biscuit-cakes, and put some into a paper bag for her daughter.

The young fellow might have chosen the highroad, but the sun-dappled path through the woods drew first his eyes and then his feet. Everything was in motion there, tilting and waving in the light breeze; dewdrops glittered still under the leaves; brilliant bits of insect life started out of the sun-warmed loam and rustled with many-legged creepings in last year's dry leaves. On the way he cut a length of hickory, from which the sap-loosed bark could readily be taken, and walked on more slowly, shaping a whistle with his knife, and thinking of Easter, and their days in school. She was not so old as he by several years; perhaps she was not quite sixteen. He had scarce awakened to full perception of her girlish comeliness, but he admired her nervous agility and grace in play. She could run and climb, and play coo-sheepy and hat-ball, as well as any of the boys; that was his way of putting it to himself.

The spring was a dark pool, walled with rock and housed with a structure of logs and hand-riven clapboards. It had a shelf all round below the surface level, on which jars of milk stood in perpetual coolness. Easter, having finished her task, was nowhere to be seen; her churn stood outside, and new butter floated in a maple bowl of water, set on the rock to cool. Having tested his whistle and found to his delight that it would pipe three or four notes, the boy bent over the water for a while, his eyes caught first by the reflection of his own face and then by the leaping and stirring of sand and tiny pebbles where the vein rose through the bottom. He laid himself flat and drank deeply of the bluish cold water; then, closing the door of the spring-house against stray "razorbacks," he began to look about in the woods. Once he called timidly, "Easter!" but the sound of her name in his own voice rather frightened him, inasmuch as he was not sure he ought not to put a Miss, or some such foolish handle, before it; and he proceeded uncertainly into the maple thicket below the spring, not knowing where to search. Then a gleam of blossom flashed between the boles, and he guessed that she would be there.

It was a white-flaming mass of azaleas, delicately rosy as mountain slopes of snow splashed over with the pink of dawn. In the midst sat a girl, drinking the overflowed sweetness of that dripping and blowing blank of flowers: now fingering single branches that lifted into the tender foliage their crowns and pompons, and now drawing all together down against her face in a sheaf of cool, pure petals—drowning her young senses in perfume. She had taken off her coarse shoes to plunge her feet into the dewy freshness of those ferns that in such maple-shaded hollows keep the azaleas company. Easter was too old to go barefoot, but not too old to delight in the feel of the ancient soil beneath her feet, and in the shining dewdrops on her instep's blue-marbled satin. In after years, when the burden of responsibility bore heavily on her shoulders, she remembered that intermission among the flowers as her last taste of care-free pleasure, her last moments of childhood.

Suddenly, with a soft crash of rending growth, the boy parted the underbrush and came toward her. She gathered herself together with a swift instinctive modesty, tucking her feet under her skirt. "Howdy, Allison?" she greeted him, and "Howdy?" he answered, thrusting the bag of cookies at her by way of accounting for his presence.

She smiled in an embarrassed fashion as she took the poke from his hand. The thought of her bare feet made her unable to rise. The big boy dropped to the ground beside her. He delivered his message and watched her read the note.

"Air you goin'?" he asked, eagerly. "Hit's closer to our house. I ain't seen you since school broke up."

"I reckon so," the girl answered him. And then to relieve the situation she offered him cakes. At that he remembered some May-apples in his pocket and produced them with the awkwardness of big-boyhood. Each was still child enough to enjoy the tasteless fruit of the mandrake simply because it was wild; and to him, moreover, it had all the exaggerated value of a boy's trove. Easter shared her cakes, and theirs was a feast of Arcady. So, too, might the Arcadian shepherds have piped among their flocks; for he tried his whistle again, and she must needs have it in her hands to blow upon it also.

Directly she glanced up and her face brightened. "There's a hominy-bird," she whispered ever so softly. Following her gaze, he, too, saw the tiny creature, swift and brilliant, a flying dagger, more like an insect than a bird. They turned to smile at each other, and as quickly turned away. It poised over flower after flower with a hum as of some heavy double-winged beetle; and ere it could be drunk with sweets a new sound possessed the stillness.

The morning had been vividly many-colored with bird notes. The thrush had waked first, his passionless strain cool as the very voice of dawn; the rest had all carolled of nests and mating, of their lives that were hidden overhead in that trembling world of semi-lucent leaves: keen struggle of life with hunger, brooding tenderness of care for the young, wooing, and quarrelling and fighting, the thousand tiny tragedies and comedies unperceived by human eyes. But now it was a mocker who set the dim, deep-lit shadow a-ripple with the pulsing of his own great little heart, in such wild song as could only come from the wild soul of a winged life—a song of world-old passion, of gladness and youth primordial. Oh, troubadour, what magic is in your wooing? Is it the vast and deep desire of Earth for the returning Sungod—her joy in the year's unutterable glad release, her yearning to the most ancient of Lovers ever young? . . .

Allison drew himself nearer to the girl, and laid his hand over hers. The mating instinct awakens early in the young people of the mountains—cruelly early; we cannot tell why—as a sweet pain that overtakes the exquisite shyness of childhood unawares. She neither looked toward him nor shrank away. Slowly her hand turned until its moist, warm palm met the boy's; and before he knew it he had kissed her—anywhere, any way.

A kiss is a mystery and a miracle. Easter sprang up, dazed and thrilled, regardless now of her bare feet—conscious only of a choking in her throat and an impulse to burst into the tearless sobbing of excitement. Allison, frightened perhaps even more than she, stood half turned from her, flushed and tingling from head to foot.

At last he found his tongue. "I won't do that no more! I just don't know what made me. . . . Easter, won't you forget hit?"

It was all he could say.

She barely glanced at him. "I won't tell hit," she murmured, and, snatching up her shoes and stockings, fled away, and left him standing so, rebuked, condemned.

Once alone, she flung herself on the ground and hid her face even from herself. This it was, then, to kiss a boy? "Oh dear, why is it like this?" she wept, and crept closer to the ground.

But she had not promised to forget.

When Easter Vanderwelt went to "stay with" her married sister, she planned to come home in time to enter school when it should open, the first Monday in August. There was the half-formulated hope of seeing Allison somewhere, sometime during the term, even if he did consider himself too old to attend. So she stacked her six or eight books in the loft room over the kitchen, with an admonition to her brothers not to disturb them in her absence. She had always kept them neat, and the boys should have them when she had learned them through.

But Cordy's baby was a fretting, puny thing; Easter finally consented to forego the summer school and stay on till frost, when, it was hoped, the little ones would improve; and the round of toil soon drove out every other thought. Or did it? Four-year-old Phronie and Sonny-buck, his father's namesake, scarcely out from underfoot, the ailing baby to be tended, preparing cow's milk, washing bottles, wrapping a quill in soft, clean rags to fit the tiny mouth—looking after these was the task of a wife and mother; Easter could hardly devote all day and every day to them without figuring to herself a future of such, shared with—whom?

The children fell ill and needed to be nursed. There were the walls to tighten against winter with pasted layers of old newspapers. Hog-killing time brought its extra burdens. Cordy, a fierily energetic housewife, would set up a pair of newly pieced spreads and get two needed quilts done against winter. In the midst of it all she got an order for rug-weaving from a city woman, and begged Easter to stay through the cold weather, with the promise of a new dress from this source over and above her wage of seventy-five cents a week.

Easter's lot was little harder in her sister's house than at home, and there she had no wages; yet she was glad when at last she could shut the three dollars and seventy-five cents in her hard, rough, red little hand—she had accepted a hen and six chickens in part payment—and set her face once more toward her father's house. Catching the hen and chickens and putting them into a basket made her late in starting. The sun was high when she turned out of the shortcut through the woods into the big road, and she found herself already tired. If a wagon would come along now, with room for herself and her small belongings—and, sure enough, before she had walked "three sights and a horn-blow" along the road, a wagon did. Who but Allison on the seat, and all by himself! She felt rather shy, this being the first time they had met alone since the morning he kissed her, under the swamp honeysuckles: she wished he had been any one else, but when he greeted her with, "Want 'o ride?" she clambered in over the wheel.

He stowed the basket under the seat. "What ye got thar?" he inquired, for the sake of conversation.

"Hit's a old hen that stoled her nest and come off with these few chickens," she answered. "What y' been a-haulin'?"

"Rails to fence my clearin'," he told her with pride. He had recently worked out the purchase of a piece of land. "Hit's got a rich little swag on one ind, and a good rise on the other, in case I sh'd ever want to build. Hit fronts half a acre on the big road, too," he added, shyly, looking from the corners of his eyes at the girl beside him.

Talking thus, as gravely as two middle-aged people, they rode across Caney Creek and into the ridges. "Gid up," he gave the command to the team from time to time; but there was no haste in the mules; their long ears flapped as they plodded, and the wheels slid on through the dust as though muffled in velvet. He began to tell her of his hopes and plans, tentatively, without once looking at her.

"If I'm so fortunate—maybe next winter . . . I've been spoken to about a position in a hardware store in town, and . . ." He did not finish that sentence, but presently went on: "One man told me last week that he wouldn't hire a single man—said they was always out nights, and no good in the daytime."

Now Easter knew that Allison was never out at night to any ill purpose, and she smiled a bit wisely to herself. His favorite pose was that of the cosmopolitan, the widely experienced man; but that was pure boyishness. There was a rough innocence about him, despite his every-day familiarity with all the crimes that lie between the moonshine still and county court. What of evil there was in him seemed to have grown there as naturally as the acrid sap of certain wild vines or the bitterness of dogwood bark. The freakish lawlessness of even the worst mountaineer seems in some way different from the vice and moral deformity of cities, as new corn whiskey is different from absinthe.

Under her sunbonnet the girl inquired, demurely, "Why 'n't ye stay here?"

"Oh, I'm jist restless, I reckon . . . I would stay if I had a home here."

That word "home" laid a finger on their lips for full five minutes. Again he ventured, flicking nervously with his whip at the roadside weeds:

"And Mavity wants me in his new saloon. I seed him when I was in Fairplay last week. The wages is good."

She spoke now quickly enough. "Don't go thar, Allison! I don't want to be—worried—'bout you."

He turned away to hide a swift change of countenance, slashed hard at the inoffending bushes, and jerked out, in a husky, boyish voice, "What makes ye care?"

She dared not be silent. "Because I know how good you air. Because I don't want to see—a boy like you go wrong."

"I ain't good!" he cried, almost roughly. Then he turned to find her looking at him serenely, silently—not quite smiling. . . .

That was all, but it was almost a betrothal to the two. From this moment she tried to imagine what life with him would be like. The picture she saw clearest was of a low-browed cabin in the dusk; through its doorway, glowing with red firelight, a glimpse of a supper awaiting a man's return.

Mrs. Vanderwelt was as glad to see her daughter home again as was Easter to rejoin the family, but that did not prevent her levying on Easter's wages. The dish-pan had gone past all mending, and the water-bucket had sprung such a leak that it was no longer fit for use except about the stable. The lantern globe was broken. So Easter reserved for herself only the price of eight yards of gingham.

"Ye're jist in time for the dance over to Swaford's," announced her younger sister, Ellender, when, after the supper dishes were washed, they sat down to tack carpet rags. "They're goin' to give one a-Sata'day night."

"You 'uns a-goin'?" asked Easter. Of course the boys would be there, and all the youngsters of the countryside—Allison, too. There are never enough girls to go round in a frolic in the mountains.

It transpired, however, that Ellender had no dress—at least, none that could appear beside Easter's contemplated purchase. So Easter was forced to consider the means of providing eight yards for her sister as well as for herself.

This was on Monday. The sisters walked two miles to the store next day, and chose the double quantity of cheaper goods together. It was white with a small pink figure printed at intervals, coarse and loosely woven as a flour-sack. They stitched all day Wednesday, and finished the frocks Thursday morning. But on Thursday evening they received a letter recalling Easter to her sister's house.

Easter's trembling hands dropped in her lap.

"Cain't you go this time, Ellender?" she pleaded.

"Maw says I ain't old enough to do what Cordy needs. She says you ain't—sca'cely," the younger sister protested.

"You-all act like you wanted to git shut o' me," Easter almost wept. "Cordy can wait three days. I'm obliged to go to this dance."

But she knew it was not so. Only in her pain she struck at what was nearest.

Easter's return found an ominous tremor and strain in her sister's affairs. At first her girl's mind groped vainly for the cause. There was the endless toil of spring house-cleaning and truck-patch, of chickens and cows, with the ailing youngest to tend, and Jim Hallet going softly, outcast by his wife's displeasure, while poor Cordy sat at night mending and freshening all the coarse little garments, scarcely outgrown, putting them in readiness for an expected use.

Oh, it was hard, it was hard on Cordy, thought the girl, pondering this thing of which she had no experience. It was hard; but she had as yet only the outsider's point of view.

Next week she had a surprise. Allison brought his team on Saturday evening, and asked her, "provided she didn't mind ridin' a mule," to go to the dance with him. It was a long way to Swaford's Cove, and she would be fearfully tired to-morrow, but she was accustomed to pay dearly for every bit of pleasure, and did not hesitate. So he came again Sunday week to walk with her to the church at Blue Springs, and later took her to the close-of-school entertainment, where she had the pleasure of seeing Ellender speak a piece, clad in the frock that was the counterpart of her own.

In the midst of corn-planting time the baby died. The weak life flickered out one night as it lay across Cordy's knees. Such was her exhaustion that the physical need of sleep came uppermost, and her grief did not reveal itself till next day.

The little body, cased in a rude pine box, was taken in the wagon to the untended graveyard by the Blue Springs church. Easter and Cordy rode beside Jim on the seat, and three neighbor women were behind in the wagon, sitting in chairs. These, with the Vanderwelt boys, who had helped dig the grave, were the only persons present at the burying. Cordy asked that one of the women should offer a prayer, but they protested that they could not.

"I never prayed out loud—afore folks—in my life," said one. "I wouldn't know what to say."

"If one o' you'll hold my baby, I'll try my best," faltered the second, after some hesitation. "He's cuttin' teeth, and may not let nobody tetch him but me."

So it proved; and the third, a poor creature of questionable reputation, burst into hysterical sobbing, and answered merely that she did not feel fit.

"I cain't have it so," whispered the poor mother, desperately. "I cain't have my pore baby laid away without no prayer, like hit was some dead animal. Ef nobody else won't say ary prayer—I will."

She stood forth, throwing back her sunbonnet, clasped her hands, shut her eyes tight, and gasped. One could see the working in her throat. They waited. Easter stared at the open grave, shallow, because its bottom was solid rock; the impartial sunshine on the crumbling rail fence, and the little group of workaday figures; the rude stones of other graves scattered through the tangle of briers and underbrush. Then Cordy drooped her head, and whispered, with infinite sadness:

"Lord, take care of my pore baby, and give hit a better chance than ever I had."

"Amen!" Hallet's deep voice concluded with a dry sob, and the three women whimpered after him, "Amen!"

The earth was hastily shovelled in, and the woman who had accounted herself unfit to pray began crying out loud. Presently Jim led his wife back to the wagon.

She spoke but once during the ride homeward. "An' I've got no idy the next'll thrive any better," she said, dry-eyed. Easter, sitting in one of the chairs back in the wagon, held her peace; so this was what life might mean to a woman.

All next week the bereaved mother went about her work muttering and weeping, until both Jim and Easter began to fear for her reason. But presently the work compelled her thoughts away from her loss. She began to take interest in the milk and the chickens; and she noticed Allison and Easter. She told her husband one day that those two would make a good match.

Far from a match, however, was the present state of affairs in that quarter. The mountain people have an overmastering dread of attempting to cope with a delicate situation in words, insomuch that the neighbor who comes to borrow a cup of salt may very likely sit for half an hour on the edge of a chair and then go home without asking for it. And Allison had never kissed her again. But both knew, without having discussed the matter at all, that Allison wished to marry Easter, and that she, although Allison was undoubtedly her man of all men, could not obtain consent of her own mind to agree.

Why?

Cordy awaited her sister's confidence, and at last it came.

"I'm afeared," the girl said, and her eyelids crinkled wofully, her mouth twisted so that she was fain to hide her face.

"You don't need to be afeared," said Cordy, slowly, staring straight ahead of her. "You'd be better off with him than ye would at home, wouldn't ye? Life's mighty hard for women anywhars."

"Well, I don' know," said Easter, doubtfully.

But when, some days after, Allison did formally ask her in so many words, she gave him the same reason for her uncertainty.

"What air you 'feared of?" he demanded at once.

She was silent, terribly embarrassed.

"What is it you're afeared of—dear? Tell me. Won't you tell me?" He put his arms around her. She hid her face on his shoulder and began to cry. "You know I'd never mistreat you?"

"Hit ain't that."

"What, then?"

"I'm just afeared—afeared of being married."

He took a little time over this, and met it with the argument, "Would you have any easier time if you didn't get married?"

She tried to consider this fairly, but there was not an unmarried woman in all her acquaintance to serve as a basis for comparison. Most girls in the mountains marry between the ages of twelve and nineteen. She saw, however, that it was a choice of slavery in her father's house or slavery in a husband's.

Then Allison made a speech; his first, and perhaps his last. "Dear, dear girl, I'll just do the very best I can for you. I cain't promise no more than that. You know how I'm fixed. I've got nothing more to offer you than a cow or two, and a cabin, and what few sticks o' furniture I've put in hit; but that's more'n a heap o' people starts with. Hit's for you to say, and I don't want to urge ye again' your will an' judgment. But I've got a chanst now to go North with some men that'll pay me better wages than I ever have got, and I won't git back till fall; and I—want—you," he said, "to be my wife before I go. I want to know, whilst I'm away, that you belong to me. Then, if I was to happen to a accident, on the railroad or anywheres, you'd be just the same as ever, only you'd have the cows, and the team, and my place. Won't you study about it?"

Easter thought of that for days, in the little time she had for thinking. But she thought, too, of the other side of the picture. Poor child, she had no chance for illusions. Sometimes she felt that she would be walking open-eyed into a trap from which there was no escape save death.

She thought of Cordy at that tiny grave. She dwelt upon her sister's alienation from her husband. Would she, Easter, ever come to look upon Allison in that way?

Yet the time drew near when Allison must go with those who had employed him. The thing must be decided. There came a heart-shaking day on which, clad in a new dress of cheap lawn made for the occasion, and a pair of slippers, Cordy's gift, she climbed into his wagon beside the boy, rode away, and came back a wife.

"But I mighty near wisht I hadn't," she said, thoughtfully, as she told her sister of the gayety of the impromptu wedding at home.

He wrote every week, some three or four pages—a vast amount of correspondence for a mountaineer. At the end of a month he sent her money, more than she had ever had before. His pride in being able to do this was only equalled by hers as she laid out dollar after dollar, economically, craftily, with the thrift of experience, for household things. He had given no instructions as to how the money was to be used; so she bought her dishes and cooking-pots, a lamp, a fire-shovel, and, by way of extravagance, a play-pretty apiece for Suga'lump and Sonny-buck, and even a tiny cap for Cordy's baby not yet arrived.

Then, one day, taking the little boy with her, she went to Allison's cabin to clean house, put her purchases in order, and make the place generally ready for living in on his return.

She chose a fair blue day, not too warm for work. White clouds lolled against the tree-tops and the forest hummed with a pleasant summer sound. She brought water from the spring and scoured the already spotless floor, washed her new dishes and admired their appearance ranged on the built-in shelves across the end of the room, set her lamp on the fireboard, and then spread the bed with new quilts. She stood looking at these, recognizing the various bits of calico: here were scraps of her own and Ellender's dresses, this block was pieced entirely of the boys' shirts, this was a piece of mother's dress, this one had been Cordy's before she married; others had been contributed by girl friends at school. Presently she went to the door and glanced at the sun. It would soon be time to go back and help Cordy get supper, but she must first rest a little. Seating herself on the doorstep, she began to consider what other things were necessary for keeping house, telling them off on her fingers and trying to calculate their probable cost—pillow-slips, towels, a wash-kettle; perhaps, if Allison thought they could afford it, they would buy a little clock and set it ticking merrily beside the lamp on the fireboard, to be valued more as company than because of any real need of knowing the time of day. Her mother had given her a feather bed and two pillows on the morning of her wedding; Allison would whittle for her a maple bread-bowl, and a spurtle and butter-paddle of cedar; and she herself was raising gourds on Cordy's back fence, and could make her brooms of sedge-grass.

Thus planning, she felt a strange content steal upon her weariness. It was borne strongly in upon her mind that she was to be supremely happy in this home as well as supremely miserable. She ceased to ask herself whether the one state would be worth the other, realizing for the first time that this was not the question at all, but whether she could afford to refuse the invitation of life, and thus shut herself out from the only development possible to her.

Little Sonny-buck toddled across the floor, a vision of peachblow curves and fairness and dimples. She gathered him into her arms and laid her cheek on his yellow hair, thrilling to feel the delicate ribs and the beat of the baby heart. He began to chirp, "Do 'ome, do 'ome, E'tah," plucking softly at her collar. Easter bent low, in a heart-break of tenderness, catching him close against her breast. "Oh, if hit was—Allison's child and mine—"

On reaching home she kindled the supper fire and laid the cloth for the evening meal of bread and fried pork and potatoes; and it was given to her suddenly to understand how much of meaning these every-day services would contain if illuminated by the holy joy of providing for her own.

She fell asleep late that night, smiling into the darkness, but was awakened, it seemed to her, almost at once. Cordy stood before her, lamp in hand, laughing nervously; her temples glistened with tiny drops of sweat, and her eyes were dark and strange.

"It's time," said she.

When it was over, and they could, in the gray morn, sit down for a few minutes' rest before cooking breakfast. Easter saw Jim approach the bed on tiptoe. His wife smiled, and raised the coverlet softly from over a wee elevation. Tears came into the girl's eyes, and she rose hastily and went to build a fire in the stove.

Beside the wagon road that was the sole avenue of communication between the Blue Spring district and the outer world, Easter sat on the mossy roots of a great beech awaiting her husband's return. Her sunbonnet lay on the ground at her feet, and she was enjoying herself thoroughly, alone in the rich October woods. She was now almost a woman; her abundant vitality had early ripened into a beauty as superbly borne as that of a red wood-lily. She had walked a long way among the ridges, her weight swinging evenly from one foot to the other at every step with a swift, light roll; she was taking time for once in her life to rejoice with the autumn winds and the riot of color and autumn light. How much of outdoor vigor was incarnate in that muscular body of beech towering beside her! Easter's eyes ran up from the spreading base to the first sweep of the lower branches, noting the ropelike torsion under the bark. A squirrel, his cheeks too full of nuts even to scold her, peeped excitedly from one hiding-place after another, and finally scampered into safety round the giant bole. Then through a rent in the arras of pendent boughs she saw her man coming.

His grandfathers both had worn the fringed hunting-shirt and the moccasins; and though he himself was clad in the Sunday clothes of a workingman, he moved with the plunge and swing of their hunting gait. Such a keen, clean face as she watched it, uplifted to the light and color and music of the hour! His feet rustled the drifting leaves, and he sang as he came.

It seemed but a moment's mischief to hide herself behind a tree so as to give him a surprise; but the prompting instinct was older than the tree itself—old as the old race of young lovers.

. . . Suddenly they were face to face. He never knew how he cleared the few remaining steps, nor how he came to be holding both the hands she gave him. They laughed in sheer happiness, and stood looking at each other so, until Easter became embarrassed and stirred uneasily. He drew her hand within his arm as she turned, and, not knowing what else to do, they began to walk together along the leaf-strewn roadside, but stopped as aimlessly as they had started.

To him a woman's dropped eyes might have meant anything or just nothing at all. He scarcely dared, but drew her to him and bent his head. And somehow their lips met, and his arms were about her, and his cheek—a sandpapery, warm surface that comforted her whole perturbed being with its suggestion of man-strength and promise of husbandly protection—lay against hers.

That kiss was a revelation. To him it brought the ancient sense of mastery, of ownership—the certainty that here was his wife, the mate for whom his twenty years had been period of preparation and waiting. And the tears of half-shamed fright that started under Easter's lids were dried at their source by the realization that it was her own man who held her, that he loved her utterly, and that her soul trusted in him. She lifted her arms, and her light sleeves fell back from them as she pushed them round his neck.

"Oh, Allison, Allison, Allison, Allison!" she murmured, as she had said his name over to herself so many hundreds of times; only, now she was giving herself to him for good or ill with every repetition.

Before them lay the vision of their probable future—the crude, hard beginning, the suffering and toil that must come; the vision of a life crowned with the triple crown of Love and Labor and Pain. Their young strength rose to meet it with a new dignity of manhood and womanhood. In both their hearts the gladness of love fulfilled was made sublime by the grandeur of responsibility—by the courage required to accept happiness in sure foreknowledge of the suffering of life.

The squirrel ran down the beech and gathered winter provender unheeded; and yellow leaves swirled round them as through the forest came a wind sweet with the year's keenest wine.

two

The Broken Urn

From *Putnam's* 5 (February 1909): 574–80; illustrated by Alden K. Dawson

Continuing the theme of woman's common lot, "The Broken Urn" opens with two small girls already playing out their expected gender roles in their rock playhouse: cooking and cleaning; piecing quilt patterns from discarded quilt scraps; and talking shyly of eventual marriage. But as adulthood approaches, their choices take them in different directions. Sarepta, the quiet beauty of the pair, remains in the mountain community and marries her childhood sweetheart. Nigarie, the adventurous one, leaves the mountain in the company of her husband, the hotel proprietor's son. The contrast in their adult lives provides the conflict around which this plot turns and offers an explanation for the author's choice of title: "The Broken Urn," after the quilt pattern that serves as metaphor for the story.

Above the cabin, in the edge of the clearing, stood a great irregular block of sandstone. Gaunt and barren it may have been, as first fallen from the

cliffs that towered behind the forest; but centuries of weather had made it a thing of friendliness and comfort. Succulent grasses, rooted in the loam accumulated by the yearly drift of fallen leaves, sprouted from every crevice; ferns trembled over its edge; the fence led only to the rock on either side, so that its bulk interposed to spare the mauling of several dozen rails; a hollow scooped under it on the woodland exposure afforded shelter in winter to any number of pigs; and beneath the overhang facing the valley two little girls had built a playhouse. Here signs of frequent occupancy were not lacking: the ground was lightly printed all over by slim bare feet, and the rock was smudged with woodsmoke above a tiny furnace of stones. No real playthings were visible, but the rock shelves were stocked with potsherds and broken crockery, and there were tin pails and even little skillets and cookers, cleverly fashioned from old tin cans, for the making and serving of real bear-grass salad.

It was, however, too late in the season for bear-grass. The tide of young summer had brimmed the valleys, and came rushing up the slopes to burst along the bluffs in a high-flung surf of laurel bloom. The two small friends were seated now on the grassy top of the rock, shaded by a great arching tupelo; they were piecing quilt patterns. They had laid out for comparison on their knees and about on the grass, the Eagle, the Dream, the Texas and Kentucky Stars, the Crazy Ann, the Tree of Paradise, and three or four varieties of brick-work and log-cabin. The pattern under immediate consideration was the Broken Urn.

"I been a-studyin'," said Nigarie, the sprightly, dark one, "whether hit wouldn't be the prettiest to piece the urn out whole."

"Let's try hit that-a-way," agreed Sarepta, a child with an angel's face.

Against nature, the beauty was also the worker, and Sarepta's small skilled fingers swiftly cut and laid out in pink and brown calico the design they had mentioned, her big gray eyes shaded by sumptuous lashes, brooding full of tender dreams above a tangle of flaxy-gold curls falling about the down-bent, intent face, pure in outline and tint as a pearl.

Even loquacious Nigarie sat acutely observant, scarcely speaking, her three-cornered kitten countenance with its hard, round little cheeks under the beryl-green eyes puckered to disproportionate anxiety, till the urn was an accomplished fact, so absorbed were they both in this, their one avenue of artistic expression.

"Hit's some like grandma's Vase of Friendship," commented Nigarie, drawing a long breath when it was done.

"We could call this the Friendship's Urn," suggested Sarepta, timidly. Nigarie usually did the suggesting for the pair.

That small person now ran a reckless hand to the bottom of her basket and plowed up her collection of scraps. "This rosebud sprig's the prettiest I've got. Hit's a piece of Easter's weddin' dress," she volunteered.

"I've got one block all pieced outen scraps Easter an' Ellender given me," Sarepta showed it.

"*I've* got one made all outen the boys' shirts, and some over," Nigarie tossed her braids. "Harmon's and At's, and this pink stripe's Macon's, and this 'n's Joel's, and here's Mart's; and hit's set together with Sam Stetson's."

"Sam Stetson's!"

"Cert'n'y; I reckon Sam Stetson ain't none too good to have a piece of his shirt in my quilt if his pappy does keep the hotel, an' he is goin' to school in the settlement. I wish't I could swap you out of that blue gingham, Sarepta. I want hit to go with this sprig weddin' dress."

"I'll—I'll let ye have it all for—for that one." The gray eyes glowed as she indicated the pink striped scrap from Macon Kinsale's shirt—and she cherished it tenderly, tucking it jealously deep in the bottom of an orderly basket when Nigarie willingly exchanged it for the blue gingham.

The trade effected, they sewed busily.

"That's goin' to be plumb pretty," commented Sarepta at last, leaning to look at her friend's work. "Do you reckon you 'n' me 'll ever—make us a weddin' dress?"

The sweetest imaginable color crept over both little faces, and shining eyes were bent swiftly to their needlework.

Sarepta's fingers stole toward the pink striped scrap in her basket.

"Mine'll be silk," said Nigarie confidently.

It was even so. . . . All through the years, Nigarie was shielded, favored. As an only child, she went to school while Sarepta was fulfilling at home the duties of the eldest girl in a large family. Work was found for Nigarie at Stetson's summer hotel, and when she came home it was to make ready for her marriage to the proprietor's son, Sam Stetson. Sam was in business now in a flourishing little city, and doing well. Nigarie promised to write often to Sarepta; but soon the letters became fewer, and after a time they ceased.

Even while there was communication, Sarepta had slight understanding of Nigarie's social evolutions, as described in occasional newspaper clippings enclosed. Statements about refreshments, decorations and costumes conveyed little meaning to a mind accustomed to clothe its thoughts in the antique dialect of the mountains. But she made out that the wedding dress and several others were indeed of silk.

She was not disturbed by that, for she could dwell on her own wedding, when she came down-stairs, shining with a mysterious happiness, in her lawn and cheap ribbons, to find the big log sitting-room filled to overflowing with her kin. She had tremblingly given her promise to love, honor and obey, and had kept it, with a willing spirit if not always to the letter. But Macon's "protect and cherish"—well, as a true wife she never permitted herself to form any conclusion as to whether it had been forgotten five minutes afterward. Macon had done the best he could; as time went on she reiterated that to herself almost fiercely. He had done the best he could!

After the first infare with their meagre furnishing to a cabin on his uncle's land, they had moved, in seven years, nine times, from shack to cabin and from cabin to shack, hounded by poverty and circling like stags as close to home as possible. Macon had indeed done his best; but Sarepta, whose wants were so few, had to pinch in ways she considered hardly decent. She had always lived on little; she learned now to live on next to nothing. She ate food which she had always regarded as fit only for pigs or chickens. Her mind was occupied, not occasionally but constantly, with problems that were like gravel in a shoe, as insistent as they were contemptible: "If I divide this inch of pork, will it season Macon's potatoes for supper and again at breakfast? If I pick a mess of sarvices to-day, have I got sugar in the house to make a cobbler for Sunday dinner? Can I, by piecing Macon's shirt sleeves, and lining the yoke with flour-sacking, get enough out of this gingham to make me a sunbonnet?"

Women always get the worst of poverty. And Sarepta was no miser by nature. Some wives eat the biscuit end of the pone and the skin of the meat because they are afraid no one else will; she chose them because she could not bear that any one else should have to.

Again and again they strained every nerve and sinew to win a shack and clearing of their own, only to be disappointed. Every time, just as the signing of the deed seemed a probability of next week, something happened—a drought on the garden, a murrain on the cow, or another baby. Three of these had come—and gone—leaving no more visible impress than a little less elasticity of Sarepta's figure, a little deepening of the shadow behind her beautiful eyes; for each, after a few weeks of ineffectual striving to digest the cows' milk which the poor mother was obliged to give it, had quietly straightened out in her arms and died.

The fourth was three weeks old and already ailing, on the day of Nigarie's return.

Sarepta heard the news from a neighbor woman who shared her tubs and huge pot and did washing for the hotel people. Nigarie's fat baby, her airs and her summer wash frocks were subjects of an intermittent conversation that went on all morning below the spring in the hollow. The mountain woman's beauty one might almost say was undiminished by her hard life. In the limp unlovely frock it shone out a luminous, incongruous fact. No one seeing her, pounding away at the bat-block and replying with mild monosyllables to the rhapsodies of the other, would have guessed that she was almost sick with terror lest this last puny life slip also out of her grasp. A woman must learn to chatter of other things, lest the gods take notice and in pity slay.

It was the first of April—beautiful weather, but the hard time of year, when the hungry winter has gnawed the last scraps of pork rind from the smoke-houses of well-to-do farms, and the small fruit and truck-garden have not yet begun to relieve the poor. Sarepta was dreading the approach of hot weather on the baby's account; yet she was wondering how to round out a good dinner for Macon from bulk pork and meal. As she carried the last of the wash up to hang it out on the fence, she saw the flicker of a white dress moving along a woods-path. Some one was coming to see her—some one fashionably attired, yet carrying a baby on her hip like any mountain woman! Then she recognized Nigarie.

She stood and trembled, without a word to say, abashed not at all by Nigarie's finery, but because she did not know on what ground the visitor would meet her.

Transgressing all mountain custom the new-comer flew at her with a little laughing cry and kissed her on the cheek.

"My, ain't you pretty yet!" she said half enviously as she entered the cabin. "I've been to the bear-grass rock—remember, Sarepta?" Nigarie's bright eyes were full of misty recollection as she untied the baby's cap. "It's just like it used to be," she said thoughtfully. "Funny how things stay, and we change. I filled Sammy's apron full of bear-grass; shall we have a sallet for dinner? Where's your baby, honey?"

With a catching of the breath that was almost a sob, Sarepta brought out the thin little occupant of her cradle. Without a word she laid it across Nigarie's knees.

The little creature began to wail feebly, and before his mother could take him and hush him, Nigarie, moved by what impulse of immortal compassion who can say, lifted him to her breast.

"Why, he's starved most to death," she said gently. "I reckon you ain't been able to nurse him. I wish I could—why couldn't I?" She broke off and laughed in her usual elfish inconsistent fashion. "Sammy pesters me most to death," she said with apparent irrelevance. "There ain't any fun stayin' at a hotel with a baby. I'll bet I'll never try it again. As soon as he's old enough I'm going to leave him with Mother Stetson. He's so spoiled he wouldn't do anything but holler if you put him down."

But skilled Sarepta had taken the fat little new-comer with his royal airs of kinghood and disposed him on a quilt upon the floor. Smilingly, silently, she furnished him with a green switch, and attracted the cat's attention.

"Well, you are a wonder," Nigarie said—"but then, you always were. I'm sick of the hotel—do you reckon you could board me for the rest of the time I want to stay? It would be like the old days—and you could take care of Sammy when I wanted to go somewhere."

Sarepta on her knees looked up at the ruling spirit, sitting above her, nursing her baby, and a mighty gratitude, a wordless emotion which she could not for the life of her have expressed, shook her from head to foot. Here, then, was the answer to her prayers.

"I'll make you as comfortable as I kin," she managed finally to say. "We're mighty poor folks—but you know that—you heard it over at the hotel before you ever put foot in this house. Oh, Nigarie, if you would only stay with me a while!"

And so the butterfly woman, the little cuckoo who never wanted a nest of her own, folded her wings for a season in this humble place. She nursed Sarepta's baby as she nursed her own. The envious eyes of the mother were on her as the little fellow's thin body rounded, and the puny limbs grew stronger. To Sarepta it seemed almost a miracle from heaven, and the little cabin a holy place.

The days were filled with a deep peace and vital joy. Nigarie was happy in having some useful work, or rather in being herself actually necessary to the daily welfare of others; Sarepta, in watching her child grow, in the presence of a dear and merry companion, and in seeing Macon take that long-looked-for "start." For he, profiting by Nigarie's presence, secured work with a valley farmer, and began working out the purchase of some two acres of land. He came home every Saturday night, carrying on his back provisions for the coming week, and left before day on Monday morning. Hence Sunday was the white milestone of the week to both women; for Macon was gifted with temperament and charm.

Sarepta's kitchen outfit was hardly less crude than that of the playhouse had been, yet she always contrived a little feast for his day at home. Talent he had, too. All the long still afternoon and after the moon had climbed above the mountain he sat on the porch, his chair tilted back against the house-logs, and played upon the banjo. He played, and set the whole fragrant night throbbing, until their only neighbors, among the pines far up the height, sat listening too, in another cabin door; played until the two mothers, the long-continued rhythm going to their heads, sprang up, took hold of hands and danced together like two girls over the shaking puncheons; played until the spiders peeped out from the roof-boards to hear, and the whippo-wills came right up to the fence and thrilled the night with their wild jodeling. And in truth his music was hardly less eerie than theirs; a barbaric jangle, interspersed with strange rocking whoops and calls, and elaborated with curious fingerings—snaps and slides and twangs unknown to banjo-players outside the mountains.

There were in it tone-pictured incidents of cabin life, and echoes of the larger enfolding life of nature—murmuring undertones as of drumming rain, ghostly half-whispered minors, and long chuckling meditations mellowed as if by the product of hidden stills. He sang too in the excellent baritone of the mountaineer—not the elder ballads which girls delight in and mothers croon, but man-songs—real folk-song of raid and foray, rollicking drinking-songs, with boast and challenge, and peculiar baying rhythms that reached a climax in the long-drawn hunting-yell.

Some of this music was known to his hearers; some, unacknowledged, was his own composition or improvisation. Nigarie had heard better in theatres, of course, but this was knit in with her earlier recollections. To this every fibre of her being responded as to the dramatic element—breath of sweet keen frost or exultant storm.

She had not known such contentment since she left the mountains.

"We've been everywhere, Sam and me," she remarked one evening as the three sat together in the dark. "I've lived at the sea-shore, in the West, and we had a winter in New York; but I always wanted, I think, to come back here—on a visit," she added the concluding words hastily, for she knew that no place on earth could hold her long.

In the fall Nigarie Stetson returned to her own life. Those restless, wayward, eager feet went back to seek new paths—and yet new ones. Sarepta watching her departure through tears that were not all bitter, a round, rosy baby on her shoulder, knew somehow that the visitor would never return. And she wondered at herself meekly. Where was the bitterness of loss, where the canker of envy she had once thought to endure when this moment arrived?

She turned a thoughtful face and kissed her child. She entered her small dun dwelling and looked about at smoke-browned beam and rooftree with new eyes. She began to realize that in the unhurried, intimate conversations of those long summer days she had come into an understanding of the quiet, unassailable dignity of her own position, and learnt the intrinsic worth of usefulness as contrasted with the false value of unearned riches. She felt dimly and half unwillingly, as she contemplated Nigarie's lot, that there was something almost disgraceful about being "kept" in soft and delicious idleness. Even the remembrance of the three starved babies was no longer a bitterness. Surely it were better to have borne and loved and lost them, every terrible, precious memory of them, than to bear the burden of feverish apprehension which Nigarie evinced toward motherhood itself; to speak continually and openly of the baby as an unearned burden.

She established her boy in his cradle, preparatory to taking up her work. She was suddenly full of a zest for life to which her days had long been stranger.

Macon, having completed his purchase of land, was now busied near home, hewing logs for a cabin of their own. By way of doing his best he had come into the house, ostensibly for a drink, but really to try a new tune on his banjo. At some political meeting the phrase about "dipping the pen in gall" had caught his fancy and suggested to him a new couplet to which he was tentatively fitting an air:

> "I dip my pen in golden ink, to write my love a letter,
> And tell her that most every day I love her a little better."

The nearly perfect monogamy of the region renders it unlikely that a mountaineer compose verses in honor of any but the one woman. As his wife came in Macon tossed the new song at her with a half humorous, but wholly gallant bow.

She laughed, as it seemed to her, immoderately—there was so much to laugh at! She turned once more to the babe in the cradle; how rosy he was, and how he laughed, too. She went, on feet that love made light, to prepare her dinner of herbs.

Later, she might lose sight of the vision somewhat, for we are all as incapable of holding constantly to great thoughts as of putting such definitely into words; but when the trailing glories paled, here was a child, gloriously alive, to remind her that she had once been inspired with the profoundly rational courage of seeing things as they are.

And on the cradle, pieced by Nigarie in the summer mornings while both babies slept, lay a little quilt of the pattern they had named the Friendship's Urn.

three

A Dark Rose

From *Harper's Monthly Magazine* 118 (February 1909): 426–33; illustrated by Lucius Wolcott Hitchcock

Averilla Sargent, the pampered village flirt in "A Dark Rose," leads young Luther Estill, a budding country preacher, on a merry chase as he woos her to be his wife. Thinking that the constriction of a preacher's life is not what she had in mind for herself, Averilla declines initially, but then she accepts him and declares herself ready to be a preacher's wife with all the "goodness" that entails. But the conversion perhaps comes too easily for Averilla and causes the reader to suspect her sincerity. Other questions arise as well: Is Miles deliberately presenting Averilla as an unreliable narrator? Is she positing this character as an archetype of the Appalachian woman who must play a role of subservience because she has no other option in the patriarchal culture she lives in?

Five preachers, in the intervals of a brush-meeting on Puncheon Camp Creek, were enjoying the hospitality of Brother Zack Lowry, whose big log house was near the place of meeting. Aunt Sa'Jane, the house-mother, quick and tireless as an ant despite her fifty-odd years, was clearing the

dinner from the table in the open entry, and the men, sitting on the long porch, told stories of past revivals.

Luther Estill, youngest of the group, was not listening to the stories; neither was he watching the movements of Aunt Sa' Jane, who, ever since he was cast, a lonely little lad, into her hands, had mothered him. He heard only Averilla in the room beyond. The Sunday "singin'" was really over, and the other singers dispersed to get ready for the evening meeting; but she, who never had any pressing work to do, and seemed always ready for any occasion, lingered alone at the organ. One is supposed, in respect, to sing only hymns or pieces of a religious nature where the preacher is a guest; but this girl was choosing songs strange to Luther's ears. "Hick's Farewell" he knew; the "Cowboy's Lament" he had heard; but these ballads, centuries old, of poignant yearning and regret, he had never heard before. Aunt Sa' Jane and his far-away mother had crooned to him—but this new manner of singing, this heart-expression, drew him strangely.

The old voices on the porch droned on, with occasional feeble laughter; but her contralto filled the echoing room with its pleading minors and cadences of passion. What was this that had come like a red flame searing his consecrated life?

From the overheard conversation of several boys, who had been loath to leave Averilla at the organ, he had gathered that there was to be a dance that night, a "frolic," at the very hour of the foot-washing—an open defiance flung in the face of the Church, at the climax of its campaign against the devil. Averilla's father, Lark Sargent, had been for years the arch-enemy of the few forces that made for righteousness along the Sourwood Mountain circuit. Now they were soon to be rid of him, for he had sold his land to a mining syndicate and given out that he, with Averilla and her brothers, would move to the Settlement, a valley town, to live; but before they were ready to leave the district he was not averse to firing a parting shot. He was flush with the recent sale; there would be plenty of cards and whiskey. Let Averilla break up the meeting if she could.

When the song was ended, the singer came out on the porch, swinging her sunbonnet by the strings. Her dark gaze swept the four elderly preachers' indifferently, but met young Luther's with a smile.

"Who's goin' to conduct the meetin' to-night? You?" she asked, pausing before him. The watchfulness of the four was turned aside by these words, and under their resurgent buzz of talk she added: "Come a piece with me. I've got something to tell you."

He hesitated a moment; then, with a kindling of his dreamy face, took up his hat and followed her out of the yard, while the other preachers looked at one another.

This house had been his home until, being "called to preach," he had ceased to have need of a home. Strange that in all those years he had never really seen this daughter of a neighbor! What was this change wrought by a few months in him—or her?

"I wish't I was a little boy, and could go barefooted in the road again," he said, overtaking her outside the gate. "This white dust feels like velvet."

The powerful scent of mountain-mint and bee-balm came to them, called up from the roadside by the evening air; and fainter, finer breaths came at intervals out of the forest. All afternoon a procession of dazzling thunderheads had been sailing slowly along the horizon toward a mellow rolling of distant thunder, as marching to the seat of war. Now they were piled, sierras above sierras, opposite the sunset, flushed with pure color from base to peak, and glowing from time to time with a silent excitement of lightnings. Passing the mounded bush that almost buried Lowry's gate, the girl had plucked a belated rose; it glowed now in her musky, heavy hair, matching the vivid softness of her mouth. Each time she turned her face to him in talking, her eyes sang; and she moved with a buoyancy unlike the gait of the ordinary mountain girl, who is apt to be weary in the cradle from her mother's killing toil. She was all music, the lovely thing! Luther was like to forget his office. But along with the duteous performance of ancient rites had descended to him something of the austerity of priesthood. He presently broke upon her rippling chatter, bethinking himself to speak sternly.

"I guess I know what you're aimin' to tell me. I heard Bark and 'Vander and them a-talkin'. You're goin' to have a big dance to-night."

She persisted, however, in speaking as to the boy who was walking a "piece" of the way with her. "Yes; don't you wish't you was comin'? Can't you, anyway?"

He tried to counter with a rebuke—"You'd do much better to come to the foot-washin'"; but he saw it fall on stony ground.

"Come, and we'll learn you to dance," she challenged.

"Why, you know that I'd be turned out of the church next day!"

"Well, you're too young to be a preacher; you've never had your life. Just think, you'll get old and die before you've had any playtime!"

Had not his own heart told him so in the night-watches but lately? Ah, the cooing, lilting singsong of her voice! the bubbling gurgle of throaty laughter! her velvet beauty!

"I wouldn't for anything!"

"Come up awhile and look on, can't you?—after you've been to the meeting."

"No-o; I can't think of hit, Averilla."

Of what use to say no to one who would not take it for answer? His refusal only changed her mood for the worse; her tone became one of raillery, without, however, detracting from the warmth and dearness of her presence.

"How many chickens did Aunt Sa' Jane kill for all you-uns to-day? Two to a preacher is what she 'lows, I think. Let's see"—she pretended to count on her fingers—"all but one of ol' Top-knot's early brood! La! just think how lonesome he'll feel a-flyin' up to roost to-night!

"Wherever these feet-washin' preachers go,
They never leave a chicken for to crow-crow-crow—
They never leave a chicken for to crow."

She peeped around into his face with sweet mischief, laughing; and he could but laugh with her. Tossing her head on her rounded neck, she began to dance along the road before him, singing through the tinted twilight:

"It was the Lady Alizonde
Looked forth from her dark tower;
She saw the stranger minstrel ride
That came to be her wooer.
If you love me as I love you,
There'll be no time to tarry.

"She from her casement lightly cast
A rose as dark as sin;
Your sign of sure defeat, although
Against the field you win!
If you love me as I love you,
No knife can cut our love in two!"

"Do come down for awhile—just to hear Alf King play the banjo—just a little while! You don't hafto be a good boy all the time. Here's your short cut back to Uncle Zack's barn."

He said good night, but he heard her song all the way back to Lowry's through the dusk of the summer woods:

"If you love me as I love you,
There'll be no time to tarry—"

There had been a conference, or business meeting, earlier in the day, setting in order the church's affairs; so that now all who sat forward, ready to take part in the foot-washing, were approved members in good standing. But out of Luther, who was wont to throw himself into this work with glad abandon, the joyous sense of fellowship with them had gone and could not be rekindled. He sat only a little apart from the rest, yet as far away in thought as if lost in those caverns of shadow cast by flaring pine torches under the woods behind him. A sibilant buzz of gossip rose above the whispering leaves, for the service was not yet begun. That distant rolling of thunder was coming nearer, though it had brought as yet neither wind nor rain.

So many people gathered here, all bound to him with what he had been taught from babyhood was the highest and truest bond of which humanity was capable—and yet all insignificant, all suddenly worthless, because Averilla the alien was not present. He was astounded that his life's endeavor should have so played him false. He felt that he stood at the parting of the ways, that a choice lay before him—to serve his Lord no longer, or to see his love no more. He would not have been the youngster he was, chosen and flattered for a gift of tongues in things spiritual, if he had not put the matter to himself in somewhat magniloquent phrases.

"Gittin' along todes time, ain't hit?" suggested a brother, after glancing across the space to see that the crowd was "about gathered in."

"Reckon hit'll come up a rain?" asked another. They all peered anxiously at the black sky, but were unwilling to forego the service.

"Maybe the storm ain't comin' here; hit may go round an' swing off down the river. That roarin's mainly the heat on the Side."

"Looks like the devil's bent on whippin' us out if he can," said Brother Brock, who was chosen to conduct the foot-washing. "Hit's done rained us out two meetin'-nights this week." But he took his place—a seat on the rough platform; he crossed one leg over the other, threw back his head, and began to sing:

"Go, preacher, and tell it to the people,
Pore mourner's found a home at last."

He was joined by the "leader" and other singers, and there were not three voices in the crowd that had not caught the strain by the end of the second verse. Like most of the hymns they employed, this one was a sort of incantation, a repetition of a half-dozen lines over and over indefinitely. When Brock had heard enough he rose, and the people became silent, awaiting his direction. He announced in measured ministerial tones:

"We don't aim to protract the meetin' any longer, except that there'll be a baptizin' in Puncheon Camp Creek to-morrow at nine (nine o'clock, didn't you say, Brother Barlow?). Yes, at nine o'clock; and I want you all to come and bring your families to see these twenty-two dear converts dipped and brought into the fold. And let us all sing and praise the Lord; yes, we'll aw-aw-awl sing and praise the Lord. I further announce that there's to be preachin' in the Blue Springs Church by Brother Rogers tomorrow night, and a experience meetin' Wednesday night; and after that Brother Estill's to take charge and preach there the second Sunday in each month. I reckon that's all the 'nouncements I have to make. Now let us throw ourselves heart an' soul into this meetin' with all sinceriousness; let us not be disturbed nor distracted by the powers of darkness nor the thunder; the Lord will take care of us. Brother Rogers, will you lead us in prayer?"

As a matter of fact, three or four prayed together, at the top of their voices. Luther caught scattered phrases of reference to the "pleasures of the weekend," and knew that the frolic at Sargent's was present in all minds as a lure of the enemy to destruction, with Averilla as chief beguiler. Songs followed, a big-lunged, swinging chant in which every soul joined with good will. But to Luther, under the spell of another voice and music in expression of a different aspiration, it seemed for the first time to have no meaning, no immediate connection with anything of vital importance in his life.

> "Oh, we'll lay down the Bible and go home,
> Yes, we'll lay down the Bible and go home,
> We'll lay down the Bible and go home,
> Bright angels standing at the door,"

mechanically he sang with the rest; but even while the chapter ordained for this sacrament was being read, the boy was trying to remember the weird and moving melody of the ballad of Lady Alizonde which he had heard that evening. Averilla's words were in his mind all during the sermon—an exhortation the fervor of which well-nigh exhausted its deliverer, and wrought the nerves of the listeners to a keen tension. There was still no rain; but the thunder was crashing now, and the lightning outlined the tossing boughs more vividly at every flash.

"Even so ought ye to wash one another's feet," repeated the preacher again and again. Between the threat of storm and the proximity of Sargent's dance, it was inevitable that a note of antagonism should ring out from time to time. "And what did He do then—yes, what did He do then? He girded Himself with a towel. Yes, He girded Himself with a towel." Here Brock knotted a towel about his waist. "You hypocrites and sinners in the back o' the camp can jist laugh if you want to; if ye do ye're a-makin' fun o' what your Master did; I'm a-doin' jist what He did now—yes, I'm a-doin' jist what He did now."

But there was none to smile at the quaintness of the old ceremony, for all except the faithful and those under close parental or avuncular surveillance were half a mile away, dancing to the banjoes. The bread and wine had been passed, and they had begun to sing,

"In all humility we now
Each other's feet do lave,"

when the storm came upon them in earnest, as if by the personal malice of a living thing. Light javelins of rain shot through the tree tops, sounding a patter on the leaves; then heavier spears pierced the roof of the brush shelter. A few drops struck the faces of the sleeping babes, who at once woke and added their wail to the clamor. No mountain man minds a wetting, but among the sisters there was a hasty readjustment of sunbonnets and shawls. Several began to shriek hysterical triumph:

"Glory, glory! My soul's happy!"
"Glory to the blessed Lamb!"
"Amen! O sweet Saviour!"
"Glo-o-ry!"

Brock saw that he must take command of the situation. Not for nothing had he been a competent shepherd for thirty-five years. He held up one hand and shouted: "Let us all walk to Brother Lowry's house, singing as we go, and thar continue the sacrament. Brother Rogers," he added in a lower voice, "if you and Brother Lowry'll holp me, we'll carry these pitchers an' things over." He headed the procession with a torch-bearer, both voicing hallelujahs on the way.

Luther intended to follow with a torch; but such a tide of emotion was surging up in him that he wished intensely to be alone for a few minutes at least. He fell back unobserved into the threshing woods; the darkness, wild now with rain, concealed him instantly. He leaned against the trunk of a big tree that afforded some protection from the force of the wind. But almost before the shouting of the congregation in the distance was covered by the roar of the rain on a million leaf-drums, his feet were bearing him in an opposite direction.

"Where am I going?" he muttered; but he knew. "I am weighed in the balance and found— Send the thunderbolt, O Master!" He bared his throat and looked into the eyes of the storm, thinking how death would be better than the blight that must follow his course. But he felt the tide rising, steady and certain, its current saying always below the thunder, "Averilla—Averilla—Averilla." He must see her face again—he knew, in the very instant of prayer, that he would see her. The rain lashed forward, screaming; the wind got beneath it and lifted and waved it like a sheet; and so he stumbled on, whipped by desire—now the crash and the torrent! Except for the changing play of colored lightnings through the blaring rain he could not see an inch of the way. The earth under his feet trembled to a short, deep booming, nearly continuous—suggestive of close range, of breathless fighting, of the short-arm jolt, of clinch and break away. He breathed deeply, and was glad of the rivulets that coursed over his shoulders and chest. At last he reached the plain road and fell into the swinging stride of the mountains. At the same time the downpour softened to a steady drumming, and the night became a little less dark. He hastened on until he saw the red glow of light from the doorway of Sargent's cabin.

The revel was now at its height. Rain had driven into the porch all the lookers-on, and he was able to peer unobserved in at the low, square window by the chimney. Already flung far off his usual pivot of thought and feeling, he was still further unstrung by the ring-tamp-a-tankle of the banjoes and the singing fiddle. His blood bounded to the rhythm of the dancers' play. There was Averilla with 'Vander Bolton, who was dancing with the Indian-like intensity of the mountaineer. Ah! Her dress, her hair, her gleaming face! The perfume of her flesh, the music of her every motion, the warmth and color and charm of her! . . . And he had neither part nor lot in her life. But, oh, if she would only come out—come with warm hands and ripe lips and a tender word—come out to him! If they two together might leave the merrymakers, and the congregation, too, and go utterly away from both! . . .

Some fellows who had been across during a slack in the weather to the jugs in the "little timber," returning noisily to the cabin, half recognized the face at the window and spoke to him. Instinctively he drew back out of the light; and they, deeming now that they must have been mistaken, filed into the house.

Luther did not return to the window; he was unable to endure the sight of Averilla dancing with the other lads. Instead, he cast himself face down under the rose-bushes. Something gleamed pale in the wet grass here—aces and kings of an unlucky deck flung out in the wrath of a loser; he felt an almost physical repugnance toward these symbols of wickedness. But the elder roses, rain-weighted, shattered in a purple drift across his hot temple and cheek, and their scent was that of the dark one in her hair.

Something rustled in the crape-myrtles near him, and he warily got to his feet. Her voice called his name, ever so low. Through his body passed a soft, swift, tingling shock, as if one had touched him unexpectedly. He did not answer at once, but she had seen the movement, and laughed a little.

"Bark 'lowed he seed ye, or somebody powerful like ye, at the window. I'm sure glad you came! I can't stay out here with ye—there's hardly girls enough to make up a set, and they'll come lookin' for me; but you come on in—a little while! Come dance with me." She even drew his arm.

He was able to answer her with firmness, "No." Yet he lingered. And she. Presently he went on, and his voice rang tense, but truly toned on every word:

"I have this to say to you—you come with me."

She looked at him, wondering.

"The meeting breaks to-night, and to-morrow I'm going on into the other valley."

"You'll be back to the baptizin'."

"I'll not be back to no baptizin'."

"You'll preach at the Blue Springs church."

"I'll not come back to you again, never no more."

"Then," she pouted, "I'll go to town with pap, and never come back here no more, neither."

He was silent. Averilla pursued an imaginary advantage.

"If you'll stay, I will. You hate to go!"

"I've got a work to do."

"Ah, what's that? Why?"

But it was his turn now. "Come with me. We'll be married at Uncle Zack's after the foot-washin'."

He stood, his wet hat crushed in his hands, awaiting her answer. For all his strong words, he felt weak as a babe. And Averilla, for all her pretty hesitation, knew her power. She shredded a rose with her lips and fingers before replying. The rain had melted to a drizzling mist, a keen, clean damp that caressed even while it invigorated. The fog usual to wet weather in these altitudes stole upon them now, and shut them round with so close a curtain that they could barely make out the red square of the window. The ring and throb of the dance beat round and through them both. At last said Averilla, sulkily, vexed perhaps because he was not sufficiently jealous to be angry:

"No, there ain't no use talkin' about it. I ain't ready to be tied to any man, let alone a preacher."

It was a buffet in the face. He took it standing straight.

"Good-by, then," he said, keenly hurt.

Suddenly she leaned toward him, caught his face between her two hands, and kissed him on the mouth.

Could it be?—he thought he heard a tremolo of weeping in her "Good-by."

A week may be a fearful lapse of time under some circumstances. Seven days had passed—seven days of wandering with Brother Brock on circuit, of unavailing endeavor to devote his best strength to his chosen allegiance and the work in hand; of fits of bitter rebellion succeeded by bitter remorse; of failure—he knew well enough that the church people were saying he "never done no good sence the Puncheon Camp Bresh-meetin'." Even Brock had not quite accepted the excuse he gave them for absenting himself from the foot-washing; but no one connected the boy's disappearance with Averilla Sargent, as they might have done if he had been seen with her afterward. Instead, all those to whom he was largely responsible for daily conduct decided merely, with sighs and shaking of grave heads, that he had been withheld from taking part in a peculiar and somewhat antiquated rite by the fear of ridicule.

In a primitive social organization like theirs, the stress of daily living is such that nothing may be spared for the pursuit of pleasure. Any surplus of spirit must be turned to religious exaltation; there is no room for the graces and caprices of idleness. And whatsoever is not for must be against the one symbol of unity, the church. Where law is lax, and the elaborately linked mail of convention is absent, the only moral protection of the community is its religion. Hence the line drawn between the belle and the wanton is but slight; both are wasters of men, though the waste be only of time needed at the plough and of mental purpose that should be devoted to Bible study. A lad's opportunity is scant enough at best for getting together his meagre start of property, acquiring the rudimentary education necessary to his daily round, probably eking out some small knowledge of a particular trade or craft, and finally selecting and winning a partner for that domestic stability which is his one chance of life's happiness. He has no time to spend in catching butterflies. A man whose welfare depends on the crop of an acre is criminally foolish to sow any of it in wild oats.

But, in thus depriving beauty of excuse for being, the danger is not first and chiefly to those who undervalue loveliness and charm and so miss them out of life; the real peril is to these qualities themselves, lest, accepting the valuation, they disport themselves accordingly. Venus and Diana, when they could be no longer divine, metamorphosed into vampire and demon. Were the lilies of the field to become convinced that they were creatures of evil, they might not cease blooming, but it is certain that they would begin at once to secrete poisonous juices.

Averilla dressed herself most carefully on that midsummer Sunday morning; the shining hair was brushed to lustrous smoothness, and done in the way she knew to be most becoming; as for adornments, she waited till she could find them by Aunt Sa' Jane's gate. Any other mountain girl would have kept away from the Lowry cabin after what had happened, but no knight of old ever took more openly the path of conquest than this wearer of the dark rose. She sang as she walked, the ballad she had begun for Luther:

"'O Alizonde,' the stranger sang,
'The mortal sins are seven,
And sweetest you of all sweet sin—
What hope have I of heaven?'
If you love me as I love you,
O haste not into danger!

"'For Christian knight, my fault is dire
As may not be forgiven,
But lo, you, lady, of your rose
My soul shall pass unshriven.'
If you love me as I love you,
What need have we of heaven?"

She passed the groups of old men in the yard, noted that the boys were already pitching horseshoes about the barn, and appeared to Aunt Sa' Jane, where that matron sat shelling pease in her kitchen, still singing a little under her breath and looking about with an enigmatic expression. Aunt Sa' Jane glanced warily up. It would almost seem she was afraid of the girl. "Thank God, Luther ain't here to see her like that," crossed the old woman's mind as she got the full beauty of the glowing face and alert young figure against the light.

"Aunt Sa' Jane," began the newcomer, dropping lightly into a chair and beginning to help with the pease, "I come over to ask could I stay with you while pap and the boys goes down to the Settlement and finds out that they don't like it. I ain't willin' to leave the mountains—not yet awhile, anyhow. Will ye keep me?"

Lord, these young girls, as wasteful of time and opportunity as they were of the hearts and lives of men! Who was going to pay for Averilla's keep if she left her father's roof? Yet, in an absolutely even, almost caressing tone, the elder woman answered her.

"Now, Averilly," she began, "I wouldn't feel that-a-way about hit, if I was you. Yo' pa needs ye. There's a heap o' good friendly folks lives in the Settlement, and you're more suited like to 'em in many a way than you air to the mountain. I reckon they have a dance mighty nigh every night down thar."

The girl pouted. "I don't know as I'll ever dance again," she murmured in a sulky tone that infinitely alarmed Aunt Sa' Jane. If she was going to carry her pursuit of Luther to the extent of playing saint for a while, the poor boy was certainly doomed.

"They's an association I've hearn tell of down there, whar the best kind of young folks get together," Aunt Sa' Jane pursued, eagerly. "I don't know as they dance, and I don't know *but* they dance; yet I've heard tell that the gals has a sewin'-meetin'—sorter like a quiltin'—about onct-every-so-often, and I reckon the boys comes—town boys, with town manners. That ort to be fine."

She was decoying the girl as craftily as ever a mother partridge lures the enemy from her nest. Averilla turned away her face, feeling rebuked, disappointed, and not a little angry. But Aunt Sa' Jane, having exhausted her resources of information concerning social opportunity in the Settlement, laid hastily hold of her next artifice.

"Now, here's a way ye can holp me," she broke off, reaching a folded paper from the high smoke-enamelled fireboard. "I got a letter yistidy, and all them men's been a-passin' hit from hand to hand. But Luther he don't write none too well, and we cayn't none of us read to do any good, so we ain't made out but part of hit."

The pease were forgotten. "From Luther!" cried Averilla, springing up so suddenly that she almost overturned the pan. But when the letter was put in her hand it proved disappointing. True, it said that he was coming—that he would be here this very morning—but it requested Aunt Sa' Jane to have his few books and other belongings collected and ready, since he expected to "leave." There was no explanation of where he was going, nor why; and the sheet rattled in the girl's trembling fingers.

"Well, there now!—I reckon he's a-goin' to take the far circuit. Wants his books—and I ain't got up a one of 'em!" exclaimed Aunt Sa' Jane, determined to bring the lesson home to her hearer. "You wanted to holp me, Averilly; cayn't you jest step into the middle chamber and lay what you know to be Luther's on the big bed, ready for packin'? He's jest that-a-way, ef he's set his mind to go this mornin', only this mornin' will do him."

The spring was all out of the girl's step as she entered the middle room. There were his books on the shelf, but she stretched no hand to collect them. Instead, she sat down on the edge of the bed, leaned her cheek on her hand, and fell into a muse. Was Luther running away from her? She wondered if he was really going to take that far circuit which Aunt Sa' Jane suggested as his destination.

The inner chamber was closed against the sun glare, that it might not become heated through the summer day. A buzz of flies and the ticking of a clock sounded faintly from the main house. As her eyes became accustomed to the dim light, she made out the newspapered wall, the mirror on the old bureau, the boys' clothes, of worn and faded homespun, mostly, hung beneath the gun-racks, and their rough box-trunks ranged below. A stately cat was visible in the open loft, watching a mouse-hole, and lizards hunting flies flickered in and out of chinks in the sun-warmed roof. She looked at the four-posters spread with counterpanes beautifully woven, wondering which of the pillows was to bear Luther's head this night. For ever since Aunt Sa' Jane had knit and washed his socks, and taught him the Bible she could barely read, and made his daily life for him, Luther had slept in this room with her other boys, and worked with them in the fields by day.

From without came faintly the chatter of little ones building a playhouse, the murmur under the trees, and now and again a brief and delicate warble of wrens from the nest beneath the eaves. Once there was an angry gobble, followed immediately by the yap of a scared puppy, and general laughter.

Then, abruptly, the heavy wooden shutter was pulled open and a dark rose flung in smote her cheek and dropped softly in her lap. After it a banjo was passed through the unglazed window and laid carefully on the counterpane. She caught her breath, for she thought she knew the hand holding the instrument. Learning forward, she whispered only the name—"Luther!"

Instantly his face appeared in the window. There was a silent moment of hesitation. He half turned away; but Averilla was not to be so balked.

"Luther—wait, Luther," she began softly. "Aunt Sa' Jane give me your letter to read. Was you—did you aim to go away? I was tryin' to get a chance to stay here."

He turned startled eyes upon her. "To stay here?" he repeated, almost harshly. He studied her down-bent countenance intently, then put one hand on the window-sill and leaped in with a clear spring. Once where he could reach her, he turned her face up to his own, and, holding it thus between his palms, began his interrogatory.

"What did you want to stay here for?"

"You," responded Averilla, almost under her breath.

He laughed out suddenly. "And I was goin' to the Settlement after you," he told her, without reserve or modification. "I can't live without you, Averil. I can't forget you. I ain't no 'count for man nor preacher if I can't have you."

He dropped his arms down about her waist, and she laid her head on his breast. "Well," she said, softly, "you've got me, Luther. Does that make it right?"

"Yes—yes—yes! It's bound to. It makes everything right. I ain't no 'count for a preacher, anyhow. God knows I never meant to fail at . . . but this—this is stronger than I am. You can learn me to play cards and dance, Averil. I—we've got to be happy."

The beautiful head came up with a start. The girl stared at him with dilating dark eyes. She put a hand where her head had lain and pushed him away from her.

"No—no—no!" she cried, as if in answer to her lover's speech. "Oh, you haven't understood. You've got it all wrong, Luther. I'll go with you when you're to preach. I'll lead the singin'. Everybody shall see that here's one soul you've saved. Oh, Luther, I can be good—for you."

A moment they clung together, trembling. The room was very still. Summer sounds from outside wafted through its casement. Whatever had been of misunderstanding, whatever seemed foreign in this change that had entered their lives, melted away. This was the supreme moment. They were not mere man and woman—they were mates.

four

The Home-Coming of Evelina

From *Putnam's* 6 (May 1909): 233–37

In "The Home-Coming of Evelina" the central character is a mountain woman whose lot in life is to be constantly moving from one house and parcel of land to another. As a girl she had the misfortune, in her mind, to be born into a family where her father frequently saw new opportunities in new pieces of land to clear and cabins to raise. He made a successful living at these endeavors, even though his family lived in a perpetual state of uprootedness. Anselm, the man Evelina married with the hope of finding a permanent home, unfortunately fell into the same pattern, not because he profited from repeated moves but rather because he was no manager and thus moved of necessity. Taking place during one of these laborious journeys, the story traces Evelina's anguish over her displacement and her longing for "home." The epiphany that comes to her just before dawn is a typical Miles ending. Miles herself experienced multiple lateral moves in her married life for much the same reason as Evelina. The author may well have been drawing from personal experience here.

She was aghast at this last failure of her long-nourished hope. As she plodded beside the pitiful stack of battered and rusty household gear—home-made for the most part, and the rest indescribably cheap and ugly—Evelina Kell, with her babe at her breast, found herself muttering and moaning over and over: "Oh, I'm sick of it—I want to go home. I'm sick, I want to go home—I want to go home." Tears at last blinded her eyes so that she stumbled. Her husband turned from his team with a kindly admonition.

"Now, mother, you'd better hush that, or you'll make yourself sick sure enough, goin' on so. Ride, honey; git up an' ride—the nags can stand it. Whatever air ye grievin' so about, anyhow? Look what a sightly evenin' it is—red—we'll have a fine day to-morrow."

She listened with a bitter, discrediting half-smile. This year, what with Anselm's illness and a fire, the stack of household goods had dwindled until there was room for her to ride beside the children. The baby was now old enough to sit by her instead of being carried—"though there'll be one in arms before the next movin'," she said bitterly, communing with herself under her shadowing sunbonnet. Moreover, the team and wagon, such as they were, were this time Anselm's own. "But there, we had to sell the cow to git it. Oh, I wish't I could just go home . . ."

She climbed submissively up. Jolting, swaying, sweltering, powdered thick with dust, the forlorn little group moved along between the ridges, stopping now and again to rest the mules or to drink of the wayside water. It was Samples' Mill they were going this time, and with every mile the country became wilder, more heavily wooded. Evelina scarcely spoke as they rode along; the little ones drowsed, or sat in apathetic silence, only at intervals pointing out a rock or a bird's nest amid the undergrowth. Anselm, seeing the general despondency, tried to cheer his woman as he ploughed through the dust, by assuring her of the tight shack and level truck-patch he had rented, and telling her how the mill men had offered him a chance to buy both. She murmured yes and yes, without interest. From having sojourned in many shacks she knew about what this one would be like—windowless, hot in summer and cold in winter as a paper shell, filled with fleas by the stray hogs that had slept under its floor, and impossible to render clean or attractive. As for the chance of buying—that, too, was an old story.

"Anyhow, I'm glad," said Anselm, fumbling for hold on his wonted cheerfulness, "that we decided to come out here instead of holin' up in Freefight for the winter."

The wagon jolted and rattled over the stony road. Anselm was a sunburned, lithe fellow, with a good-humored, three-cornered face that held structurally a hint of mirth in it. His wife resented that look just now. Both the children were whimpering, and she addressed their father with a querulous tremor in her voice.

"I'm plumb wore out with this ridin'," she said.

He could make no headway against her disaffection; he could not warm or cheer her; he began to feel piqued, and became sulky. It was some time before he again spoke, glancing at the sun.

"Well, I reckon we'll make hit ag'in dark," he observed. "The little fellers must be gittin' tired, too."

Again, when the shadows were flung far across the road: "Hit ain't more'n two mile furder. Our place is right on the p'int o' this ridge."

All drew a deep breath, and shifted position on the creaking, clattering load. Then, without warning, the off forewheel dropped into a chughole. There was a lurch, a strain, a crash of splintering wood; the children shrieked, the team plunged for a moment while their driver shouted and plied his whip. Then the calamity was quietly accepted, and all began to scramble into the road.

"Haf to take this wheel to the mill blacksmith's," said Anselm, tapping the smashed rim and tire with his whip-stock.

"And us camp here!" exclaimed the woman; but that was the extent of her outcry. Oh, well; it was of a piece with all the rest. Her lips were drawn as she went about unloading the needed bits of furniture, while her man unhitched and fed the mules.

"I'll go down into the breaks yonder," he proposed, surveying the land with an experienced eye, "and see if I can find us some water afore it's too dark. You know where them matches is at?"

She set the little ones to gathering brushwood, and presently on wayside bush and weed shone the shaken brightness, as ruddy a blaze as ever graced a hearth. But while the woman sliced the salt pork for their repast she was moaning softly, under the sound of crackling and bubbling, "I want to go back home"; and, though the children raced to her in delight over the find of a quaintly freaked box-terrapin no larger than a coin, and though Anselm appeared next moment with brimming buckets, having had the luck to stumble on a good spring not a hundred yards from the road, her heart lay like a stone.

All her life Evelina Kell had belonged to that portion of the mountain people who, sometimes through restlessness, sometimes driven by dire poverty, are continually shifting their habitations. Her father, Daniel Beaver, was not poor among his neighbors; he was only a type in which the instincts of the settler are forever conflicting with those of the rover. His way was to choose a piece of wild land, clear and fence a few acres, open a well-spring, build a cabin and a stable or smokehouse, raise his own cow-peas and truck for a season or two—and then, almost before Bess and Piedy were thoroughly assured of the whereabouts of the milk-pap, he would swap the whole for a larger piece of wilderness somewhere farther back, and begin the whole task anew. By this means he had owned, at one time or another, nearly every tract of arable ground on Sourwood Mountain, and, with the help of his strong sons and willing neighbors, built some twenty cabins. There is a tradition in the coves of Sourwood to-day that old man Beaver had a raisin' every fall and a barn-raisin' every other fall, his wife having a quiltin' on the off year. It used to be said that his dog, on seeing the wagon backed against the door, waited no commands, but ran at once to hustle in the chickens—all save one knowing old rooster whom some wag described as meekly holding up his legs to be tied.

So Beaver grew old in the full content of usefulness. In that land of pioneers he had been of inestimable service to his kind—like the historic Johnnie Appleseed of a more northern region. That the fruits of his husbandry must be plucked by others—that strange footsteps trod the puncheons of his hewing, and the laughter of babes unnamed by him echoed along the timbers he had mortised—this troubled him not at all. He made a good living and, with his five sons, enjoyed the almost nomadic life. But he wore out two wives in the process; and all his eight daughters had married pathetically young, hoping to escape, like Noah's dove, to the solid ground of a permanent home.

In Evelina's case the hope of haven proved a mirage. She had indeed married a man in whom the domestic instinct was dominant, but Anselm was no manager. He tried work in the mines "yon side the mount'n," and was at one time a hand on the valley railroad; he had tended the grist-mill on Caney's Creek, and there turned occasional pennies by fashioning bread-bowls of maple wood and baskets of oak splints. He had once set up a primitive jug-factory among the creek beds of pale-blue clay; and in season he helped with sorghum-grinding, cotton-picking, and fruit-packing on the valley farms. Shreds and ravellings these of any proper calling; yet Anselm was so hard and willing a worker that he always kept bread in their mouths and a roof over them. Evelina's sorrow was that the roof should be so frequently changed; for he never attained their common desire of a four-acre plot and cabin of their own. Something always happened just when they seemed about to settle—he lost his job, or learned of a better one elsewhere; the water failed, or they became convinced the place was unhealthy. Whatever the reason, the fact was that every year, sometimes oftener, they "shut the door and called the dog." To Evelina that proverb was a hateful mockery. Her part in the moving inevitably meant three or four days of hard work and exposure to the weather. The children seemed always fretful and ailing on moving day. Sometimes their scant bedding became damp with mountain mist. Often on the steeps they had to unpack the load and carry it piecemeal over a difficult pass. Once night overtook them stalled in mid-stream where Anselm had mistaken the ford. If they had a cow she was sure to break loose somewhere along the route and lead them a weary and anxious chase before they could start again. The children were all so nearly of a size that, until the last two or three moves, no one could be trusted to secure another on their precarious perch atop the bedding roll. And upon their heads was the summer sun and dust, or else the cruel frost, or a searching rain that might turn at any time into needles of snow. To-day's moving, in fine spring weather, was an exception.

The sun was gone behind the woods. Azalea fragrance floated in great waves from out of the hollow, and the whippoorwills began calling. The road, white as if covered thick in meal, and printed over already with little bare feet, ran straight into the green tangle and was lost; butterfly-peas and centaury roses bloomed beside the way; fireflies sparkled in the shadow. Between the oaks was a glimpse of a blue hill like—well, she could not quite remember what blue vista, far in girlhood, was like to this one. But that blossoming chestnut tree, with its clear, vibrant hum of bees in the honeyed dusk, reminded her of the one at . . . no; again, she could not fix the memory.

"This place feels like hit used to at home," she sighed, when the supper was over and the children asleep on a pallet spread under the trees.

"Which home?" queried her husband, and awaited no reply. The moon glimmered through the boughs, and the camp-fire slowly faded to a skein of pungent smoke in the darkness. "We gotta get up early. I want to have that wheel mended at the mill forge afore breakfast, and git a soon start if we can."

So a second pallet was prepared, and on its hard, uneven length they stretched their weary limbs.

For a time she was wakeful, while the deep stillness and loneliness of the forest night took hold upon her heart. She lay breathing quietly, lapped like a lifeless thing in a sadness too great to be altogether of a personal quality; the weight of the world's pain was in it. Dark, still and chill with dew, swept by an unknown wind from the unshapen, empty homes of the air, the vast night hung over her—Night, older than Time.

She waited, not caring ever to rise to a new day, praying only for the passion of tears that should bring relief. Then she slept. It may have been about two o'clock when Evelina awoke from a beautiful dream. She tried not to wake; her spirit strove to grasp the golden thread and follow into the enchanted country it had quitted, but roused itself in striving. However, the charm remained like a perfume round her.

"I was back home," she whispered to herself in the darkness. "That was it. I was back home." Overhead the night-wind was swaying the treetops slowly against the stars. She heard the whispered counsel of the leaves. "I was back home."

She tried to piece together details of the dream picture. There was a blossoming orchard, of that she was sure. An orchard all light and bloom, aquiver in the sun—the one at the old Dease place, of course. Yet it could not have been springtime, for she was picking blackberries, and a cornfield rustled beyond the fence.

Also, by the absurdity of dreams, with the rustle was mingled a drumming undertone of rain as she had used to hear it on the dear low roof by Caney's Creek, and framed by the dark entry-vista above the purple-misted range she remembered from one of her first childhood dwellings. Through the house a shadowy, beloved presence—was it her mother, or sister Lib or Em?—had made itself gently felt; yet surely she glimpsed the sunny head of her little boy that died.

Where was it, then? Where and when was it, this home, the centre, the very core, of lifelong desire and remembrance?

Suddenly, with a soft, swift, tingling shock, as of a hand laid on her in the dark, Evelina knew. She became fully awake, and saw the truth as clearly as she saw the stars. This home for which she yearned was no place to be reached by any road of earth. What she seemed to remember was no single definite locality, but the ghost of fair, perished days in many dear places—a lovely composite of all the hours, perfumes, and pictures past,—essence of all she had known of love and youth and the joy of life.

Over her head a bird broke the deep silence with a brief and delicate nocturne keyed like the falling of drops into a lonely pool. On the instant, as if at a signal, the frogs' orchestra began. From the marshy little hollow below the spring a few piped severally at first; then followed a chorus of tinklings and flutings and trillings and tintinnabulations. All were bent on achieving rhythm and unison, and all, as usual among the frogs, gave up just when success seemed imminent. And then the awakened treetoads took up the strain, in long cool tones, half a dozen trilling at once in as many different minors. Occasionally a deeper note rang vibrant and heavy—the bass-viol of a bullfrog. Every littlest tinkle was given its full value, held separately afloat on the ocean of silence. Evelina, listening, felt the old bitterness fall from her like a broken chain. So the frogs' music had rippled, clear and merry, from so many marshes through the summer nights of her life; wherever she had lived—in the ridges, at the foot of Sourwood, or on the Side, by the river, or on the breaks of Caney—she had heard them without fail each year. And so the thrush foretold the dawn; so the chestnuts bloomed ever in the engulfing forest; so the treetops fanned the quiet stars. And all were hers, for she loved and remembered all. These, not one particular lintel, were her home and her children's home.

She turned, and drew a deep breath. Over the oaks a rim of gold began to widen toward the zenith; the thrush's harp-note rang from the creek below. She felt her soul adrift on an infinity of perfect peace and wholesomeness. The great secret had been whispered to her in the night. And though she might not put it into words, she felt that she should put it into life—a larger life than she had ever known. At home everywhere! It was given her to perceive, in a simple way, that this frame of mind was the greater gift, outweighing the ancestral acres, the broad hearths and strong-raftered roof-trees, of women she had envied. Here was her mansion, canopied by God's blue.

Day broke through the highland forest; and, with the pacific confidence in herself and trust in the blessed everyday world of men and things which is faith in God, Evelina arose among her sleeping household, for the first time in her life a woman at home.

five

Mallard Plumage

From *The Red Book Magazine*, August 1909, 670–80; illustrated by F. de Forrest Schook

"Mallard Plumage" introduces a young wife, Roma, locked into the stifling restrictions of a forced marriage to old Preacher Guthrie. In a daring display of female rebellion, she runs away with Atlas, the young man she loved before her marriage, only to find that she is pregnant with her husband's child. Though a "fallen woman" in the eyes of the world, Roma is not an unfeeling one. Demonstrating compassion toward old Guthrie, who has pursued the runaways and suffered a serious injury in the process, Roma and Atlas take him in and nurse him. In keeping with the formula of local color fiction, Roma and Atlas display "hearts of gold" in their final actions toward Guthrie, and he reciprocates.

I.

Waked in the night by the first thunderstorm of the year, Roma sat up, suddenly restless. The rain sounded hollowly, with a noise as of drums on the roof of the big log house, and she could hear how the wind exulted through the tossing forest. Slipping out of bed, she opened the window and leaned across the sill. The drops whipped her sharply in occasional gusts. She stood breathing deeply the lightning-sweetened air, almost ready to yield to the spell of the storm—to run out into the downpour with mad laughter, to shout with the wind.

To run out into the storm and be part of it! Behind her there was the even breathing of a sleeper on the bed. She was like a thing with a leg chain, she might run but so far, then the clog she dragged would catch in some barrier and throw her on her face in the dust.

"To fly away, like Atlas," she murmured.

She was thinking of one wild as herself, with whom she had once taken shelter from such a storm under the Hanging Rocks. While the lightnings flared pale green and blue and rose, he had piped for her on his hickory whistle; they sang together, "Oh Brother Green;" and once after a tremendous peal he made her laugh out by shouting, "Whoop-ee! Blow again, Gabriel; there's some of 'em ye'll have to dig out!"

And the bitter aftermath of that escapade; how the gossips' tongues had wagged, and her own people talked and talked till she felt herself a thing disgraced. Atlas Cleaverage went West to escape their petty persecution; and she had been persuaded into marrying the gray haired preacher, Boaz Guthrie. They had no reason to watch her now; she was hedged about with righteousness—and hated it.

She was not unaware of the comfort and distinction of her position. In a locality where most women, especially those newly married, still prepared their meals on the fireplace, it was something to own a cook-stove, a reading-lamp, a sewing-machine, and any number of ducks and chickens. That these had been the property of a former Mrs. Guthrie did not lessen their value. There was, besides, something newly bought which counted more in Roma's estimation than all other possessions; her organ, whose twenty stops and square of mirror now gleamed dimly through the dark.

Yes, the organ would have been worth giving up much for if she could have been left to enjoy it in her own way; but in the preacher's house no music was permitted except that of the church. Roma was forbidden the dance tunes and ballads learned at home, and provided with a number of books containing the religious rag-time her husband admired. Having learned these, she became passive hostess of a series of "all day singin's" at which the neighbors spread a basket-dinner on the grass of the big front yard, and sang with fervor till evenfall. On these occasions Guthrie, throned in a rocking-chair and beaming on the guests, had flattered himself that he knew better than most how to treat a wife so as to keep her contented and happy.

And after such days there were apt to come nights when Roma sat, as now, gazing sometimes at the dim bulk of her organ and sometimes at the world outside. Once, among her Pekins—fat, milk-white creatures who demanded not even swimming water—she had reared a mallard. She loved its dark plumage, the very turn of its alert head, the sweep of its powerful wings. But the wild one joined the first flock of its kind that flew north in the spring, and she never saw it again.

If a door were open to her like that! If it were only to join a flight of her kind—and away!

She sat, until the storm blew over, and the pallor of coming dawn outlined the rifted clouds. Then she dressed herself and went to get breakfast.

It was a Sunday morning. Attired in a new print, with a ribbon at her throat, Roma fared to church on a blanket-square spread on Buckeye's croup behind Guthrie's saddle. She sat through the hours of meeting, distrait and rebellious. More than once she caught herself "faulting" the want of sense in her husband's argument. She knew by heart his round of phrases. References to "the cold-bleak-and-icy mountain of sin!" or "the teeming millions that have out-stripped us," rang as familiar on her ears as the cracked church bell. This was not the first Sunday that she had preferred to recall memories of unregenerate days rather than give heed to the sermon; there was no real coincidence in the fact that there sounded from the woods, at that moment, Atlas Cleaverage's own peculiar yodel.

A patent stir went through the congregation, though the call was faint and musical and far away. Guthrie, recognizing the note, took it evidently as a direct personal challenge from the powers of darkness. He plainly began to gather his forces for he knew-not-what conflict with Apollyon.

When, after a few minutes, Atlas' figure filled the doorway and then slipped into the nearest seat, the rambling sermon concentrated its fire upon him. All eyes but Roma's were turned, more or less openly, for a glance at the prodigal come back so tanned and muscular; and curiosity having prompted a first look, his mallard beauty, with its color of unguessed romance, was sure to draw a second. He sat quietly attentive and very straight in his place, showing no resentment at the preacher's personalities. The same old neighborhood, he was probably thinking, the same group of inextricably intermarried double-cousins, fenced in with no mental occupation but the gossip which inevitably runs into back-biting; forever brooding trifles and hatching mischief!

Atlas Cleaverage come back, and sitting in the church with her husband! Roma's inconsequent girl's mind had never conceived this conjunction. She strove only to bear herself as one unconscious of anything strange in the situation. When, after the service, she with Guthrie passed the newcomer in the yard, her cheeks were burning, her eyes down-bent, and her limbs trembled. He gravely took off his hat to the preacher's wife, which innovation caused the lads around the threshold to catch their breath.

"Reckon you come back to the mountings to get ye a wife?"

The leading question was put to him curiously as the young fellow lingered among his former cronies after service.

"I—well, there's no denyin' I did start with that notion," Cleaverage hesitated. "But some things back here has turned out different from what I expected, and I reckon I'll take my money and buy me a loggin' team, and stay around here for a spell."

Yet the next week, and the next and the next, Atlas did not come to church. Finally the preacher, unmindful of that portion of Solomon's wisdom, which in effect bids a man let well enough alone, rode Buckeye down the creek to the sawmill, where Cleaverage was at work, and flung him a bidding that was a challenge to attend next Sunday's service. Atlas had laughed at the news that he had been made the subject of a special intercession at a recent prayer-meeting; but at this summons to show why he should not be utterly condemned for contempt of church, he straightened himself, looked the elder man in the eye, and answered:

"Very well, sir, if you say so, I'll be there."

Guthrie's main reason for calling the interloper out to church was that during these weeks he had thought of many more effective things which might be hurled at him, and the sermon was pretty well devoted to the shortcomings of a certain fool who had flouted the faith of his fathers and gone west into heathen lands. Atlas received the charge almost smiling, with that look under his eyelashes of an inner light or knowledge which fascinated and daunted the duller witted. Roma, shivering in her seat, dreaded the collision which she thought must follow. But young Cleaverage had learned better ways of fighting for his own. At the close of the sermon, he asked and received permission to make a few remarks. Instead of rising in his place to address the congregation, he walked the length of the room and took his stand on the low platform that served for pulpit. Guthrie sullenly stepped down and seated himself in the amen corner, unwilling to endure the withering comparison of standing beside the younger man, yet quite unconscious of that fact.

"Friends, kinsmen, and neighbors," Atlas opened in unknowing plagiarism of a greater speech. At the first word the houseful felt the thrill of the unexpected. That he should begin, unhurried, unabashed, without singsong or gesticulation, to address them as he might if they had met him on the open road, riveted their attention; the stature, strength, and beauty of the man, and first and last the deep, bell-like *timbre* of his voice, held and swayed them.

"I aint here to defend myself against old charges or new," he said, half smilingly. "Time has cleared my name of mighty near all I was blamed with. You all know who poked Brother Guthrie with a stick through a crack durin' the big meetin' in this church two years ago. I reckon you can guess, yet nobody says much about it, seein' the man's dead, who it was that shot through the church-house door at Shiloh. As for the story of my playin' cards all night in the loggin' camp, that's neither here nor there; I was run out from this neighborhood by tales that seemed to be hurtin' somebody else worse than they could ever hurt me—an' I was a fool to go. Nor I'm not goin' to apologize to you for never havin' been baptized, neither. I've lived out yon where there's room for men of my religion, and a free life for all, and if I hadn't got to honin' for something I'd left behind me, I reckon I'd been livin' there yet."

Roma bent low her head over the hands close-gripped in her lap. The color ebbed swiftly from cheek and lip and abruptly returned when Guthrie rose, put forth a shaking hand, and interrupted the discourse.

"Oh, no," objected Atlas, coolly. "You've had your say, Brother Guthrie. Leave it to the folks now. If they want me to hush and set down, I will."

The easy confidence of this proposition won the instant suffrages of a people who prize courage above everything. Of the entire assembly, Roma only could follow the speaker's thought, and she less by reasoning than by the answering leap and thrill of kindred instinct. At no point did the round of their contracted lives touch the greater circle, which he now tried to make real to them; yet they were eager to hear. It was not his statements which charmed and carried them with him, for they were incapable of logical thought and set no value upon it. It was not the interest of a novel point of view, for novelty is anathema throughout the region. It was the sense of sweeping, elemental occurrence—of winged life—of wind and rain, and snow and hail in the hothouse, which startled and enthralled them.

"Go on, Brother!" cried three or four men at once; and Guthrie sank back in his place silenced: whipped out in his own kennel, ashamed for his congregation, and jealous of the figure he cut before his young wife.

Atlas spoke at length of his life in the West, his longing for the mountains (one heart beating with guilty rapture guessed what that longing meant); and finally asked his old friends to come forward and shake hands with him. They were moving up by twos and threes, all singing, Cleaverage's clear baritone leading the tune, while the little windows shook to the clang, when the preacher came to an understanding that his meeting had been fairly taken away from him.

It was Roma herself who had to remind him with a soft touch on his shoulder that it was time for the formal dismissal of church.

His bearing at home during the ensuing weeks was hard for a wild young creature like Roma to endure. All day he sat brooding in his big chair on the porch and allowed the farm work to lie. The mantle of dignity seemed to fall from him, leaving him a sulky, irritable, old man. Once when the girl could endure it no longer, she flung out at him in reply to some bitter taunt of his own.

"Is that yo' religion?" she asked. "Atlas Cleaverage has mo' good will in his little finger than you have in yo' whole body. Is that yo' religion?"

He turned upon her with a sort of snarl. "You mad at me because I don't fellowship with that there—that—" The fit epithet was wanting in his vocabulary, and he went on: "I shake hands with no man that's got neither beliefs nor principles—that's not even a member of any church!" But after a heart-sick pause he added, staring down at the floor, "I may be a mighty ill somebody to live with, but I think a heap o' you, girl."

"I know hit," she answered scarcely above her breath.

She did know it, and to her cost, for every day it was coming more bitterly home to her that she had sold her birthright of young love and a mate of her own feather; bartered it for ignoble peace, for a cook-stove, a lamp-shade, an organ with a square of mirror let into the top. And from this time on Atlas inevitably strode into her dreams and her waking thoughts, strong and vivid, a creature of sun and earth and air, the embodiment of the life from which she was shut out.

II.

So passed the summer; and the season drew nigh when the great migratory instinct should again send the wild birds South across half a world. It chanced that Boaz Guthrie was much from home about this time; the young wife was idle, thrown upon her own resources, and this perhaps was not well. Returning from an appointment at the head of Sequatchie Valley one day, the preacher found his cabin shut and locked, and Roma gone. There was no message nor writing left for him, but inquiry among the neighbors soon showed that she had fled with Atlas Cleaverage in his wagon, the pair striking out across country.

Guthrie lost no time in determining his course of action. Was he, after all, so greatly surprised at the outcome of things? Had he not, from the first, looked for just this? He had married a wife less than half his age, on impulse, as most men marry; yet with him the impulse ripened to a passionate attachment—that almost embittered devotion of the old for what is young, and full of life, and beautiful. Now his faith taught him no scruples against vengeance, nor did his church "think strange" of his armed pursuit. Atlas and Roma had a week's start; but at first he did not grudge them a day of it, deeming the cumbrous wagon easily traced.

Where love and tenderness must carry a little home of comfort with them, naked and single vengeance could follow swiftly unincumbered. Taking only his gun, a shirt or two, and what ready money he could get together, from camp to camp, by creek and gap and break and ford, across Sequatchie County and up through the Cumberlands into Kentucky, Guthrie followed. But he was delayed by one mischance and another—a rumor of change in the wagon's course, a strain of Buckeye's withers, a flood where Atlas had forded safely the day before, an invitation hardly to be refused, to preach in return for hospitality; and the sixth week found him still on the trail.

Whither were the fugitives heading? To the coast? Was it their plan to sell the team and wagon there and take passage on a ship? The thought staggered Guthrie, for to the mountaineer's consciousness the world beyond the water looms almost as dim and unreal a shadow as it was to the aboriginal inhabitants of his land. No; more likely Atlas was tending toward the place of his childhood near the Carolina border. There might be some fastness of the ranges known to him alone, some little valley enclosed by walls of rock, some "jug" cave defensible by one against an army. That the pair he pursued might be in mere, aimless, mallard flight, wing and wing, snatching each day's delight from under the sword, did not occur to Guthrie.

The strain told on his years; but he lessened the distance between himself and the team by a little almost every day. At the same hour when he camped miserably in Kell's Cove on what he began to fear was a blind trail, Atlas, only five miles away across the range, was purchasing a coop of a dozen chickens from a huckster, because Roma said she must have better food.

That huckster met Guthrie next morning, and replied to the haggard stranger's question:

"Why, yo' man mout a-been in with a gang o' traders that come thro' here with a string o' mules three-fo' days back. You mout ast some o' these-yere folks livin' along the road 'at seed 'em go by. I *did* meet a feller'n 'is wife yen side the ridge, but they was settlers here. They wasn't gwine to'ds the coast. He 'lowed he aimed to put 'em up a shack some'ers hereabout. Couldn't a-been yo' man, I don't reckon?"

"No," said the preacher, never guessing how Atlas could have altered his plan overnight. He thought it not unlikely that the pair should have joined the traders' camp for better protection, the more as they must be nearly penniless by this time, and Atlas' skill of horseflesh might in such case stand him in good stead. He made inquiries as the huckster had suggested, and was told that there had indeed been a couple among the "gypsies" answering the description he gave.

He overtook the traders at Nashville. There, in the jockey-lot, sick with disappointment at having wasted weeks on this false scent, he collapsed with "the winter fever." His mind, fiery with the lust of vengeance, was wearing out his body; and through the long weeks when he lay "tended on" with rough kindness in the gypsy camp, it haled him back upon the track and showed him pitilessly where he had played the fool in passing by the squatters of whom the huckster had told him. It was mid-winter when, disregarding all remonstrance, he again took the road.

Back into the Cumberlands he headed, clamoring upon the only God he knew for that wild and blundering justice which was his sole notion of Right; but every mile and every moment put behind him set his revenge further away. Although his heart was still hot, it began to be that he was pursuing a phantom. The constant endeavor to reach an understanding, in order to forecast the fugitive's probable course, unwittingly bred something like sympathy with his enemy's mind. For weeks he had continually asked himself, "Now, if I was Atlas, what would I do, and where would I go?" That this persistent question must result in some harmony and consequent final agreement between pursuer and pursued he had not the insight to foresee. He could not realize that under his anger, day by day, his purpose was ebbing from him.

After all, were they not kin by birthplace and tradition? Had Atlas been quite incapable of religious passion, he could not have so overpowered and humiliated the preacher that day in church. And had Guthrie felt no stirrings of an untamed nature, he would never have been so determined to marry a madcap girl.

III.

Title-deeds in the mountain-country read "from the bluff" and "to the bluff;" but the bluff itself is, like roads and rivers, Public Domain. Atlas had, in common with many mountaineers, an indistinct and limited knowledge of law, but an unbounded faith in the Government's good will towards men; it was perhaps with some idea of placing himself and Roma under Government protection that, when she could go no farther, he chose their habitation, like an eyrie, half way up the mountain-wall. The great cave at Wolf-Pen Gap had hidden many a refugee aforetime: the red man, or those who fled from him, scouts and spies of older wars; now it became shelter of this wild pair during the first frosts and storms of the year. But ere winter locked the Gap, Atlas sold the team and wagon, and managed to erect a tiny cabin on the wide-arched ledge at the cave's mouth. He worked now and then, when the weather permitted, for a farmer in the valley, walking to his toil before day, and carrying provisions home on his back at night. At other times he fished and hunted and trapped. Their walls were half covered with drying pelts. Roma broiled venison and trout and pheasant over four stones in the middle of the hut, since there was neither floor nor chimney to their dwelling. The smoke-escape was an opening in the roof.

It was the life of their dreams—of their dreams. And yet, dreams have a cynical trick of coming true, clipped, shorn, presenting the semblance and denying the substance. Roma had said to her companion in the first day's ride:

"I do love you, Atlas; but if ever you tech me ag'in my will, I'll leave ye; I b'lieve I could kill ye for hit; I'd never look on your face again."

And now, at the end of their wanderings, she was farther from him than ever.

A flaming autumn had swept the mighty slopes, and the long rains followed, extinguishing the last sparks of the splendid conflagration. November handed them over, along with the woodland creatures, to the hungry winter; but unlike their lesser brothers in fur and feathers, this pair was cut off from even a diminished natural food-supply. Then one blow after another was dealt them by the weather: it turned warm to rain, turned cold to snow, and cleared with a sunshine that only mocked their eyes through the glittering air. They ate food that neither had ever before tasted, things they had dreamed unfit for human consumption. The mountains towered about them pitiless as if built of white metal; the valleys might be open, but at that altitude the snow lay thick. All day, in the frozen forest, stripes of blinding silver changed places with shadows of steel.

And yet from this strange companionship, the love that was in them, the wild free zest for happiness that was common to both, wrung a taste of joy. The home in the cave's throat was a nest of kindly human warmth. In the long evenings, by the torches and the red hickory blaze, they achieved a dear comradeship in spite of the sword Roma had laid between them. They sang together, all the songs they knew—old ballads handed down by word of mouth for centuries, and new ones, quite as wild, of their own composition and rhyming. And they talked, like Indians, in voices low and even as the rain upon their roof, with long intervals of meditation. Roma, at least was happy. The dull emptiness of her other life was a thing of the past. Atlas could always interest her with tales of hunting, herding, or trading. His keen humor, and the swift, strong, level action of his mind, even more than his grand build and strength, made him seem bigger and freer than other men. She felt she could have gone with him to any fate.

The man, taught a little in life's school, kept wondering how it would all end, hearkening ever for the footstep of that change which would put a stop to the strange, impossible situation. But even so it was unexpectedly that the avenger came upon them.

Guthrie, circling where he lost the trail months ago, heard of the couple keeping house in the cave, and in the face of a sleet-storm walked, from the valley farm, up a path which Buckeye could not travel. He knew better than to attempt such a journey at such a time; everything was against him: failing strength, bad footing, wind and weather; the paths obliterated, and at best a way he did not know; but there was that in him that drove him forward.

The rain, freezing as it fell, thickened on every twig until the trees hung heavy with their burden, groaning aloud as the strain neared the breaking-point. Now and then a sapling bowed slowly to earth, or a big branch snapped like a shot in the tense stillness. He wandered, stumbling and sliding, along the talus of the bluff, where hand-hold and foothold were varnished with ice. It was too late to turn back even had he wished, and he would not relinquish the gun that hampered him dangerously. The low sun broke through the clouds as he scrambled, and for a moment the forest flamed with more jewels than Aladdin's garden. In the fading light he saw the clouds run scattering, driven by the whistling scourge of the wind that now began to search his vitals. The preacher was wet, sick, and disheartened. But at last he descried, on the heights above him, a moving light as of a pine torch carried in some one's hand.

Relieved that he had not passed the Gap in the dark, he began to climb heavily, this way and that, over the rocks. Almost impossible, he knew, was the ascent as he had attempted it. There was only one pass here, and how was he to find it in this black-diamond night? Still he climbed. It was his intent to burst open the door and cover the hut's interior with his gun.

But he was not destined to enter so. Quite near the cabin a young tree, loosely rooted in a crevice overhead, heavy now with the storm's burden of icy despair, let go and crashed down upon him, breaking what bones he could not tell, and burying his gun. Because his knife still remained to him he ground the suffering between his teeth. Slowly he freed himself, and dragged his broken and nearly exhausted body to the cabin door. Here, lying in the withering cold, he raised himself at cost of torture to a chink from which the firelight issued; and he could see.

Roma, thinner and yet more lovely than he remembered her, sat by the fire with something in her lap. The heart of the watcher leapt at sight of the tenderness in her face, and leapt again, as she bent to the little bundled thing she held.

For the first time he wished that he had not come.

He could not see Atlas Cleaverage from where he lay; the bit of warm, smoky brightness held only mother and child, like a madonna in a niche; but the man's voice came out to him shaken with strong feeling.

"I can't stand this no longer," Atlas was saying, evidently in continuance of a conversation. "I tried to leave you oncet before, honey—the time I was out huntin' for so long you 'lowed I was killed. I said to myself hit was nothing but a torment to live with you this way; but I found hit was a worse torment to think you might be sufferin' an' me not here to do my part. I had to come back. I can't leave ye; I can't live on with ye this way. I don't know what to do. If there was any neighbors, or if I was fixed to provide ahead for you and the little feller until such time as Boaz Guthrie could git here, I'd go back and give myself up. I've studied a heap about it an' that seems to me the only way."

"I don't want to go back," said Roma gently, glancing across the fire to some point out of Guthrie's view.

"I don't believe," the man continued, in a voice that shivered with feeling, "that people ever get what they want in this world."

"*I* believe that if they be patient and do the best they know, they're liable to get something better in place of it," she answered half musingly.

"I never wanted anything on earth but you, Roma," burst out the man's deep tones; "you know that; and you're not mine—you never have been. I see now you never will be. And nothing could ever take your place."

The listener outside sank down unconscious. When he came to himself he was lying in the hut on a bed of pine boughs and blankets, and Roma was chafing his hands while the baby miaowed faintly from another couch.

"Let me see hit," were the preacher's first feeble words. "Mine," he whispered to the top of the downy head. "Pore little soul—mine!"

They gave him whisky and an atrocious liquor of boiled pork rinds as the best they had. All the next four days, while the pass was chained with sleet, he lay with eyes closed or watching Roma and his child. Atlas was out of ammunition; but coming on Guthrie's gun tangled in the branches of the fallen tree, he dug it out and with it killed some rabbits, that the injured man might have broth. Yet as he lay, tended upon faithfully by these two whom he had come to destroy, tasting the nature of their life and beliefs as would never have been otherwise possible, Boaz Guthrie felt his end draw near on steady foot.

"Sing something," he whispered once; and Roma sang a favorite of his, "One Day Nearer Home;" but at its close he only said, "No—some o' yore kind o' songs—somethin' you like."

So she sang to him of the "Ladye Bright" and of "Wearie's Well," and the ballad of "Roma" for which she was named. When he lay quietly listening, she ventured on love-songs quaint and foolish with wild minors of refrain. Whether they carried aught of meaning to the dying man she could not tell. Tears gathered in her eyes as she sang.

Near the end Atlas, in answer to the reflection of a wish on the graying face, put out his hand. Guthrie took it and held it.

"Yo' fo'give me?" asked Cleaverage, choking.

Guthrie's quiet eyes went from one vivid young face to the other; they traveled about the smoke blackened interior of the rude nest Atlas had built for her.

"I wont say I forgive you two," he whispered at length, "beca'se I see some things different now. I don't consider that you done far wrong; an' I'm a goin' whar a man travels lighter if he casts out hate. Send for a preacher whenever the ice melts, and have me buried right; and if you will, best have him say yo' ceremony after mine."

He spoke no more.

By and by a puff of wind shook open the rude door and sent the smoke and white ashes whirling about the hut. It was turning warmer; and the new day shone in upon them.

six

The Dulcimore

From *Harper's Monthly Magazine* 119 (November 1909): 949–56; illustrated by W. Herbert Dunton

A mother-daughter struggle occurs in this story, the title of which highlights a mountain musical instrument more commonly spelled "dulcimer." Selina Carden has high aspirations for her beloved Georgia; she wants her to leave the community, study music, and find a life away from the harsh mountain environment. Georgia, however, has become enamored of Return, the young blacksmith with whom she has played since childhood. When he whittles a dulcimore for her, her fate is sealed despite her mother's protestations and heart-wrenching revelations about her own courtship and marriage. As genesis for this story, Miles may well have been recalling the struggle she engaged in with her own mother when she was contemplating marriage to Frank Miles.

The mounting summer had at last escaped the grasp of the April chill, and the season's growth came on with a headlong rush. The forest was one rustling loom of life-stuff, everywhere thrilling to million-tinted glories

of summer beauty and abundance. Between twin hills that lay against the sky, dark and softly rounded as the breasts of a slave-mother, the old smithy nestled. It was a log structure, low and windowless, and lighted like a grotto with blue and greenish reflections from the hot sunshine outside.

The young giant in the leather apron was clanking steadily on with his task, albeit he had a visitor. Straight from trysting with the wind among the blossoming laurel on the hill, she came into this place of grime and toil, with perfume yet on her garments, and her dreams in her eyes. Georgia Carden, daughter of old Jared Carden and his wife Selina, who lived on a good farm under which coal had been found in fairly profitable quantities, was a noted figure in her environment.

"She sha'n't go with the young folks around here," her mother said, half fiercely. "Let her roam as she will; the woods'll be all lumber and tan-bark soon enough; let her enjoy them while she can."

In the twenty years of her wifehood, which began with galling poverty, Selina Carden's pride had never faltered, yet she had not been so foolish as to prefer utter failure to makeshift. She adapted herself in order not to die, and she had so managed that all her children were actually rich. For each babe that came were the clean changes, constantly forthcoming on demand, that she could not afford for herself. For the new babe's sake she forbore cruel toil a while. Later, she furbished her early knowledge to set them in the way of permanent riches, by teaching them what she knew of their immediate world, supplementing the crude schooling which was all they could have, to fit them to enjoy a life which had never been hers. But the Carden lads, as they grew, would have none of such impalpable possessions. Georgia alone, on the opening of the coal veins beneath the farm, asked the reason for the dainty fern-prints in the shale. Her brothers echoed only chance-caught information about freight rates and comparative values. Was it strange that the girl, her youngest, seemed of all Selina's children peculiarly her own—that the usual mother-dream of a relation to endure indefinitely was here intensified?

"Howdy, Return," the girl spoke from the doorway, her light lawn dress blowing about her, the sun at her back, facing the shadows. Her mother's indulgence had given her years of faerie wanderings and dreaming to remember; and now any day that dawned might hold ere sunset the hour of the Prince's coming, the morning of love, with music and white light. The consciousness of this imminence was aglow in her face as she flitted across the earthen floor and perched moth-like on the work-bench, where scraps and broken tools were piled in rusty confusion.

By way of welcome the young smith fetched her a drink of cool spring water in a dripping gourd. There was something about him that seemed near akin to the silent, incomprehensible, tireless earth itself. Toward her freshness and sweetness all his being drew with a yearning like that of the tides heaving moonward from unsounded depths; though one looking on would never have guessed it.

"I'll fix you a better place to sit," he said, and his voice had the sweetness of bees droning in honey-drunken meadows. It was an odd, murmuring speech, coming and lapsing like natural sounds, but very pleasant to hear.

"I can see better from here," Georgia argued, tucking one foot under her. "What's that you're making? I want to watch you work."

"Jist a cow-bell," replied Return Ritchie. "Man up the valley's got two heifers might' near alike, and it's his notion to bell 'em as near the same as he can; so I'm aimin' to match this here." He showed his model, and sounded it so that the clear tone filled the cavern of liquid-cool shadow. They smiled at each other, and he turned to blow the forge fire. A red flare shot up and illumined the smoky walls.

With the big pincers he drew out of the coals a thin sheet of iron cut into the required shape. She watched him bend it round the anvil's beak and deftly seam the sides before the metal darkened. Afterward he riveted the seams, fixed a staple rivet in the top to hold the clapper, and added a bar through which to run the collar strap.

"Now it's ready for brazing?" she inquired, with interest.

"Now it's ready; only brass has got so high that they mostly have to be brazed with copper; and copper's copper these days, let me tell ye. You never see one made afore, Georgie?"

"I never did. You're always making things; that's why I stopped in—that and to see Aunt Lucy." She looked on while he laid the bits of copper over the outer surface, wrapped them in place with a wet rag, and packed the whole bell inside and out with clay. Then he fired the mass, pulling regularly on the bellows.

"Now, when I take it out the fire," he told her, "the copper'll be run in a thin coat clean over hit—all ready to put a clapper into and hang on the cow. This one here's been coppered—see?—and the copper's all wore and knocked off." He leaned that she might take the old bell from his hand.

"I expect it's travelled many a hundred miles through these woods, along of the cow, into wilder places than ever I've been," said the girl, holding it up. "Listen! Don't it ring sweet?—Do-re-me-faaaa! Return, can you read music?"

"Any Jack can read them songs they've been learning at the Blue Springs church," he allowed. "But without shaped notes I'm liable to git lost. I can't read the words any too well yit."

"I told poppa I was sure I could pick out tunes if he'd only buy me an organ; I'd love to have all-day singing at our house, and so would mother. But you know he calls all instruments 'inventions of idleness.'" She laughed deprecatingly. "If I even had a fiddle, like yours—Could I play that, Return, you reckon?"

"You could learn. I'll learn you." If the words sounded gruff and ungracious, it was because he was taken unawares by the sudden opportunity. Here abruptly was the opening for which, all through the spring months, he had planned with such quiverings of hope and trepidation. Now the way was easy for presentation of his gift. Yet he found it necessary to make his approach obliquely, mountaineer fashion.

"D'you ever see a dulcimore?" he began, after a silence.

"One or two."

"How would one do, instead of a organ?"

"It would be music."

"I've—I've got one."

"You— What say, Return?"

"I've made ye one—a dulcimore." The new bell was imperilled while he groped into the recesses of his tool-box. Presently he held toward her a queerly shaped instrument of three strings, a little larger than a mandolin. It was whittled with innumerable patient touches out of dark-brown oak, unvarnished, the head resembling a fiddle's, but curiously carved in an attempt at ornamentation—a thing fitted only for the wild minors of native airs.

She took it and jumped to the ground; silent with surprise, she stood holding the dulcimore in both hands.

"I sent back where Aunt Lucy was raised, in the other valley, for the pattern," he said, uneasily. "They've got lots of 'em there. . . ."

"Did you make this for me, Return?"

He pulled at the bellows, and made believe not to hear.

"You did make this for me?" she asked again, slowly; and at her tone a tremor of joy went over his averted face.

"I knowed you liked music," he muttered, as though offering an apology.

Still wondering and admiring her gift, she seated herself in the main doorway, on the sill white with road dust, and began to draw the strings into the weird and plaintive harmony of which they were capable.

Without letting go the bellows, he tossed into her lap a triangular plectrum of smoothed bone.

"You pick hit with that," said he; and, meeting the girl's eyes, was suddenly mastered by the laugh of utter delight that he had been trying to restrain.

A gray little figure appeared in the opposite doorway, which connected with his home cabin and truck-patch.

"I 'lowed I heared some music," quavered Return's only relative, the old aunt who had raised him. "Oh, hit's you, Georgie. Howdy, honey?" She came into the smithy, and the young man brought her a broken wagon-seat. She settled herself to look over a lapful of wild greens she had gathered.

"Eh, law!" she commented, when the dulcimore had been explained to her, "and that's what he's been a whittlin' on all winter. Whar I come from the young gals used to sing to them things." She sat nodding and smiling, tapping the floor with her foot while Georgia coaxed a shadowy melody between false starts and fumbled fingerings. It was but a little time before impatience got the better of the air, and *Barney McCoy* fell away into faint monotonous chords.

"Well, I must be going," the girl said finally, rising. She cherished the little brown dulcimore in tender fingers, slipping her hands softly over its rough whittled sides as though she smoothed a child's tousled head. "Return," she said as she turned away, "if it's clear to-night, you come up to the house and bring your fiddle. We'll tune it with my dulcimore then. Maybe against that time I'll have learned how to play a little. If the moon shines, you and me and mother and the boys can all go down to the waterfall and sing there like we used to. Good-by, Aunt Lucy."

But the moon did not shine. That same evening a terrific storm, the tail of a hurricane beating up from the Gulf, swept over the valley. Throughout the half-hour of the storm's endurance the play of lightning was almost continuous. Between the twin hills, where it was caught and concentrated as if in the nose of the smithy's bellows, it went roaring like a battle. Day broke nearly cloudless over the wreckage that strewed the fields. Wherever a twist of the wind's erratic course had driven hardest, there was ruin. Return's chimney had crashed through his roof; and the old aunt's life had passed with the passing of the storm.

For weeks thereafter Return was a man lost in his own walls. He tried to go on as usual, but every hour of the day had its peculiar strangeness, upsetting all the habits of his life. The effort to eat in solitude a dish of his own contriving choked him. He had retained from his healthy childhood a sound, simple delight in the mere round of the day; but now, from the time of rising, when the early sunbeams shone on no little gray figure by the kitchen window, with deft hands moulding the morning's biscuit, to the sunset hour of rest on the deserted porch, nothing was as it should be.

"Poor Aunt Lucy! Jist looks like I cain't get over it," he muttered again and again. The presence of death seemed ever with him in its unsupportable majesty. "I reckon that's what sets people to thinkin' about ha'nts in houses," he reflected, forlornly. The unlighted lamp, the empty rooms, were terrible to him. The silence oppressed like a weight of dark waters. He mended the broken roof and rebuilt the chimney; then he resumed regular work in the blacksmith shop, and frequently prolonged his labors far into the night for sheer dread of the gaping doors.

In these days Georgia made the discovery that she had, while awaiting the Prince, unwittingly become bound to Return. She had a period of bewildered astonishment. How could this be her lover, this man of the stony soil?

One twilight, between mocking-bird and whippoorwill, sitting by the spring near her home, she told him, utterly trusting herself and him. In their great moment the habit of proud reserve cheapened suddenly to insignificance, and the shyness of youth fell from their hearts as the clay had shattered from around the perfected bell.

"I can't leave you, never, no more than if I was your mother," she said, with quaint frankness.

The dulcimore and the fiddle lay forgotten at their feet. But the gladness she looked for did not come at once into his face.

"I used to wonder sometimes, when we was little folks singin' by the falls, if you wouldn't come to me some day," he answered, gravely, with a deep tenderness. "I've always wanted you, but I had about give up. Have you thought, girl? . . . You must talk to your folks first."

"Whatever they say can't make any difference to me, Return," she promised. "I don't mind about the others; but mother—I'm afraid she's going to take it hard."

"I would do the very best I could for you, sister; you know that. But she'll think it's not good enough . . . It's not good enough; but—"

Beyond the word there stood something too vague for expression, something great enough to face all opposing considerations with perfect calm. He wrinkled his big brows. "People have to put up with things sometimes," he brought out finally.

"And I couldn't see this coming," moaned Georgia's mother, as the two sat on the porch at twilight. "I could not see. I was afraid, too, for you to keep that dulcimore he made you; but music seemed to be your happiness—and your father wouldn't let you have the organ. Oh, I ought to have guarded you. But I never dreamed that such a man could have any attraction for a girl reared and taught as you have been. Why, Georgia, it can't be more than a passing fancy. Don't, don't think of it longer than you can help, dear, and it'll go by. You can't mean to ruin your life!" And fear stood in her eyes.

To her, Return was little more than the freckled urchin with ready grin and a missing front tooth who had used to thank her for cookies. Georgia saw him transfigured by a light of dreams into something finer than he would ever appear to his fellows. He was still the barefoot playmate, but he was also in some way the Sungod. Which were the truer estimate, let him say who has dwelt longest in that unearthly radiance. Into the mother's mind flashed two conflicting urgencies—the need for prompt action if she would save her daughter, and the fear that one ill-considered word might fumble her slipping hold. Already she felt her grasp loosening, moment by moment, as Georgia before her eyes became a woman.

Her little girl!

Afraid to leave the subject where it had fallen, she hurried on: "Georgia, dear, you shall go down into the Valley—to the Academy—and have some music lessons. You've always wanted to; now you shall, honey; I'll manage it somehow. And time you come home I'll make your father buy you an organ. I can. I've never asked much of him; but I can make him do that."

"Music lessons—an organ!" echoed Georgia, piteously, "Why, that couldn't make any difference, mother—though I'd love to have them, to play for—him."

Her face expressed only wonder and pity. Poor mother! Did she believe the whole world of music would count for a minute against Return? There was no hesitation, no complexity, in the girl's mental processes. She had given herself to love—to her lover—she was wondering now how best to comfort her mother. It was as simple as a plant's attitude toward the sun.

The mother, leaning forward, clutched the slim wrists of the girl with both her dingy, toil-maimed hands. In her extremity she sought for help whence help had never come to her.

"Has he asked your father for you, then?" she inquired, huskily. "And you never spoke one word to me about it! Georgia, my poor child, this is worse than ever I thought. Oh, put it out of your mind. If you are too young to realize what is due to yourself, try to think, dear, is nothing due to me, your mother? I was nursing you and slaving for you when Return Ritchie was riding stick horses!"

"Yes, he asked father," the girl said, gently. "He says poppa told him I could do as I pleased. Poppa likes him." A little wistfully: "I'm sorry Return spoke to him before I named it to you."

"You're blinded," spoke Selina, heavily. "You can't see now; but when you wake up and find yourself dragged down to the level of his people, it will break your heart."

Looking into the young face, its roseate velvet all atremble with new emotions, the mother felt as though striving in a nightmare with bending, splintering weapons. She had reason to know that she was impotently dashing herself upon no human adversary, but one of those laws that seemed always arrayed against her, always defeating her heart's hopes, always crushing her pitilessly. Had she not fought this same losing fight once before? She had never forgotten the days and weeks before her own marriage; the struggling, resisting, calling to her aid all habit and tradition, all maidenly reserve and family pride—in vain. She had suffered in withstanding; she had suffered in yielding; and her suffering had not mattered in the least, would not matter now. Oh, the big blind forces, the dark brute powers! Why was it allowed, this stupendous cruelty? Who allowed it? She was near to arraigning the great laws of the universe.

Yet she gathered herself for the battle. Before, it had been to save herself from she knew not what; now, with experience behind her, she would fight to save her daughter from a fate all too bitterly certain. She would appeal to Return also, to the rude and genuine good heart of him. There, if nowhere else, might be a chance. . . .

"Oh, listen to reason, Georgia, before it's too late. You don't know—" Her tongue ran into wild and futile repetitions. She became conscious of them and caught herself up. "Dear, you can't see what is ahead of you, or you would not think for a moment of doing this thing. Only let me tell you what it has been like with me. I never would let you know—I hoped I should never have to tell you. Just listen to me . . ."

She poured it all forth now, the story of the bitter years. . . . "And they don't care," she whispered. "They don't know. Nobody knows but your own self. You never saw your uncles. My brothers wouldn't visit us. When things were at their worst they wrote and wrote, urging me to come back, to leave him; offering a home, offering work, offering to educate the children—anything, if I only would. Seemed like they couldn't give me up to lead such a life. They don't write any more now, of course—but then . . . One baby after another. Yet the babies were all that kept me alive. It's a miracle any of you got through; we hadn't any decent—arrangements. Oh, I suppose I was all that kept them alive, too—my body held between you-all and death. You look as though you thought that was something glorious! I tell you there's nothing romantic about cooking three meals a day with a teething baby on one arm and your face tied up with neuralgia. Nothing heroic about washing overalls, or following your man to the barn with a lantern at two o'clock on a February night to tend to young lambs, either. And look at me!" She stood up, a scarred and darkened ruin. "Look at me! It's what you'll be; it's the best you can hope to be. You that I slaved for—you that I nursed—the only one that is mine! Georgia, daughter, tell me you won't do it!"

"I won't, mother!" cried the girl, the heart wrung out of her by grief and compassion. "I'll stay with you. Return will understand. I'll take care of you—"

"No! I won't have you sacrifice your life for me any more than for him. Oh, you don't know. . . . It would be easy enough to die for a man; it's hard to live for him—to give him all your life just when you want it most yourself. And when you think you have given the last that is in you, comes a new demand. You can't back out; you've got to meet it. Why, I've done things I can't talk about even now—things any woman will tell you she can't do. I had to! Take care of me? Why, I'm easy now; I've reached the best life holds for me so far as rest and plenty are concerned. The hard work is over, and the long pain, and the cold. And the worry. But the disappointment will never be over."

She was striving for self-control now, overcoming by main strength an impulse toward the hysteric crying of despair.

"And it's no use! I see by your face that it's no use talking. Was it for this I have stood between you and the work and the hardships—have I carried the burden for years on my own shoulders only to see you take it up at last? Oh, I've waited and watched, praying for a chance to send you away—to lift you out of such a life. I want you to have a chance. . . ."

Poor woman! she had meant to be all in all to her child, at least until the coming of larger opportunity. And now here lay her treasure on the quicksands!

"But—Love?" whispered the girl, blushing exquisitely. "It was you, mother, taught me what love means. I—I used to wonder how you could bear—poppa's ways, until I came to see that you accepted them as parts of him, like his voice and hair; and you accepted him twenty years ago. People think their children don't notice; but—it's beautiful, beautiful, mother."

There was a wonderful light in the eyes she raised timidly, pleadingly, to the elder woman in the soft dusk.

"I taught you?" Selina's voice was hard. "Well, then, I can teach you the better, maybe, that this feeling you have now—won't last. It can't last. You believe it will, but it can't. Do you suppose I didn't have it? Ah! you think it lasted—for me?" She laughed bitterly. "Georgia, if you throw yourself away, I have lost all that made life bearable." Her face fell into lines of gloomy reverie as she looked away.

"She is remembering," thought the girl. "She had love once; she was young; she hardly knew what trouble was or pain. Now there is only heart-ache." She called up in her own memory as much as she had known or guessed of her mother's trials, and her eyes filled with tears. Yet it detracted nothing from the mysterious splendor of her own fate that its terror must be set over against its beauty. The glamour which invested her lover's figure would be no less bright if her crown promised to be one of thorns.

"Love," the woman's voice touched the word as though it were something hot which burned. The eyes of her spirit seemed to glance at it as though its brightness seared. "Love— Oh, Georgia, you don't know." Her tones sank, her head drooped forward; but she spoke again. "When I first came here, to teach the little school in the cove, I was as full of dreams as you are. I had money saved to finish my education; I wanted to be somebody. But I waked up and found myself married . . ."

The girl cried: "But you don't have to live so! What makes you?" Swift indignation at the man who had claimed all this possessed her. Less wise than her mother, she did not see past him to the eternal law, the Way of Things, of which he was but an expression.

"What makes me?" A dull interrogation showed through the blank and beaten face.

"Why don't you go to your people?" pursued Georgia. "Why haven't you gone long ago? Back to your own life!"

Selina stared for a second, and then threw out both hands with a motion as of casting something from her.

"Oh, I couldn't do that," she wailed. "Georgia, what would become of *him?*"

The girl's eyes, already wonder-filled, widened and widened as the full significance of these words went home.

"You see!" she breathed.

"See what?" queried the elder, tonelessly, detecting a low note of something akin to triumph in the cry.

"Mother!" She clasped her warm young arms round the bent and quaking shoulders. "Mother! Don't you see, now—" The rest was a whisper. "Now you *have* showed me—what love is, what it means to us women."

Selina sobbed on uncomforted for a time. At last she became quiet, and leaning her head on her hands, sighed wearily.

Dusk had deepened almost to night about them, sparkling with fireflies and throbbing to wilder songs than are heard by day. From the turn of the lane, where all the sweetness of the blossoming earth was being evoked by the dew, came suddenly the cooing of strings beneath a bow's caress. The girl's eyes lighted softly.

"I don't know," said Selina, without raising her head. "He's not fit for you. But . . . he will always be a good man. And"—nervelessly—"it's the only way to live, I suppose. Maybe—by and by—I can be reconciled. But—My poor daughter!"

The strings sounded again, nearer, and as though at the touch of the unseen wapentake the girl rose. She looked long down the shadowy vista with that light upon her face that can shine but once in a lifetime; then turning, she reached from its shelf within the house door the little dulcimore that held all of music her life would ever attain.

seven

The Breaks of Caney

From *The Red Book Magazine* 14 (March 1910): 824–34; illustrated by Hermann C. Wall

"The Breaks of Caney" offers a glimpse into the complexity of family relationships as young adult siblings take on the role of looking after one another and their ailing widowed father. The plot revolves around a personable moonshiner's wooing of Orphy, an older sister who spurns him, while Zaraldie, a younger sister, secretly pines for him. Prentice Roark's choice of occupation is but one of the factors that complicate his relationship with the Farris family. The community doctor and extended family members who have moved to "the West" become important players in the working out of the drama of familial responsibility and romance.

The house smelt like a tar-kiln from the billet of pitch-pine that blazed on a rack of two iron strips driven into the wall. The log next above was half charred away from having many times caught fire. The whole bare wall was richly darkened with smoke; goblin tags of soot depended from a

ridgepole inaccessible to the sedge-grass broom. A freezing rain drummed on the cabin roof: the sword-song of the wind over the chimney was mocked by the joyous roar of the fire. Drops falling made little explosions in the embers and tinkled on the lid of the bubbling pot.

Dad Farris, for once perfectly sober, was basking in the warmth and radiance, and Orphy turned to him her steady eyes and good brown face all alight with eagerness. She had chosen this evening to discuss with him and Zaraldie and Man her project of seeking work in town.

The younger sister was seated on an oaken block directly in the rich light, a creature small and lovely like a bird, with dark curls falling on the rose-velvet of oval cheeks. Orphy, coming to stand behind the block, drew Zaraldie's hands back and held them so in a half-unconscious clasp.

"Looks to me," she said, "hit's the only way. We've tried our best to all stay together and at home, but ever' year gits harder."

"Hit's a long ways to the Settlemint," objected Man, from the shadowed corner where he had curled himself on a sheepskin. He was entering his teens, but was still "Little Man," having been christened "Jesse Edward" too late to oust his milk-name.

"Hit is so," agreed Orphy, swinging gently the hands she held. "But when there's only one thing to be done, why, there aint but one thing *toe* be done, and no multiplyin' words—"

"Why, howdy!"

They turned as the door swung wide, letting in a great gust of chill and storm. It was only Bud, the elder brother, come home for over Sunday; the plashing of the eaves had covered his approach. He walked in without greeting, threw a sack of provisions into a corner, and spread his hands to the blaze. When he became warm he drew a plug of tobacco from his pocket.

"Here, dad—and there's shorts and potaters, and a middlin' o' meat, in the sack. But that'll hafto do you'ns, now, until next week," he warned them, glancing round.

"'Taint nigh as easy livin' somehow as hit used to be here," complained the old man.

"That's why I feel obleeged to make a new shift," Orphy reopened the subject for Bud's benefit. "We got to look furder away for a livin'."

"I don't see how us folks'll git on without ye here, Orphy—let alone Prentice Roark," said Bud, covering a deal of affection with a jest.

For the first time a quick shade of impatience crossed the face of the older girl.

"I don't care for you-all knowin' here and now, " she cried, "that Prentice Roark's one main reason why I aim to leave here the first day I can git ready to go."

They looked at her, standing proud and sweet in her warm youth and womanhood, daring the known and the unknown together, and they turned their gaze to the fire again, helplessly.

Orphy began to set the table for supper.

"Hit's strange she never has liked Prent Roark like the rest of us do," said Zaraldie, a week from that evening, after all farewells were said and their sister had adventured forth. "But ne'er a one of our folks ever wanted to leave home, either, did they, Dad?"

"Your Uncle Ed," the old man reminded her. "He's West som'er's."

"Prent he jist bothers her; he's bound'-determinated for her to have him," explained Bud. "Well, hit a-goin' to be hard a-gittin' along without her, but I don't believe she'll stay no longer'n the water gits hot."

He took the trail to the valley farm, where he worked for a weekly portion of provisions and his board, and Zaraldie bravely assumed her sister's duties at home.

After a few days of it she cried to her father, sitting futile though sympathetic in his place:

"Well, dad, if Orphy had sech a time as this—"

"She did; ye nee'n'to think otherwise," he replied. "You know, she had you two chaps besides, at first; your mother left Jess'-Ed'ard a baby in arms."

He bent forward, trying to assist in the rescue of the dinner, which the pot had turned out on the hearth.

"Why, here comes Prentice to fill up ol' Tiger!"

Old Tiger sat in state on the fireboard, a sleek and shining presence, and young Roark was wont to see to his plenishing. Prentice's clear and merry gray eyes recommended him to the lads, and this week he won a welcome by saying, as he helped to set up the pot:

"Well, I seed Orphy when I was in the Settlement yesterday. She's workin' for Dr. Lewis' wife—housework and cookin'. She hoped you-uns was well, and aims to come out and see ye whenever she can git away."

Zaraldie took the apparent message at face value, though she might have guessed that whatever Orphy had to send them of help or cheer would come through the far off mountain postoffice. But it was quite true that Prentice had not permitted the girl of his choice to escape him by merely going to town.

“I’ve got business thar pretty frequently,” said he.

His confidence in the discretion of these friends was such that he did not mind their unavoidable suspicion that his business was in the interests of a still concealed under the breaks of Caney.

He continued a frequent visitor at the cabin, but what with bad weather, manifold duties, and the heavy winter roads, it was near New Year before her household saw Orphy again.

She came to them at last like a mother bird, bringing in a basket the substance of a holiday feast.

“But what makes ye look so worried, Orphy?” demanded Bud.

“I’m a-studyin’ about you-uns,” she answered. “Man looks peakid to me.”

“Why, he’s been well all along,” said Dad. And the boy supplemented gruffly, “Aw, I aint sick.”

“Well, another thing’s worse, and that’s Prentice Roark. He’s been a-comin’ too often.”

“Not often enough,” cried the owner of Tiger in sheer bravado.

Orphy, not wishing to spoil anybody’s appetite, said no more at the time, but once abed the sisters talked it over.

“Bud spoke to Prentice,” admitted Zaraldie, “and he laughed and ’lowed that so long as Dad’s got obleeged to have liquor, hit mought as well be from his hand as anybody’s. I think myself that’s about the rights of hit. He—he—brung me a right pretty pin from the store a-Christmas, and I didn’t want to take hit. He told me that he was aimin’ to be a brother to me as soon as he could, so hit was all right.”

“He knows good and well there aint a true word in his mouth when he says that,” Orphy assured her. “I aint able to think well of him, Raldie; and I do wish he’d stay away from here.”

“You don’t have no idy, Orphy, how lonesome we git with you and Bud both gone, and Prentice is good company,” pleaded the little maid, loth to lose at once a hope and an ideal.

“I’m old enough to know my own mind, sister. There never was but one boy in the world for me, and I don’t never expect to see him no more.”

“Well, I’ll give Prent back his pin if you say to.”

“You better—and have no more to do with him.”

Next morning, Orphy, more than ever uneasy, cornered Bud.

“Why’n’t you notify Prentice to stop hangin’ round our house?” she began valiantly.

"He don' hang round enough to bother me. Good Lord, sis! what have you got agin Prent? I'd have a fight on my hands right now if I was to send him a word like that," countered Bud.

"You'll have wors'n a fight if you don't look out. I'm afeared for Raldie; she talks as if he was much to her. Our little sister! I don't like hit."

"Shpppp! That all? She's only a little switch of a gal. Now don't you worry; me and Dad's enough to look out for her. If you feel anyways bothered, you'd best think better of what you've said, and take him yourself."

After parting with Raldie, who had "walked a piece" of the way with her, Orphy left Bud's well worn trail to the valley and turned into a fainter one that led across the creek.

By the dark sheen of frozen pools, past filigrees of the spray and drip of little cataracts woven over night, through the shivering trackless woods she descended, mile after mile, following the waters of Caney.

Prentice, in the rock-house that sheltered the still, had just got his fire going in the primitive furnace. Two other men, joint-owners with him of this industry, had left him in charge for the morning, and had gone to haul a sled of corn. From time to time a noise of squealing and trampling came from the thick brush down-hill, where his hogs in a pen were awaiting their share of the waste after boiling.

"Condamn your thick hides," he sent good-naturedly to their address between tasks. "Want to call up ever' revenuer in Tennessee?"

Suddenly, with an access of squealing, was mingled a clear young treble, singing an air that he and Zaraldie and her brothers had sung together round the cabin hearth not a week ago. He straightened himself and stood, gun in hand, with puzzled eyes on the trail.

As the girl's blue-clad figure came gradually into view through the semi-transparent maple brush, he drew a breath of relief, although his face still expressed considerable anxiety.

"Well!" he greeted her blithely, striding forward with lowered weapon. "I make you welcome, Orphy; but you've took a good deal on yourself a-comin' here! If ye hadn't a-sung that song, I'd a-took a shot at ye. Git to the fire and warm. We set on that boulder." He threw his coat over it for a cushion. "I been tellin' 'em this here place wasn't well hid."

"Tellin' who?"

"Oh, my shotes down yonder!" he laughed. "Why, you aint clumb all the way down Caney to find that out, have ye?"

"No, nor to look at shotes, neither."

She had laughed with him, but had not accepted the proffered seat, and now faced him with hands clasped before her.

"Prentice," she said, "wont you please stop a-goin' to our house?"

"Why, Orphy! whatever's got ye now?"

"Well, I've got a special reason for axin' sech a thing, or I wouldn't. Hit would please me mightily for you to promise me you'd never go there no more."

"Now, Orphy, s'fur's the old man's concerned, you know he's nachally got to—"

"Oh, don't say that to me!" she cried sharply. "That's what they all told me at home. Hit's something else I mean."

"I aint, honestly, doin' you-uns any harm that I know of."

"You know—"

She began in a low voice, halted, and then rushed on:

"You know I never have thought so much of you as my folks do; and I don't want Raldie to think too much of ye, neither."

She had chafed so against the necessity of asking anything of Prentice that now her impatience and confusion betrayed her into unguarded speech.

The young man stood looking at her flushed face, and thinking of what she had said.

"Oh," he said, quietly. "Why, I reckon the little trick likes me as well as I like her—for a sister. And I bid her to look at hit that way, too, because I'm always a-hopin' hit'll come to that yit!"

"Well, *I* let her know hit'll never be!" cried Orphy, exasperated.

"Whatever made you do that, Orphy? Couldn't you see that only made bad worse? She aint been studyin' about me noways but as a likely brother, and now you've fixed things so hit may change."

"But if you was to never go about her any more," urged the girl.

"There's an easier way, you know," he suggested, coming closer. "Jist change your mind, Orphy. Make me her brother. Oh, now, don't fly off. This is the first time the woman I want has ever sat by my fire. Jist think of hit. I won't stay away from yourns' house—not for sech a reason. Don't—don't send me away. Whilst I'm in this business there's but few I can trust, and I've got no folks of my own. I'd fur ruther give up distillin' if that'll move ye," he begged.

Her face softened as she thought upon his plea. It was true, there were few houses he could enter with confidence. Yet she had waked the weary night thinking of Zaraldie; she must not weaken now. Even should Prentice sever his connection with the blockade still, she would have but little to offer him.

Sadly she propounded the immemorial triangle:

"But if she was to care for you and you for me, and I care for—"

The incompleted sentence maddened him.

"Finish that sayin'," he demanded harshly, pouncing on her and catching her by the shoulders. "Finish hit! Who do you mean?"

"Nobody," she answered doggedly.

"Tell me!" he insisted.

"It was a long time ago," she at last confessed. "I aint seen him for years."

"I knowed there was some reason I couldn't make no headway with you, but I never had thought of that. Mart, wasn't hit—the boy your uncle raised? Shucks! we was all chaps-like when they went West, and he's likely enough dead or married long ago."

They stood silent, gazing out across the wintry gulch. At last she despaired of attaining any adjustment in this way, and turned to go. Her errand had failed.

"Aint ye goin' to give me a answer?" he asked softly, turning with her into the woods.

"You've had your answer long ago. What you can want of a gal that despises you, I can't see!"

"Maybe because I've followed ye so long; maybe because I've told folks hit was to be; maybe because I'm jist that kind of a feller, but want ye I do, and have ye I will." He spoke earnestly and without bravado. "I'll let ye know how Raldie is, when I come to town next week."

"You'd do well to go slow!" she retorted. "I give Bud what I thought about it, and he promised to look after her."

Prentice would not let her see how deeply he was hurt by this; but under the lash of her defiance and suspicion he struck without taking thought:

"Oh, Bud's all right. He's a-learnin'to take his liquor like a man."

As he turned back to stoke the rude furnace, and indeed all the rest of the week, he was haunted by the white shocked face she turned on him before vanishing round the rock.

When he again visited the cabin Bud showed him a letter from Orphy. Its cry went straight through Prentice's armor:

"Bud, will you tell me, for God's sake, is it true that you are drinking? I can't sleep since I heard that. Let me know what could have started such talk."

"I wonder who told her that tale," was the boy's comment.

"You write a answer and I'll take hit down with me," Roark advised, a little uneasily. He had not meant to be cruel.

He found Orphy, as he had feared, more than ever defiant, flung a little off her usual self-possession.

"I jist come to see if you'd changed your mind," he began. "And to tell you that Raldie aims to keep that pin for a while, anyway. You don't never know for certain."

"Oh, Prentice, I'm might' near sick. What makes you do me so? Didn't Bud git my letter? Oh, of course you'd not know. I ask ye oncet again, wont you stay away from our house?"

She laid down the knife with which she was scraping vegetables, and looked steadily at him over the big pan in her lap.

Prentice folded and refolded his soft hat between his hands.

"Orphy, I can't see for my life what makes you take on so. I've got a letter for ye from Bud; you can read hit right here. I was mean to tell ye what I did, but you'd riled me till I wasn't fairly at myself."

She reached for the letter, but he held it back.

"Tell me first," he begged, "that you'll give me a note to Raldie takin' back what you've told her. Orphy, I aint sech a bad one as you believe. I jist want your word that you'll marry me or nobody else," he insisted.

"Oh, I'll give ye that."

"And you'll write to the folks to say so?"

"Yes, yes; give me my letter!"

He came close to her, keeping the letter in his hand, looking in her face.

Orphy had risen, and now sprang back crying:

"Don't you touch me, Prent Roark—give me my letter!" and he obeyed.

Eagerly Orphy scanned the lines in which Bud assured her that the only liquor he had taken was when he caught a chill from being out in the raw winter rain. He could tell her, he would never love liquor; he "knowed too much about it now for his own peace." This was quite enough to set her at ease about Bud.

"If hit does you any good to know it, Prent, I hate you worse than ever for that lie," she declared, folding the paper slowly.

"Don't say that. Give me the writin' to the folks, now, and I'll go. I'm satisfied for the present to know that no man gits you if I don't."

So word went to the cabin home that sister had changed her mind and would some day "have" Prentice. But when the young wild-catter explained to Zaraldie that she might now wear his pin, she answered that she did not care for it any more—he could have it back.

It required resolution of a high order to remain away from home under the circumstances, but the wages that supplemented Bud's earnings were not to be lightly foregone, and the woods were dark with summer ere Orphy came again. Dr. Lewis had planned for a few months' vacation in Colorado and this allowed her a considerable stay.

July days are doubly long in the silent, beautiful loneliness that broods over Caney. All the blue, drowsy afternoon the girls sat on the porch and the boys sprawled in the shade in the clean swept yard. They held little speech, satisfied to be together under the home roof.

But here was a grown-up Zaraldie, quiet and reserved for all the old impulsive affection. Orphy thought she perceived a shadow on the young face beyond what a few months of responsibility should cast.

"Have you been worried about Man, honey?" she inquired.

"Why, I never noticed he was poorly till you spoke of hit," replied the girl with some compunction.

"I reckon what you need's a tonic, Man; but they tell me might' near all of them's got liquor in 'em, and I don't want to commence givin' ye that."

"Prentice might have let me have some o' his'n," said Man, "but when I named it to him he 'lowed he wouldn't hardly dast to with you promised to marry him. He told me he aims to quit makin' liquor this month, anyway."

"He's 'lowancin' mine," was Dad's contribution.

"Would you go to see Dr. Lewis before he goes West, Man?" she asked.

"Aw—I don't know."

The doctor's office was no dragon's den to Orphy, who had often put it to rights in the morning; and she was able to partly overcome the boy's trepidation. It was decided that Bud should accompany his brother to the Settlement next day.

But Zaraldie's trouble was beyond medical aid. That night, while the whippoorwills wailed in the edge of the woods and the garden sparkled with fireflies, Orphy was aware of her sister's wakefulness; she could not be sure whether there was a tremor of inaudible sobbing.

At last she could no longer keep silent.

"Honey, what ails you? I can't stand it not to know. Tell sister!"

She crouched beside the girl, on the patch work wrought by patient hands long dead, and speaking as to the child who a few years ago had been content, on waking from some terrifying dream, to find that sister's breath still stirred her hair.

But she knew it was a woman who answered:

"I want to go away. I'm tired, tired of hit."

"Where you want to go to?"

"I'd like to git me something to do, like you did. I can cook good now. Why can't you and me jist change places?"

"I don't see how we could do that, Raldie," said the maid-mother, knowing how different was the work in town from everything learned in the cabin, and sure that Zaraldie among strangers would wither like transplanted mountain-laurel. "You see, when you said you wasn't goin' to school, I promised Miss' Lewis I'd go back and stay with them another winter. But I wont promise for no longer, so you can get away next year."

"Next year. Oh!" and Raldie's voice broke.

"The boys and Dad couldn't make out without us, or I'd jist take you with me."

"Aint ye goin' to git married and settle down?"

"Not this year," temporized Orphy, weakly.

The days drew forward, slipping one by one, beads of a golden rosary, but threaded on a triple strand of pain.

One night as they dressed for a play-party in a neighboring cove, Orphy inquired, as she was about to fasten Zaraldie's collar:

"Where's your pin?"

"What you axin' me that for?" flashed Zaraldie. "You still mad cause Prentice give hit to me?"

"Why, I jist thought hit would look pretty on you. I wasn't never mad about it," said Orphy, in surprise at the outburst.

"I done lost hit long ago."

And Raldie fell to brooding.

That evening, in the course of a game, Prentice chose Zaraldie for a partner—Zaraldie in a white dress, curls, and string of beads, sweet and warm as a velvet rose. "Fire on the mountain, fun, boys, fun," he sang, dancing all over with the mountaineer swing, his head just clearing the rafters.

As he took the girl's hand to lead her through their part, suddenly Orphy knew. That flushed, sweet face, with a dark-eyelashed twilight of modesty veiling its starry happiness, could mean but one thing.

It was Prentice who, on the way home, let her know how he and Zaraldie had been together at a number of frolics during the past winter.

"She's good company oncet she gits a-goin'. And I think, seein' she's to be my sister, you nee'n'to object. I do think you treat me scandalous."

Orphy was baffled, wordless. Prentice never presumed on the promise she had given him, but she felt bound by it to a semblance of friendliness. There seemed nothing she could do.

As the summer went on, her knowledge of Raldie's poor, little, unconfessed love became a wall between the sisters. Neither was able to speak of it; neither could think of anything else. Prentice's appearance in the low doorway at any hour sufficed to set both girls acutely on the defensive.

And he caught himself more than once watching Zaraldie, or doing small services and offering small services for the glance of warm thanks she could not forbear giving him. Zaraldie was being happy while she could. Orphy had promised that she should go to town when Prent was married; but "I needn't go; it will be the end of life to me," thought the young girl; and meantime, "Nobody need know that I care." Yet sometimes, when she and Prentice were alone together, a current of emotion flashed from one to the other; their speech fell away into silence, and they smiled at each other with trembling lips.

"If Orphy would only look at me like that!" was his longing.

One day, when the blue and gold of September was inclining toward the richer purple and scarlet of autumn, Prentice hauled a load of apples to town. As Orphy was now ready to return to her place there, he offered her a seat in his wagon.

"If Man'll help me load 'em he can ride over the mountain with me, too, and see that doctor again. My Limber-twigs is all honest produce this time," he added, laughing. "I'm out of the liquor business oncet for all."

Almost the look he craved rewarded him.

When Man came home he sat till far in the night recounting what the doctor had told him of the West.

"He seed our uncle Ed out there. Says you can ketch feesh with your hands in Uncle Ed's errigation ditches. And he raises, I don't recollect what all; you ride over his land a hour before you git to the house. And when he heared the doctor was from this part of the country, he axed about us, and Doctor Lewis he told about me, and—and he 'lowed he aimed to send for me to come out there."

"What did the doctor say about that?" asked Bud.

"He judged hit might do me a power o' good, and he hoped how soon I'd go."

November spilled the year's wealth upon the land in wild frost-sweetened fruits and mast and chestnuts, and Bud's hearth-fires grew in glory, fed with fat knots and roots of pine—flowing over logs, licking round the kettle, whirling against the soot-mossed back of the fire-place, displaying rainbows of strange colors, and pouring finally into the black throat of the chimney as a waterfall disappears into a sunless gorge. No stranger can ever know the real beauty of this red heart of home, which mocks the old north with its low, cheery music—with soft roar of burning, with laughing sparkle, with flicker and blue flutter, with the fusillade of hickories, and the "treading snow" of brands half-consumed, and the last clink of the falling ash at sleeping-time.

Into this radiance came Prentice one evening, his lungs and his garments filled with the breath of the keen clear night.

"Hit'll frost to-night," he said, nodding all round. "Like a young snow."

"I make ye no less welcome, Prent," complained Dad Farris, "but hit's a on-disputed fac' that I aint had a drap o' good whiskey sence the last you give me. This here boughten stuff's a sin to the lizards. I cayn't drink hit."

"Sorry," laughed the young man. "I'll show Raldie how to make persimmon beer, and we can all drink some. But I got shut of that business in a good time," he continued, seating himself in one of Orphy's new chairs. "You'ns aint heared about the raid?"

"We never hear anything 'thout you or Bud tells us." Dad's tone was still aggrieved.

"Well, they sure made one to-day. That marshal must be a devil-yarker! Went right down Caney alone, and slipped up on 'em in the still—ketched 'em makin' a run, and slipped between them and their guns and covered 'em. They got rattled and run spang into his arms. Got 'em both."

"Oh, I'm proud you was out of hit long ago," breathed Zaraldie.

"I am, myself. Orphy she'll be glad to hear about hit. You can write her."

They told the thing over and over, and discussed all its aspects again and again, fixing it well in mind. Afterward the conversation turned to Orphy; where was she, and when would they see her again? Was she growing too fond of staying in town? Or was she, on the contrary, unhappy with homesickness?

Bud and Prentice were upholding one balance of probability and Raldie and Dad another, when again the door swung open, and Orphy herself appeared.

"I was hopin' you'd all be settin' up together!" she cried joyously, before any of the startled occupants of the room could frame a question. "Dad, here's Uncle Ed come to see you. We walked out from town together."

A tall man stooped through the doorway behind her—a man browned with many summers and grizzled with many snows, yet in appearance younger than Dad.

"Why, how're ye, Jesse?" he rumbled, genially. "You're gray as a rat. What y'been a-doin' to yerself?"

"Are you Uncle Ed? Are you Dad's brother?" screeched Man in delight, dancing on one leg all round the hastily quitted circle of chairs.

The two men shook and shook both each other's hands; then the Westerner caught the mountaineer by the shoulders and shook him; then they fell to shaking hands again, Dad reiterating all the while that he was indeed "powerful weak, powerful weak, Ed, but hit does me a world o' good to see you."

"Well, I aint so surprised," said the newcomer, standing back at last, "not when I look at your family, and think Ann's been dead this many years. This Bud? Howdy! Man ever' eench. Orphy's been a tellin' about him as her and me come on. Raldie, honey, come and give your ol' uncle a kiss. They been skase things in my time. Like sis Betty, aint she, Jesse? Here's the boy that's goin' home with me? Looks to me you must have growed too fast, Man. They ortn't to have give ye sech a name to live up to, and then ye might have took your own time to hit. You can read and write, can't ye? That's right. I always 'lowed there ought to be a few scribes in amongst sech a bunch o' Farrisees."

Dad slipped his word edgewise. "This here's Prentice Roark—old Arch's boy, Ed. He's e'en-aboyut one o' the family," with a nod toward the fireside where the two sisters stood.

"Howdy, boy. I'd a-knowed you was Arch's by your looks. So you and Orphy's promised? Well, well—she never named you to me, and I was jist a-fixin' to tell her what Mart said. You recomember him, do ye? He 'lowed if she wasn't married he'd be glad to hear from her. He's in with me on the sheers."

"Mart!" breathed Orphy. "Is he—how is he?"

"He's all right. He's turned out well, honest and stiddy, and smart with hit; jist the man for any gal, be she free. Good thing for Mart he don't know ye like you air now, or he'd be powerful disappointed."

They fell to planning for Man's going away; then Uncle Ed must hear the news of old neighbors, and the others must be told of the wonderland West. But Prentice sat silent, drawn back into the corner. He looked from one sad girl face to the other, and bethought himself of a way to lighten the shadow on both.

But like the Indian who inhabited his forests aforetime, the mountaineer moves with caution until the moment to strike. The hickory log had burnt to a bed of coals ere he finally spoke the word that freed them all from a false position.

"You're mighty right I aim to be one o' the family," he stated abruptly, "the first chanst I git, but you're mistaken in the gal."

Uncle Ed, unaware of the sensation aroused by this seemingly innocent explanation of a very natural mistake, talked on.

"I had good luck takin' one boy to raise; I feel considerable encouraged to try another. And if so be you aint promised to nobody, Orphy—well, I wouldn't let Raldie put me to dance in the kettle if I was you."

But all the young people, at least, knew what Orphy meant by her murmur as Prentice took his leave:

"I might have treated you better, Prent."

"That's all done and forgot about," he answered.

The light of the embers reddened moment by moment on the group of happy faces, and the brave housegear that Orphy's service had introduced. A hoarsely jubilant chorus of cock-crow arose from the chimney shelter outside.

It was Zaraldie who flung open the door for Prentice; and they two stepped forth to say good-night beneath the black-diamond stars.

eight

Flyaway Flittermouse

From *Harper's Monthly Magazine* 121 (July 1910): 229–35; illustrated by W. Herbert Dunton

Though Miles is known for her love and concern for children, "Flyaway Flittermouse" is her only story in which a toddler is the main character. Flittermouse epitomizes innocence and trust as she wanders by herself along a country road. She charms each local traveler she meets and brings about good will, all without effort, guile, or awareness on her part. This story had its origins in an actual event. On a hunt for huckleberries in July 1909, two-year-old Kitty, Miles's youngest daughter, became separated from her siblings. When the child was discovered missing, her family and neighbors launched a search. According to the account Miles recorded in her journal, Kitty's eventual savior was a neighborhood lad headed out to see his girlfriend. Hearing the child crying in the berry bushes, he delayed his journey long enough to carry her home. Kitty's adventure served as inspiration for the story of "Flittermouse," Emma's pet name for her baby girl.

Ever since the first of the week, when the elder children started for school, with a basket of biscuits and fried pork and a First Reader among

them, Flittermouse had been lonely. To-day it was worse than ever; for not only had Pappy left to work before she waked in the morning, but even Mother was almost inaccessible through the malignance of a headache. As for little Man-alive, the only playmates that interested him were his own sea-shell feet and hands.

Aunt Libby, having "drowned the miller" in making up her bread, came to borrow flour, and stayed to help with the churning; but now she was gone back home across the field, and Mother lay with tight-closed eyes on the bed. Flittermouse tried for a while to keep store, in imitation of her brothers, on the plank shelves they had arranged in the fence corner; but after pouring out the cans of water which represented barrels of oil and sorghum, and dismantling the rows of patiently moulded mud loaves and red-velvet oak tips, galls, and acorns which made up the rest of their stock, there did not seem to be much to do here; besides, she had an uncomfortable conviction that the boys would not approve her activities when they came home.

Across the fence, in a great airy cavern of shade beneath an oak, was a playhouse of more domestic character, all aglitter with broken china and upholstered in plushy moss. She had so often slipped between the rails to play here with sister that the fascination of forbidden fruit was absent from its neat and pretty housewifery, and the two little bare feet did not linger, but only printed the ground lightly as they pattered past.

Along the dew-damp sand broad shadows lay invitingly, though the day was not yet too warm. A cardinal flashed between the trees as she looked, and, "Birdy," she greeted him, with an indescribable circumflex; adding immediately and regretfully, "Flyed away; gone wa-ay off-in-woods." She heard the *Song of the Open Road* as plainly as it was ever sung. The iridescence of wings in the azure air, the happy z-z-z-ing of gnats and honey-lovers—it was all a siren lure. She was drawn down the road's green, sun-shot vista irresistibly even before her Great Idea took shape; but once having glimmered into consciousness, it speedily became evident to her mind that Pappy was coming, somewhere yonder, probably just round the turn.

"Go'n' meet him," said Flittermouse, firmly.

Forthwith her toddle quickened to a trot. The little checked cotton frock she wore would have been for a time distinctly visible, flickering in and out of the bands of sunshine that lay across the road; but the eyes of the house-mother were so dimmed with headache that even had she roused herself to look from the window she could hardly have seen. Besides, had not Libby said that she might take the child home with her for the day?

So, all unchallenged, unhindered, a little gipsy went dancing down the green-arched lane like a butterfly drifting on the breeze. The road as it ran away seemed to laugh back at her over its shoulder; she followed it on and on. From time to time she was tempted aside by a shining cluster of berries; she stopped to gather her hands full of flowers, and to splash and wade in a rivulet rutted by passing wagons; she poked in an interesting hole, and was startled by the appearance of an exasperated toad; she squealed in delight at a jewelled dragon-fly; and once, absorbed in a phenomenon which she afterward described as "two bum'lebees rollin' a mobble," she came near forgetting her purpose. But after the minute of wonder, she got to her feet and went on, looking eagerly down the road where she expected, every moment, to see Pappy appear.

Ah—there he was! She ran forward with a shout; then her footsteps lagged and faltered as she saw that it was not Pappy, but a stranger. Out of sheer interest she came to a halt and stared. The newcomer was so bristly gray, and had such fierce eyebrows!

She kept her soft dark gaze steadily and gravely on him. That he was grim and surly she did not know, any more than she knew that she herself was the most enchanting bit of human perfection the old fellow had beheld in many a day. This was a Man, and her experience of men had not been at all disconcerting; the whole race was typified, of course, by Pappy.

But such a funny man! He was about to pass her, when she giggled, showing all her little teeth like grains of rice. The man stopped and stared in his turn, as if he had not seen her until that moment.

"Huh!" said he. Then, "Whose little gal air you?" he asked, in a queer husky old voice that matched his bristly gray hair.

She knew the answer to that question. "Pappy's."

"Huh! Where you think you're a-goin'?" came the next query.

"Go'n' meet Pappy."

He looked at her a moment, made as if to laugh, and went striding on. But his face had perforce relaxed a bit; and as he went he muttered: "Little dickens—watch them feet o' hern! Jest like Cinthi' said, young critters sca'cely knows whether they dancin' or walkin'. Eh—law—Cinthi'."

She had scarcely watched him out of sight when a murmur of voices caused her to look the other way. The two now approaching were deep in some altercation; they were, indeed, quarrelling, not with loud words or angry bluster, but in the mountaineer's way, with a growing tension of distrust. Behind their immobile faces thoughts were gathering that might separate them for life. But at sight of the little girl they dropped, for the time, whatever they had been talking about.

"D'you reckon she's lost, Jeff?" said one, using his companion's name in a kinder tone than he had employed since the question of that misplaced fence came up.

"I'll see," the other answered, peering at her from under a green corduroy cap. He bent upon Flittermouse a pair of very pleasant gray eyes. "Want to come?" He held out his hands, broad, brown, flexible, the palms calloused with field work. "Lemme tote ye home, pretty. Where is hit you live? Where's Pappy?"

"Down road. Go'n' meet Pappy," exclaimed Flittermouse, confidentially, liking the man's voice and manner. "Uh-huh; go'n' tell him—dot—szschicken for zupper."

"Oh," the man smiled, drawing back a little, "is Pappy down the road? You waitin' for him?"

She nodded. "Go'n' eat a szschicken bum'tick."

"Come on, Jeff," urged the truck-grower. "The baby's all right—ain't ye, sweetness? She knows what's she's headed fer."

Flittermouse accepted this with dignity. Here was a man who recognized ability when he met it.

The man in the green cap hesitated. "Well—I guess it's all right, and I—I ain't got much time." He appeared to be apologizing to the little stray before him. "But I declar' you do look like Clay's kid; and if that's so, you're a right smart piece from home."

But as Flittermouse continued to back away, step by step, not suspiciously, but as one who is sure of the course of duty, he decided that the child's father could not be far distant.

"If she *is* lost, we'll be apt to hear of hit a ways on." And returning to contemplation of his own thrice-vexed affairs, he made haste to overtake his companion.

They did not take up the quarrel exactly where they had left it. Instead, each cast about for something to say which would conceal from the other the fact that he was thinking deeply.

"Who was that went on in front of us?" inquired the man in the green cap.

"Old Provine, goin' down the creek to see after his sawmill," replied the truck-grower. "I looked for him to say somethin' to me, but he took it out in glowerin'. Old man's got it in for ever'body since him and Aint Cynthi'

Macklin had their last set-to over her granddaughter's church trial. That was the masterest argu-mint I ever heard."

"She whupped him out, though."

"That's what she done. 'Lowed the Good Book says there's a time to dance, and Orphy should choose her own time about hit. They let the trial go over for decision, didn't they?"

"Yes; but I look for 'em to turn the pore gal out next month." He spoke with his mind centered on something else, which sharpened into utterance in the next few steps. "Look a-here, Jeff; tell ye what I'll do. Let your fence stand, and I'll sell you the ground as fur as the mistake occurred, and take the cow in part payment. Now, that's fair, ain't it?"

"Why, yaas, that's—why, that's fair enough; and I'd be willin' if hit was any other cow, but— Well, tell ye, Riley! I've got a heifer in the woods, fraish in Feb'wary; how about her and, say, five dollars cash?"

The tension had disappeared. A play of emotion almost boyish came back into both bronzed faces; their speech was once more interspersed with chuckles. Just before they passed out of sight one glanced backward to where a little checked cotton dress gleamed against the dusty briers.

Flittermouse had forgotten them. She was intent upon a streak of black ants, hurrying to and fro on a narrow trail of their own pioneering, on mysterious, alien business. "Free, four, five-six-seb'm-eight-nine-ten-leb'm-eight-nine-ten-leb'm-eight-nine-ten," she counted. At this point she was, by the similarity in sound between seven and eleven, invariably betrayed into a circle of four numbers. When she tired of it she began building a wall of sand, and placing chips inside it. "Pigs in a pen; a-a-all fensh op. Sooey, pig! Soo-oo-ey!"

She tucked one foot under her, and grasping the other, rocked herself to and fro to the rhythm of a tuneless song: "Bat, bat, come un'er mine hat, an'—when I bake—" She forgot the rest, but the idea of baking reminded her of a certain promise of chicken for supper. She was about to rise and resume her quest for Pappy, when a shadow fell on the ground beside her, and she looked up with a start that ran all the way from her top braid, the size of an ear of wheat, to her brown toes.

A shock-headed boy of twelve stood there, grinning. He carried a pole and line in one hand, and in the other a string of four perch. He was clad in a pair of homespun breeches and a man's shirt that, through various rents and a buttonless front, let the sweet wind flow all over his sunburnt body.

"What you think you're doin'?" he inquired.

In a country where two or three youngsters count for no more than a nest-egg, and a man's mother is likely to be only fourteen or fifteen years older than he is, children lack the opportunity, among the overlapping generations, for acquiring self-consciousness. Flittermouse was accustomed to take herself very much for granted as the next-to-youngest in a considerable family—neither the trusted eldest nor the petted baby, but just an extremely small girl whose duty was to keep out from underfoot and not meddle with hatching weedies. Her world was a child's world; she was used to being fed, played with, scolded, kissed, occasionally upset and run over by Joe and Orrion and Susy. It was only by accident that she stumbled to-day into the grown-up's country.

So, angry at being startled, she spoke to the boy as she felt, somewhat belligerently. "I'm zingin' zong," she announced. "You funny at me?" And as the freckled grin flashed broader, "*No* funny at me," she cried, and scrambled to her feet for a charge. But she came to a stop a few feet from the enemy, who had himself retreated in haste, snickering.

"I'm ain't go'n' kill 'oo," she reassured him, with more than a touch of magnanimity; "I was des a-p'ayin'."

"Got a chip on your shoulder, though, ain't ye?" suggested the boy.

She followed herself round and round in her tracks, like a kitten, in the endeavor to ascertain whether indeed that portion of her anatomy bore such a decoration.

"You sure have; jist look!" he encouraged her, enjoying the manoeuvre. "Well, if you ain't the funniest young 'un I might' near ever seed! What's you' name? Whar's you' paw? Want some May-apples?" he asked, with a motion toward his pocket.

But she shook her head, growing sulky with his increasing merriment, and stood pouting, her hands behind her back.

The spontaneous generosity of boyhood was on him, however; it was positively necessary that he give somebody something. As he went whistling on his way, he decided that it would be a capital joke to drop a mess of fish into his grandmother's water-bucket when she was not looking.

Alone once more, Flittermouse reseated herself on the sand. The shadows shortened as she played, and began to creep from the opposite side of the road. After a time she heard a patter of hurrying footsteps, and turned to stare at a girl who seemed to glitter as she came through the sunshine, so vivid was her hair, so brilliantly clean her apron.

Here again were approaching the thoughts that had power to divide like blades. "I can't live with her no longer," the girl was saying to herself. "It's her contrary ways, her weecked old tongue—they ain't to be endyored. I'd do better to run away to the Settlemint; I could make out to git me a new dress there oncet in a while, anyways. The idy of her a-havin' me pick berries all th'oo the season, and not lettin' me buy so much as a yard o' lawn! 'Be shore ye git the change right, Orphy,' she says. And now I've got to pick some more again' supper. . . . I can git away, and I jist will."

Then out of the wayside bushes blossomed a living rose—a child's face, wide-eyed and wondering, but with lips curved, ready to break into laughter.

For all her haste this girl, too, paused to go through the same sequence of questions as had the other people. It was a colloquy of which Flittermouse was beginning to tire. But this time it terminated charmingly. From her pocket the girl produced a fat cooky, wide as a saucer, and gave it into a ready little hand.

"'Oo nelcome," said the baby, with such gracious promptness that Orphy was moved to reply merrily, "Well—thank you!" She scurried along the road, tittering still; but she had ceased to scowl, and she went more and more slowly. At last she almost stopped, and counted over a few coins in her palm.

"I could keep this, and git to the Settlemint all right—git a dress, and find me some work," the girl muttered. "But she worked for hit as hard as I did—and the half I leave won't be near enough for her. Maybe I can stand to stay with her a while longer. She won't have nobody if I leave. She *is* my granny—I mustn't forgit that. And she was good to take me when my maw died. And the time I had the mumps—an' then the way she stood up for me to the church folks—" Orphy laughed, and shook her shoulders. "If she'd only make up with Uncle Zeke's folks, and go visitin' oncet and again—Well, I vow, I'll stay with her a while, anyhow."

The bright future was no bigger than a flower down the green vista now. Flittermouse, having eaten her cooky, sat happy as a lizard in the broad glare of afternoon light. Overhead shone the blue day; the rustle of the woods was all about. She laughed and cooed, patting sand-cakes with her chubby fingers; she rolled over like a puppy, and sat up, shaking the sand from her plaits. Her hands were scratched and stained, her frock dabbled with mud through which she had waded.

What was there to be happy about? Nothing and everything. She might as easily have reflected that she was far from home, and found ample excuse for disturbing the peace with desolate cries. But she had, in baby fashion, the deep sense of reality that comes with joy; she felt the ocean of life beating, soft and warm as summer, strong as fate and salt as blood, all round and through her little being. Life everywhere! In the woods, the sky, the ground, it crept and swarmed, burrowed and flew; life eyeless, helpless, dumb; life of a woodland grace, or elfin-quaint as Chinese carving; life winged and swift like a soul; life, the red gift of the sun! She heard its murmur, a summer sound, as of running water far and sweet. And oh, listen!—her features became rapt; she caught her breath and sat winking in intensity of attention—the Birdy was singing! Singing to Flittermouse as if she were the world and all. He must have known that she listened, there under the rustling trees. She uttered a gurgle of happiness; he sang again. In her heart the tide of feeling swelled; it rose and rose, till it was ready to brim over into tears or ripple out into laughter, she couldn't quite tell which. She loved things so!

Something seemed to take her by the throat, as if she were about to crow, or else to cry; it just trembled in the balance—

All at once she spied on the ground a short, thick stick or root, with an irregular knob on one end, like a head. It was much the same as any other stick, and it had lain there all the time; but the little girl had had no need of it until now. From "head" to "baby" was made the instant connection of ideas; she scrambled eagerly to catch it up.

"Howdy, doll! What you be dere for?" she inquired. "'Ish is doll. I'm rockin' little doll; rocky-bye—" and before she knew it, Flittermouse had, like the bird, turned the almost unendurable tension of the moment into song. A queer song, bubbling tuneless but sweet from her plump throat, its words mixed up of two Mother Goose jingles learned from the older children:

"Rocky-bye—wind blow,
    We sha' have 'now,
C'adle rock: p-o-o-oh shing,"

over and over. She wrapped the doll in as much of her short apron as she could well get hold of, and rocked and crooned, her round knees showing like two eggs beneath the hem of the scarlet garment she always spoke of as her peckitoat. She sang to the bit of wood in her arms, but it was her own body that responded to the lullaby. It became increasingly difficult to hold the doll in its cradle. The firm earth bore her up so strongly; the sky watched her with measureless kindliness. It was as though she for once usurped the place claimed of late by little-Man-alive, and lay clasped in her mother's arms. A good spot for a nap. But this reminded her that she was sleepy, and sleep, she knew, was what ended each one of her beautiful days. She struggled to her feet, resolved to fight, this time with all her strength. She would not tamely submit to see this delicious hour snatched into oblivion!

But it was already drawing to a close. The touch of antagonism, as soon as she said to herself "I won't," shattered the whole lovely structure, like the fairy palace of frosted glasses that brother Joe had once brought in and set beside the fire. She found the same old weariness and disillusion that made sleepy-eye time coming upon her, eclipsing her happiness as usual. And she had supposed it would last forever, this beautiful runaway day!

She began to cry, heartily, as she did everything else, with a view to rousing succor from somewhere. Her way in trouble was to appeal vigorously to the cosmos; it had never failed her yet.

It did not now. From a hitherto unperceived by-path came stepping a quaint little old figure carrying a huge pail of blackberries and clad in a sunbonnet, neckerchief, and straight-gathered calico dress. A face with twinkling blue eyes peered out between gray curls—a face like a Limbertwig apple that has hung into November and shrivelled with all its keen flavor retained inside. Flittermouse ceased her wailing, and gave the newcomer a glance of recognition, not of the individual, but of the type. Through tears she even smiled, with a little gasping cry of relief, as if at sight of some one she loved. This was a Grandma.

"Why, what's the matter with a little gal, out here all by herself?" asked the old woman, in a true grandma tone. "Air you lost from home?"

"Want a d'ink!" Flittermouse offered that as the most expressible and instant of her woes.

"All right; we'll jist go and find one," comforted the Grandma. "What's yore name, honey? Whose little poppee-doll air you? Tell Aint Cynthi' yore name!"

She set down her pail, and the mite, with a confidence born of long petting, instantly attacked its contents.

"Flittermouse," the red lips replied, juicily, between berries.

"And whar's your Pappy?"

She gave the same vague answer she had given several times already. It did not, however, deceive Aunt Cynthi' in the least.

"Well, is that all the name you got? Don't Mammy call you something different when she scolds ye?"

Now it so happened that this little maid who fared forth so bravely into unknown lands that summer day was afraid of her real name. She wouldn't for any thing have attempted it. Her tongue had a trick of transposing sounds that sometimes got her into difficulties; and at best this making people understand was the most serious and complicated business she had encountered in her life. So she remained silent, helping herself industriously, contentedly, from the berry bucket.

"And how'd you git here?" marveled old Cynthi' Macklin, half to herself.

With a momentary return of the morning's exuberant spirits, Flittermouse threw her arms up and down and laughed out. "Des flyed away!" she said.

"Uh-huh! An' air you aimin' to fly back? You 'des' better fly along home with me, till I can find out who wants ye the wust," cooed the old woman, deep in her throat, fond blue eyes on the baby.

But this it appeared the tired child was unable or unwilling to do. They made two or three starts, but each time Flittermouse lagged and came to a whimpering stop.

Cynthi' was in a quandary. Neither the child nor the berries might safely be deserted, and she could not carry both. "If that triflin' Orphy was with me," she thought. "But thar! the gal's but a gal. I mind when she looked so much like this 'n' nobody could 'a' told 'em apart."

She was on the point of hanging the bucket in a tree, to be out of harm's way until she could come back for it, when she had an inspiration. At a wet-weather spring that trickled from a bank she dipped a corner of her apron and washed the dusty, berry-stained little face ("Ain't go'n' ky," said Flittermouse, heroically, mindful of past struggles), and, taking advantage of the refreshment temporarily afforded by this process and by a drink from a leaf cup, she mounted the two tired legs astride a good sized stick-horse, which pranced over the remaining distance without a sign of fatigue.

They turned in at a wooden gate half buried under honeysuckles. A house peeped at them through a screen of cherry trees beyond. For all her light-heartedness in wandering, Flittermouse went suddenly limp all over at the thought of getting somewhere at last. There were other houses in the neighborhood, of course, but they sat aloof to the right and left of the road along which she had come, wherever was a sheltered lap of the hills or a spring hollow. The little girl yawned, her mouth opening like a hollowed rose, the tongue curling up as it were a single interior petal; and "I'm zo-o-o zeepy!" she complained, toddling after Cynthi' up the path.

She was hardly able to make away with the bread and butter she presently found in her hand. Sitting on the porch, she drooped and nodded over it, only half aware that a cheery old voice was recounting a story for her benefit: "And the fire began to burn the stick, the stick began to beat the dog, the dog began to bite the pig, and the pig began to go-o!" After a while, in the big log room, Cynthi' Macklin stood looking down at a dimpled brown body relaxed in the depths of her feather bed. So heavy with sleep, so rosy and fragrant! She had almost forgotten what a bit of sweetness and tenderness a baby could be. She noticed how the long lashes swept the cheeks, how the under lip pushed the other slightly out of place, like a twisted azalea bud.

"She does favor Orphy when she's a baby; an' then agin, she's jist about the age o' Sam's Dythie," the old lips murmured, as Cynthi' bent to lay a cloth over the slumber-flushed face. "Jist about her size. Eh-law! I'll ventur' Dythie's forgot me—wouldn't reco'nize her granny a-tall. I'm e'en-about minded to go over and see Zeke's folks a-Sunday, me and Orphy. Ef hit wasn't for that no-'count boy o' his'n—they ort to put him to hoein' corn. I seed him go on this morning with a pole and a canful o' red worms."

She tiptoed away, turning to dip a gourd of water from the shelf by the kitchen door.

"Well!" she exclaimed, in astonishment. The gourd remained poised as she stared into the bucket. There, in the clear water, swam at some inconvenience a couple of shining perch.

"Well!" she said again. "That boy! . . . I will go over thar, come Sunday." A smile spread slowly across her features, twinkling from her eyes in a sapphire gleam, seaming her pink cheeks into kindlier wrinkles than Orphy, just coming in with her afternoon harvest of berries, had ever suspected there.

"H'sh, Orphy," was the grandmother's greeting. "I got me a baby in here, asleep."

"I'll bet hit's the little gal that was playin' in the road," the girl whispered, tiptoeing in to look. "Whose is she?"

"That's what we've got to find out, I reckon," the elder returned. "But see here what some one fetched us for supper! Now, Orphy, you blow up the fire, and I'll be in therectly to holp ye fix 'em."

She left the house, to lean over the front gate. Chestnut flowers were falling noiselessly through the dusk beneath the trees; old memories came to her on the perfume of these and the honeysuckles, now heavy with the approach of evening. She heard the deep brass of cow-bells, sounded from winding paths that led up out of the creek; fireflies began to sparkle in the shadowed grass. She might have been a maid harkening for her lover's footfalls, so youthful a brightness shone in her eyes.

By and by the old man whom Flittermouse had first met was seen returning at the same plodding gait. Cynthi' hailed him with a question—an inquiry that made both forget the occasion of their last meeting. John Provine responded with grave interest. No, he couldn't say whose little gal had run away; he had seen one up yon a piece this morning, but had heard no stir of searching. No, he couldn't come in, he was belated already, settling with a feller that owed him for some lumber—been around and let him have a ixtension of his note, like a old fool. N-no, he'd be late to supper—"and then like as not Sis' Betty she'd take 'n' set hit off the table; you know she's kind o'— No, thank y'. Well, I don't know jist—"

He found himself edging through the vine-bound gate, setting himself erect, and getting hold of his most stately manner. The gray curls that topped Aunt Cynthi's alert head quivered as their wearer fluttered to the house; she seated her guest in the place of honor on the porch, and took advantage of a half-audible sigh from the sleeping child to run in and slip on—a bit of youth, of tender sentiment, of wistful remembrance, made visible—the lace collar that she had worn when a girl.

"And, Orphy, honey—if you'll hurry and make up some o' your best biscuits, and set on a jar of cherry preserves, I'll—I'll git ye a new dress in time for us to go to your Unc' Zeke's a-Sunday," she whispered, through the half-open door.

"Good gal to work, ain't she?" commented Provine, as the spirited old belle settled herself in the rocker opposite of him. "She's shore goin' it lively at that supper gittin'. Her feet sounds like she was a'dancin again."

"I'm afeared you 'n' me 'll git into a argu-mint if we set here *too* long, so I told her to hurry up a bite for us," Cynthi' answered, twinkling. "Do you ricollect, John Awthur, the first quarrel we ever had?" Her cheeks were even pinker as she put the question. "We've been quar'lin' ever sence."

But there was no answering gleam of fun in his face. He made one or two efforts to speak, failed, and finally brought out: "I been sorry a thousan' times about that. You was half promised to marry me, Cynthi'—and then you went and took Macklin."

"Air you sorry you called me a witch?"

"I wish somebody'd a-whupped me right thar when I done it. I do, I do, shore. Might 'a' learnt me some sense. Cynthi'," he stole a glance at her half-averted face, "you—you're the only—"

"Thar—thar's—I do b'lieve thar's Clay Sanders a-comin' home from work," she cried, jumping up nervously as a girl. "Let's us ask him about this here baby."

So it came about that Flittermouse, feeling herself swung into a well-known resting place, was not put to the trouble of opening her eyes. She had followed the beckoning of fate that day, and traversed a wider circuit than she would ever know, carrying, all unconscious, her lamp of love and joy and innocence to light sundry dark places.

Flittermouse snuggled closer on the big shoulder, and murmured drowsily:

"Oh, Pappy, I'm des been a-coming—tell 'oo—dot sz-z-schick'n for zupper."

And Aunt Cynthi', hearing the gate close behind the pair, turned to the man beside her and asked coyly, "Do you ricollect ever seein' me wear this here collar before, John Awthur?"

nine

Three Roads and a River

From *Harper's Monthly Magazine* 121 (November 1910): 882–89; illustrated by Howard E. Smith

One of Miles's strongest stories in both plot and craft is "Three Roads and a River." She again develops a marriage and family theme, but the dominant factor experienced here is galling poverty. The proud and previously independent Hutson family suffers the loss of their livelihood when a new government bridge across the river eliminates the need for ferry service and road maintenance. Both Shell Hutson and his father, old Zion the patriarch, feel a pressing responsibility to provide for their loved ones. Each engages in actions he would never consider under normal circumstances, resulting in dire consequences. Though Miles cannot resist exercising her "happy-ending" penchant, the tension and climactic outcome of this story place her squarely in the camp of naturalists such as Theodore Dreiser and Stephen Crane.

Before the cabin ran the wild mountain stream, its dark-green water, wonderfully clear, sliding under steep banks overhung with thickets of laurel.

Just here, after fretting for miles against the bluff, its current swung wide over the shallows and rippled quietly up the shore; up to where the rude raft that was Hutson's Ferry lay idle under a leaning service-tree tasselled now with silvery bloom. The warm sweet tide of spring was rising in the valley, its line of advance visible far up the mountainside in the shapely gold-green tops of tulip trees. But for the first time in fifty springs no quickening of travel was perceptible at this centre of the fan-like network of trails that threaded the ravines and ridges. The government had last year flung a bridge across at the Narrows, where four pines stood black against the tender opalescent mists of the April sunset. And the government's new highway, unmindful of the fate of Hutson's log house and its inmates as of an unfortunately placed ant-hill, cut diagonally across the old road which Hutson's grandfather had built before the war. It shortened the distance between town and settlement by several miles; and even if it had not, what countryman laden with game or produce but would ride out of his way if need be to escape the payment of ferriage and toll?

So, instead of hailing his acquaintance from the toll-shack—which had latterly been put to use as a chicken-shed—old Zion Hutson brooded in his doorway and smoked all through the long spring mornings. The road which his son Shell had been wont for a livelihood to keep in tolerable order was rapidly becoming impassable. Thus seated, the old man could pretend to forget the woful ruin, since it was out of sight; but from the field spring it showed for a long way up the mountain, a mangy scar, worn more rutty and sidling by every rain. And farther up, he knew, the "corduroys" were rotting, and overhanging stones were being let down one by one in frost and thaw.

The winter had been a hard one for a valley in this latitude. Grandmother Hutson, unable to endure it, died of "winter fever" and lack of proper nourishment, and the old man, lost without his mate, was daily becoming feebler. "Every change o' the moon takes something out o' him," said Ona. He muttered to himself continually as he smoked and drowsed in the sunshine; sometimes he broke into curious fragmentary prayers. He was being shredded of his wits by the dragging days.

There was little to eat in the house. To old Zion, who used to kill from five to ten hogs every Thanksgiving, the fact of being without meat was incomprehensible. His mind reverted again and again to the subject, trying to account for the omission of killing-day from the winter's calendar. He seemed to believe that it was in some way Shell's or Ona's fault.

"I don't see what ever could a-went with that big barrer," he would begin, fretfully. "Last time I seed that hog was—" and he would recount time and place with circumstantial detail.

"Why, pap, I'm satisfied the pigs all died up in that bad spell in Jiniwary, same as the bees did," Shell would explain.

"Ef there'd a-been any mast last fall, they'd a-lived through." The old man always accepted Shell's view until next time.

"Yes, ef there'd a-been any mast."

"Anyhow y'uns missed hit by sellin' ol' Piedy."

Here Ona, who on her children's account needed the cow sorely, turned consoler: "We couldn't a-kep' her through, pap."

"Well," he grumbled, "ye might a-made hit th'oo Jiniwary with her on what crab-grass ye've got stuffed in them two straw-ticks. We-uns could a-slep'on saidge-grass or leaves."

They forbore to argue, and old Zion relapsed into silence.

The orchard came out bravely in its spring array, and Ona helped her husband dig up a truck-patch and plant it with the seed saved from last year's garden—beans, beets, and okra, pumpkins and cucumbers, and a larger patch of cow-peas and field corn; but seed potatoes or onion sets were not to be thought of. The meal was low in the barrel; the coffee was out. There was only a little sorghum, a little lard—salt in the piggin, and vinegar in the keg. Ona felt more frightened at this state of affairs than either of the men.

The two children alone remained outside the shadow that rested on the house. Behind the kitchen was an old Limbertwig whose branches swept the new grass in a circle round the body of the tree; and within this flowery screen they made a playhouse with piled stones and broken crockery, and moss from the spring branch, and early flowers—Sunday-shirts, fish-blossoms, rooster-fights, and wild honeysuckles, stuck into a rusty baking-powder tin. Here they frolicked as though the crumbling smokehouse contained all the plenty of former years. One rainy day they fretted at being housed, till their mother threatened to shut them in the toll-house with the chickens. She put them to bed an hour early, and sat with folded hands before the fire. The darkness was turbulent with rushes of rain, alternating with whooping gusts. Early in the evening had been far-away gleams of lightning and half-heard thunder; but now it was turning cold.

Presently Shell entered, and drawing the loose brands and the forestick forward, threw a thick log on behind.

"Now, Shell, you haul them chunks out," remonstrated old Zion from the shadows of his corner. "You know the sayin', 'A house built over stumps never stands, and a faar built over chunks never burns.'"

"Turned a right smart colder, ain't it?" asked the woman, anxiously.

Shell nodded. "Gwine to be a freeze, I'm afeared."

"Blackberry winter!" muttered old Zion.

"That frost last week only peenched the peaches some. But this here—" Shell's gaze went out the little storm-beaten window, and returned to the bed where his children lay. The danger was too grave for many words. So much depended on the orchard's yield.

Ona, in the firelight, crouching, looked up at her husband. Woman-like she took little count of her own plight; but the sight of her man ragged and hunger-bitten filled her with pity and dismay.

"I wrote to Nettie a-Tuesday," she said, abruptly, breaking a silence. "I 'lowed she'd maybe holp us out some—till the gyarden truck begins to come in."

"Well, shorely 'n' ondoubtedly she will," put in the old man. "Did ye tell her I ain't got no tobacker?"

"Why, she'll know in reason you ain't," said Ona, smiling.

"Ne'er a chaw!" said old Zion, plaintively.

"A-Tuesday—then she ort to git the letter afore this time, I reckon," said the younger man, kicking the forestick and sending up a crackle of sparks. He was ashamed to show the relief he felt at this slender hope.

"She may holp us out till the gyarden comes in."

"Yes, till the gyarden truck comes in."

"I heard Steve Miller was a-doin' well."

"Lord! thirty dollars a month, and nobody to keep but them two."

"Well, he does send some home to his mother," said Ona. "But I hope he can make out to spar' us a little."

She got up and went into the dark inner room to get a drink. Something crackled ever so faintly under the gourd as she dipped it. Was it a leaf? A dry leaf that had fallen into the bucket on its way from the spring? Forgetting to drink, she felt over the surface of the water with trembling fingers. Even then she refused to be convinced; she obtained a sliver of fat pine and lit it at the hearth.

"What you lookin' for?" asked her husband.

"I—dropped the gourd," she replied. By her miniature torch she examined the thin crystals fast forming round the sides of the bucket. There was no mistake.

"Hit's a-freezin'," she whispered, through dry lips. "Hits's a-freezin'." Extinguishing the little flame, she stood staring into the darkness. Their only hope lay now in Nettie's generosity.

"But she cain't, she couldn't keep us that long. We'll have obleeged to—move. Shell can maybe git work in town, where her man is . . ."

A knock, sounding above the drumming rain, brought her hastily into the main room. Shell flung the door wide; and, pushed by the storm, a woman staggered across their threshold. She reached the fire and crouched over its red warmth with a little moaning cry before throwing back the shawl from her haggard young face and dripping hair.

"Nettie! Lord, if hit ain't Nettie!" cried Ona.

"Why, we-uns was jist a-talkin' about ye!" quavered Nettie's father.

"You sick?" inquired Shell, briefly.

"Well, up-on my soul! what you out in this rain fur? Ain't ye might' near dead?" Ona advanced toward the newcomer, trembling, incredulous.

"I rode as fur as the nigh cut in a huckster's wagon," answered Nettie, spreading her shaking hands almost in the flame, avoiding the gaze of all. "But I got wet walkin' the rest of the way. Hit's a-sleetin' now—freezin' up everything." She folded her arms on her knees and bowed her head upon them. "I don't know what y'uns 'll think o' me comin' home like this, pap; but I didn't have no place else to go."

"Why, Nettie! what's the matter?" Ona crouched beside the shivering form and touched her sister-in-law gently. "Come, honey, git up and set in a chair."

"Steve he's gone," explained Nettie, without raising her face. "Nobody don't seem to know where. He couldn't make nothin' after the mill shet down, and he got out o' heart. I reckon he may have went to look for work som'er's. But people there got to makin' a mock o' me, and I couldn't let on no longer to know where he was at, so I come home for a while, till I hear from him. Oh, my Lord, how I suffer!. . . . I didn't have no other way to turn."

"There now! there now!" Ona patted the heaving shoulders, but her own heart sank. The wind, as always before a cold wave, made nightmare sounds over the chimney, hooting like the great ghost-owl of Cherokee myth; the sleet in a fiercer gust leaped and clawed beast-like at roof and door.

“You better fix her a bed, Ona, and a hot drink,” said Shell.

“There ain’t no coffee,” his wife reminded him, going to her store of quilts.

There was a new sound in the cabin before the close of another day—a pin-point wail stabbing the vast mountain silence, a cry of unnameable desolation, a protest, bitter and piteously thin, against the untried task of living. Ona alone tended on the helpless two. Ere the lean years had gnawed away their substance, the Hutsons had fronted their world with a gay independence, a cheery arrogance which neither asked nor gave; they would not now cry for help. And since latterly Zion had relinquished his post as autocrat of affairs religious, the three or four neighbors, a few miles up river and down, had more than ever got into the way of letting them alone. So Ona and Nettie won through the terrible hour unaided.

The sun on the evening of the birth set golden fair, but it was on a blighted garden. The orchard was a spectacle of marvellous beauty—bough after bough sheathed in clear ice ere a bud could shrivel or a petal fade; fairy gold, sure to melt with dawn. Shell broke a glittering spray and fetched it in for the women to look at.

That week saw the last of Ona’s chickens, each of which tided the family over another day and furnished Nettie a bowl of broth. Old Zion almost forgot his longing for tobacco in his joy at seeing his daughter at home; but Shell and his woman, needing every bite for their own little ones, could give scant welcome to another mouth. The situation was managed, however, with the adroitness usual to the mountaineers, and it was not until she was up and about again that, in helping with the housework, Nettie discovered their extreme necessity.

She felt bound to speak of it. The two women were sewing, having found some old things that could be cut into little garments. The light from the doorway fell upon their glinting needles; the air came in softly, as if no blade of frost had mowed the land.

“Yes—two days more, and there won’t be even pones and white gravy,” Ona confessed.

Nettie swayed gently the little bundle in her lap beneath the sewing. “Nor no more white beans like we had yesterday?”

“I borrowed that mess from Mis’ Nicklin; I’ve done borrowed of her till I’m pine-blank ’shamed to show my face there any more. Howsomever, I got obleeged to go som’er’s to borrow some for seed.”

"You got nothin' to plant again?"

"Little okra, and some beet seed, that's all. Shell, why'n't ye kill some rabbits?"

The man addressed lifted his head and stared sombrely out upon the barren field next the river. "I ain't got more'n three charges o' powder."

"Well, ketch a mess o' them little bony pyerch, then. Lord! we cain't give up."

"Used to be," piped old Zion, suddenly, "that a man here could go out and kill him a deer or a turkey afore breakfast."

Shell took down his gun from the rack over the fireboard and fared forth. All that day he was gone. When he returned, after dark, he flung down something heavy, slamming it on the kitchen table without a word. It was a shoat he had killed. It looked to Zion much like one of the Nicklins'; but the head, which might or might not have borne the Nicklins' earmark, was missing.

"Shot all to pieces," the hunter explained to the womenfolk.

There were pots full of pork and strong gravy now; but this was not the food needed by the young ones, who soon began to look puny and downcast. So Nettie, leaving her baby in Ona's care, went far and wide, foraging in all fence corners and under sunny banks for frost-nipped shoots which the sun had coaxed out afresh. These salads, deliciously contrived with salt, vinegar, and dripping, eked out their fare for many days; and meantime, as Nettie was fond of pointing out, the bean vines came apace. Only in the young mother's sea-colored eyes was a radiance of hope; her spirit was as bright against the others' moping as her hair against the smoky interior of the cabin.

Ona was frying the last of the meat (they had traded a quarter to some camping hunters for meal), when the little boy ran to her crying, "Mammy, I'm find somep'n." He showed a handful of crumpled green tips. "In gyarden."

His mother could not restrain a cry of delight. "Them white multipliers o' ma's—and pa'snips! Oh, I do hope there's enough for a mess—"

The child, elated at having produced a sensation, went to point out his trove among the dry stalks and kecksies of the unploughed field; and that day Ona surprised the family with vegetables for dinner. "Hit ain't a mess—jist a bite around," said she. But Nettie slipped her portion on to the children's plates.

It was two or three days after this that her own baby began the continuous moaning fret of hunger. She looked upon him in despair.

"I'd take 'nd wash that baby in the deeshwater if he was mine," said Ona. "That was my mammy's rimidy. I couldn't count ye the peakid babies she fattened that way. Hit's greasy, you know, and they git the stren'th of hit."

"There cain't be a great deal o' stren'th in our deeshwater," said Nettie, walking the floor with her child. She had maintained that same unavailing pace for hours.

"Eh-law!" said the other mother, watching her. "Children never pays for their raisin'."

"They do!" flashed Nettie, lifting the downy head to her cheek. "Mine evens up hits little account with me every day of hits innocent life."

That same evening Shell returned from a three days' quest for work.

"Nobody wouldn't talk to me about hit," he said. "Where I wasn't knowed at sight they taken me for a tramp. I heared the's men now a-walkin' the streets in the Settlemint, so I never went there. But a feller told me of a womern furder on that lived by herself and wanted a man to take charge of her place. Well, I went plumb on out there, and she—she—sicked the dawg on me."

He fell silent, but the two children burst into sobbing.

"Pappy—never—brought us nothin'!" cried the little girl, burying her head in her mother's lap.

Shell Hutson stood up. His face became terrible. Ona shrank away from him affrighted for a moment; but all he said was: "Oh, baby! Honey!"

Then he went out. The children cried themselves into a restless sleep. Though the two women sat beside the hearth till daybreak, Shell did not come in again.

There was meal gruel for breakfast, and in the cloudy dawn old Zion set forth with knife and basket, having bethought himself of a burnt cabin down the river where might be found yet another mess of poke salad. It was a dark morning, the sheet of cloud drawn smoothly over from the west; for all daylight a low pale illumination streamed from beneath its fringes that swept the eastward forest. Sounds came far through the heavy atmosphere; he delayed his plodding more than once to hear, with a deep despondency, the wheels of laden wagons crossing the government's bridge, like the very car of progress leaving him and his in its desolate wake.

He was not disappointed; round the cinder-strewn area stood plant after lusty plant, fresh and succulent as anything ever forced under frames for a city market. As he sat resting on the doorsill of an outhouse which the flames had spared, the glint of a bottle, thrust in a high chink and forgotten, caught his eye. Old Zion reached for it in hope of finding whiskey; but the contents turned out to be a dark fluid of sinister strength, some unknown chemical, at which he sniffed gingerly, till the skull and crossbones on the label apprised him of its dangerous nature.

"Wow! Hit's a good thing I didn't take a swaller 'thout lookin'," he exclaimed. But after he had gathered his basket full of greens he tucked the bottle carefully under the broad, glossy leaves. He had no idea what use he could ever make of it; he acted only from the ancient, half-superstitious reverence for virtues and drugs, and from an inborn reluctance to throw away anything.

"Y'ain't seed Shell yit?" he inquired, as soon as he reached home.

No one had.

"Have ye got ary bit o' meat-grease left? Poke's liable to make people sick if hit ain't cooked up good and greasy. Now, Ona, don't you go and th'ow out them stalks. You'ns have got lots o' vinegar. I'm a-gwine to make us some pickles; they'll be good again' supper-time."

The greens were bubbling in the pot, and the sun lay some hours beyond the noon-mark, when Shell came in. Then from every one of the little assemblage broke a cry of astonishment and joy; for he carried a bag of meal and a salt-pork middling.

"Bought 'em," he informed the company, shortly. His face had not relaxed since last night. Into the hand of his woman he poured a jingle of silver coins; then he dropped heavily across the foot of the bed as though he had been drinking.

"Now, by Jackson!" exulted the old man, "I want you gals to cook like ye was feedin' a rigimint. I wonder—how do you reckon Shell got—" He broke off, and his face changed slowly as he looked at the figure prone there, defeat, in this moment of seeming victory, showing in its every line. In the eager preparation for a supper feast no one heeded old Zion's staring at his son, sinking lower and lower in his chair. Finally he rose unnoticed and hobbled out-of-doors.

Nettie meantime came to the voicing of a matter which had occupied her thoughts all day.

"Ona, you think if you'ns had a cow ye could feed my baby, without me, so he'd thrive?"

"On a bottle? Why, I reckon so. Why, yes. You ain't studyin'—"

"I'm a-studyin' about goin' back to the Settlemint. I can git work there, and holp to keep us all."

"Why! you said ye tried and couldn't!"

"Oh, that was before the baby was born. I can, though, now. . . . I cain't bide here with you'ns; this little bit o'grub won't do us no time." Nettie knew that there was work in town at which a woman could always earn enough to feed several mouths. It seemed now the only way.

"Well," cried her sister-in-law, an edge put on her tone by her insistent misery, "I wisht ye'd a-said so a good while back!"

Nettie laughed and went to put the baby's small belongings in order. She must send Shell to bargain for Nicklin's fresh cow to-night, and go before the child should awake in the morning; there was no time to be lost. "Pore little man-boy! I'll come home every week, to see that they take good care of ye," she whispered to the wee shirts and frocks. All at once she lifted the blue silk cap that the baby's father had bought only a few days before his disappearance. Something else was folded inside, as being, like the cap, too dainty for actual service—the lace handkerchief Steve had given her on Christmas morning. Heart-wrung, she laid her head on the window-sill and cried her slender strength away.

It was near sundown when she again looked out of the narrow panes; and as she gazed her face brightened unaccountably, as if by some spiritual dawn invisible to the other woman at the hearth.

"I reckon I won't go yit awhile—not to-morrow," she said. "Wait a day or two . . ."

On the bank of the river old Hutson walked up and down, wringing his thin hands, swaying his head, and muttering, muttering, muttering. He was praying for a sign. He had in mind the starved wife he had buried; his daughter deserted and helpless through poverty; his son, he suspected, driven to crime. The vision of destruction clutched his failing heart like the talons of those fiends that abounded in his theology. He could not endure the thoughts that came to him. But there must be some way out, if he could but find it; and he prayed, prayed desperately, that his God would show him the way.

Overhead the clouds were breaking with the close of day. Under their flying lights and shadows the river changed, and changed again, with indescribable pale hues, colors of strange metals molten, alloys of copper and silver; now sheeted gray as aluminum without a gleam, again taking lights as of dusty gems, amethyst and emerald and beryl, with riffles of blinding silver spreading below the shoals. With eyes closed, still crying out with all his soul, he turned round and round slowly, in the midst of his unsown field, seven times. . . . Now for the sign.

He looked upon the cold rain-swollen stream. Here beside him met the crooked ways of all the world. Behind him his mother-mountain had cloaked herself in the majesty and mystery of Sinai. To him those smooth-worn phrases, names, and metaphors coined in the vanished fervors of a people's lyric passion were glorious with deathless values. The meanings he read into them, however different these might be from the intention of originators in the ports of the Levant, had through a lifetime's brooding worn, not grooves, but sunless gorges in the fabric of his mind. To one who habitually sought the imagery of the Apocalypse everywhere, cherishing even homely plants by such fantastic names as Balm of Gilead or Tree of Heaven, it was inevitable that the mountain stream should long have symbolized the River of Death. And across there, as he looked, the sudden glory of a sunset clearing after rain turned the spring-empurpled hills to rose and gold. The water flamed into glass mingled with fire; for a few moments his world lay steeped in a jewel-light. It seemed a covenant and a promise.

"Jist over, jist over Jordan," he muttered. "Hit must be so. Death 'ud be better for all of us. The Good Master never intended for anybody to live sech a life, anyhow. . . . Hit's onchristian. Hit makes women like pore Nettie and her mother; and thar's Shell's boy—ef he don't learn to rob and steal, he'll end up jist like—me. Provideth not fur his own—too old." He joined his hands and shut his eyes once more; and shaking his white hair in the soft damp wind, he concluded very softly:

"Lord, I thank Thee for the Sign; send me now the grace and stren'th to do Thy will, and receive us all in the kingdom. Amen."

The water faded swiftly to a pallid jacinth in the gray matrix of twilight.

He went slowly back into the house, and forthwith prepared his poke-stalk pickles, secretly adding to the vinegar the contents of the bottle he had brought from the burnt cabin shed. They were presently set on the table with a great steaming bowl of white gravy, and the greens, and the pones and fried meat. How delicious it all looked and smelled! The two children wriggled on their chairs while the old man asked an unusually long blessing on the food he believed to have been stolen; but he would not eat anything except the relish he knew to be poisoned, partaking with the air of one receiving sacrament. Then all ate of it but Nettie.

"I'm afeared to resk givin' the baby a colic by the sour," she objected, when urged.

Her father turned upon her, his face working. “You’re a fool not to eat ’em, gal,” he cried, in an uneven, febrile voice; then, as she shrank, he muttered, “God’s will—God’s will be done,” and said no more, evidently deeming that the matter might be safest left in the hands of his Lord. But Nettie wondered, not for the first time, if her father were mad.

Shell and his family presently staggered away to bed, curiously drowsy, leaving the dishes unwashed, the hearth unswept, and no wood brought for the breakfast fire.

“A heavy supper does make a body so-o sleepy!” smiled Ona. “What air you a-singin’ for, Nettie? You ac’ like ye had all the money in the bank to draw on.”

“I have,” answered Nettie, with the mountaineer’s inconsequent defiance. It was truer than she knew. Had she not from the first drawn upon the living strength whose source is inexhaustible?

Ona lay down without removing her clothes, and drew the coverlet up to her chin. It was Nettie who straightened the house for the night, brought chips in her apron, and went to the spring for water, singing still, with that strange mingling of content and hope imperishable in her sea-gray eyes. Night had fallen, with the blind clouds again riding swift and low; now and then one swooped to blot out every vestige of the landscape; she could not see her way, but her feet found their path a step at a time—and she could sing.

Afterward she sat before the few embers that remained of the cooking-fire, nursing her babe. The rain again set in, and she closed the door lest the damp blow on the little head. Old Zion was still nodding; his voice quavered faintly from the corner shadows, and she made out that he was trying to repeat a hymn—“Will the waters be chilly?” But the rhythm faltered and sank into muttering. “Death in the pot,” she caught; and then, “The will o’ God, the will o’ God.”

They were his last words. She laid the baby to sleep, and turned to persuade her father to go to bed. It was close upon midnight now. Something in the huddled posture of the figure in the chair struck cold to her heart. She was suddenly aware that she no longer heard the breathing of the sleepers, which had been loud when they first lay down.

On trembling knees she halted forward, her hand outstretched. “Pappy?” she whispered. “Pappy! *Pappy!*”

Her fingers touched the withered cheek. It was already cold. With a scream, she crouched back, staring; then turned and ran to the bed where Shell and Ona lay side by side, their children at their feet.

Still crying out, she grasped and shook them. "They cain't be dead! Oh, pappy—Shell—Ona—cain't you hear me callin' ye!" she sobbed, over and over. "Why, hit's only a little while sence we was all settin' at supper!"

She turned once more to the hearth, only to find the old man's body slipped sideways from the chair. The blades of Fate's shears had swung together, dividing Nettie and her child from that doomed family. As she clamored, beside herself with the sudden horror, the little creature waked and added its shrill wail to her outcry—and the others were all still and mute as stone. Catching up the babe, she started, with an unformulated intention of going for help; she did not know that she had already twice shrieked her husband's name.

As if in answer to that cry, the door burst open; fragments of its rude latch flew spinning across the room, and a man halted a moment on the threshold, bewildered by the firelight, unable at first to see what lay before him.

"Oh, Steve! Oh, Steve!" she cried, running to him, clutching the arm he put out, clinging to it, the child between them, and dragging him so into the room. In the terror of that moment she found nothing strange in his presence there.

"Nettie!" his deep voice reassured her; his big arm went around her with a sturdy support which brought comfort, even facing the stark tragedy to which they now turned.

The next day, while Mother Nicklin and the neighbors who had been summoned put everything in order for the dignity of death, Nettie lay on her bed as one half stunned. After all was over and the poor bodies laid to rest in the burying-ground on the hill, she rose and went with Steve and their child down to the river, to sit, pale and weak, on the old raft in the quiet sunshine. She had passed worthily through her great trial, and gained the peace that lies on the other side. Little waves lisped and patted upon the black half-sodden timbers; small perch leaped now and again with a happy flash; overhead the ripening service-berries hung against the new-rinsed sky. The hills were wonderfully blue, swept with a besom of rain; and up and down stream was a miracle of purple rhododendron.

She smiled at her husband over the baby's rosy sleep. He softly stroked her shoulder, though he wondered at her smiling.

"Hit was pore pappy—caused—what happened back yon," she answered his look. "I've seed for some time his mind was failin'."

The young husband agreed soberly. "Some o' the folks found a bottle," he told her. "Aconite, they called it. Your pappy must have been out of his mind."

"Yes," Nettie murmured. "Nobody would want to die. We seed a awful hard time, Steve," she added, simply. "But look like where the' was little 'uns—nobody would aim to die."

The man's brown cheek crimsoned. "Oh, Nettie," he cried, "I was comin'! I come as soon as I had anything to fetch ye. I've been seekin' for ye, up and down and all about, for two-three days, honey. I'd never been here, you know, and look like nobody couldn't tell me so I could locate the place. I was right nigh here a-yesterday, with money in my hand for ye—and them that's gone, pore souls—when a quare thing happened; some scoun'l set on me—knocked me down from behind, and robbed me of several dollars in silver before I come to."

Nettie caught her breath and looked at him stealthily. But Steve had not recognized in the shrouded and shaven Shell his assailant of yesterday, and his wife did not tell him of her suspicions.

"I never heard of a robbery in these parts before," Steve said. "But the feller didn't take my roll o' bills! Never found it, I reckon, as it chanced." He showed her the precious little hoard lying in his hand. "Now, Nettie," he glanced toward the house, then to that one of the three ill-mended roads that wound away toward the burying-ground, bent his head a moment with the air of one who makes his devoir to the dead, and went on, "you 'n' me 'll go back to Pyriton, where I've been. I can have steady work there; and we'll send this chap to school when he's older."

The wife nodded above her child's head, the wisdom of the mother-creature alight in her sea-blue eyes. "I knowed you was a-comin' back to us, Steve. I just knowed that," she murmured. "I said so to myself when I was a-singin' the baby to sleep last night."

"Last night." The awe and wonder of it grew upon the man's face. "Why, girl, do ye know, I'd 'a' turned back last night, I was that tired and discouraged, but I heard you singin'—and then you called me."

"Yes," she answered, with simple confidence, "I jist expected ye, from the time I looked out yestidy and seed the sun shinin' on the hills across the river."

ten

Flower of Noon

From *The Craftsman* 21 (January 1912): 386–94

Fan Walton, the protagonist in "Flower of Noon," proves to be a resourceful young woman who must withstand suspicion, distrust, and false accusation in the aftermath of the sudden death of Harmon Ridge, for whom she has been housekeeper and bookkeeper. Family members and neighbors of the unmarried Ridge crowd in for the wake and for information about the dispensation of his property, left, they all assume, without an heir. His sanctimonious brothers and their grasping wives believe they will inherit, only to be gravely disappointed by a most unexpected revelation. Additional layers of the plot include a love interest for Fan and a glimpse into her compassion for others. In all of Miles's fiction Fan Walton is the one woman whose promise of fulfillment in love is not compromised by self-effacement.

Although there had been for years a continual sly threading of the trails that led to his place of business in the woods, Harmon Ridge had never during his lifetime had so many guests as today. Most of the folks now gathered in the best room of the log house were voluntary strangers to its door. Women were coming and going clad in garments of hastily donned and ill-matched colors, with here and there a black waist, hat or skirt. Susan, the wife of Clifford Ridge, and old Mrs. Bivins were distinguished by whole costumes of the appropriate hue; the latter not through any peculiar depth of feeling, but because, having no kin of her own, she made a point of attending all the burials of the countryside, and for expediency had long since cast all her outer garments into the same pot of funereal logwood.

In the tidy kitchen Harmon's young housekeeper had not changed the steel-gray gingham she had worn the day before. She was occupied with straightening the dead man's accounts, which she had kept for two years. Fan Walton was a strongly built, energetic girl, standing firm in her broad shoes and breathing deeply as she worked. She always experienced a faint shock of surprise on the rare occasions when she faced a mirror, at not finding herself beautiful.

From under eyelids swollen with loss of sleep she looked up as a tall, sunbrowned young mountaineer stooped through the doorway.

"I've cut you a quantity of wood and killed them chickens for dinner, Fan," he said. He came forward and laid one hand on the table at which she was seated; his tone became almost pleading as he went on. "Now you let me start dinner for ye. You're werried out. My dad was cook for his company all through the war, and he learnt me how. I bet I can beat you makin' dodgers."

"I bet you can't," she replied; but putting away her book, she watched him deftly blow up the hearth-fire with a turkey-wing and hang a kettle over the blaze.

"I reckon," he continued presently, coming up the cellar-way with a pan of potatoes, "that's why Mr. Ridge always liked me to tend the still for him; I could generally git water to bile without burnin' it. Well—I got to look out for another job now. I'll never work for a man I like better. I do wisht I'd a-been there when—when—the rev's took him, instead of haulin' corn. Maybe if there'd been two on gyuard it wouldn't have ended that way."

She caught her breath with a great sob. "Oh, Byron!" There was something tragic in the cry that freed itself from her strained throat. "He was so good!"

The boy nodded without looking up from his potato-paring; the pathos of her position, or as much of it as was known to him, smote him to the heart. But Fan, impatient with herself for the moment's weakness, turned quickly, and rolling up her sleeves on her firm shapely arms, mixed a creamy mass of meal and butter-milk and began manipulating it into dodgers. They remained silent and busy until Grandma Bivins' shrill voice announced her entry: "Looky thar, Bar'n—that colt's a-gwine to break ever' one o' them crocks!"

The pretty, petted sorrel sprang back in a well-simulated panic at the wave of Fan's dish-towel, and an instant after was stretching an investigative nose toward the window again.

"Truelove's restless today," explained Fan as she patted the oval pones into their oven nest. "Take a chair by the door, Mrs. Bivins. I hate to shut the colt up, for I know how she feels."

"I'll go turn her in the pasture," said Byron as he put the potatoes in the pot.

In the barnyard, a half-dozen men sat around upon inverted feed-buckets, the chopping-block, the ash-gum, the bales of clapboards riven to roof the old barn—anything rather than go in the house before the activities and lamentations of the womenfolk had come to a standstill. A certain cautious restraint was perceptible in the conversation here, an edging around the subject that was inevitably the center of interest to all, of which circumstances forbade direct mention.

" . . . That's a powerful fine orchard. Might' near all Limbertwigs, ain't they?"

"Harmon Ridge took as good keer of his land as he did of his team."

"I never seed a better quartered colt than that one Bar'n Standifer's a-leadin' yonder. Her dam was a fine pacer."

But no one asked in so many words how much Harmon Ridge was worth or who would inherit the property.

In the lane three men conferred a little apart from the others; Absalom Ridge, the deacon of the Borden Springs church; Clifford, justice of the peace at Belview, affable and prosperous beneath due decorum; and with them the preacher, properly punctilious and punctiliously proper, as befitted the master of ceremonies. In the mountains a funeral sermon is seldom preached in seed-time or harvest; it may await for months the convenience of the family connection. Clifford urbanely offered the front rooms and ample porches of his house for the purpose; but Absalom, loth to relinquish the one bit of prestige life had granted him, insisted that his church should be the chosen site.

The preacher agreed. "Let 'em all bring a basket and spread dinner on the ground, Brother Ridge, and afterward protract the service into a praise meetin'."

Clifford yielded the point with admirable grace, perhaps feeling that he could afford to. "That announcement will bring out a good crowd."

"Then," continued the preacher, "how 'bout havin' it the third Sunday in next month? All crops 'll be laid by again' that time, and I haven't got no appointmints for that date." He cut a fresh chew of tobacco from the plug offered him by Clifford, and went on dolorously: "It's a hard thing to be called on to preach the funeral of a man that never made any profession of faith. I'd rather be called on for any other duty of the ministry than that."

"Hit's hard; yes," agreed Absalom sympathetically. "I'm afeared the one consolation you can set before our sorrowin' family is the fact that not one of us ac-chilly *knows* anything about pore Harmon's faith."

"You might jist mention," interrupted a new voice, "that he was honest as the open day, and the best-hearted friend a man ever had in time o' need."

They all jumped around, and came face to face with Byron; but ere they could frame a suitable reply he had passed on, the sorrel following. The very presence of Harmon's helper was embarrassing to the justice and the deacon, reminding them that the brother whose large well-knit frame and lionlike flow of beard now reposed beneath a sheet on the rude scaffolding had served the devil and defied the law for the past ten years.

Yet as they halted, staring at each other, those two suddenly remembered the warm-hearted, wayward boyhood of the rover—the brightness of his blue eyes, the reddish-brown cowlick that swept down over his forehead in correspondence to some unruly twist in his nature. After all, in those far-off days, of what had Harmon been guilty except just being himself? Only his earthborn strength had affronted the careful propriety and thrift of the one, the saintly demeanor of the other. Slowly and in silence they walked toward the group under the tree.

Indoors, the wives, under cover of putting the house in order, essayed an examination; but the attempt failed dismally as closet after closet was found to be already immaculate.

"I wonder if she does keep things like this all the time; or did she take 'n hustle everything straight because she knew folks would be in?" whined Absalom's wife, Marzela, between her prominent yellow teeth.

"Do you reckon he was prepared to go?" continued Marzela, piously. "I hoped, seein' he' lingered on for some days after—his injury, that he'd profess religion at the 'leventh hour—repent, and believe, in time. I even tried to git Absalom to ride over and talk to him; but he's always had trouble when he tried to git pore Harmon to think of his soul, and there was only them three days left of the dark o' the moon to plant in."

"The fact is we didn't none of us have any idy it was so serious; we would a-come, but we didn't look for the end so suddent; it come on us a awful shock." Susan began to weep in a ladylike fashion, rocking to and fro in the easiest chair.

The company had recourse to Scripture texts.

"And I know in reason," she continued presently, "that Harmon himself didn't expect it neither; 'r else he'd a-left some kind of a—will." There seemed some thought behind the speech which it was not advisable to put into words.

"He always thought so much of N'omi and Paul; he was good to all the children, but them two was his favor-ites." Marzela had awakened tardily.

The two women eyed each other for the first time with frank hostility. But Susan, feeling the necessity for making common cause against the enemy, resumed tearfully: "I wouldn't want to ask *her* anything about the 'last hours,' but Lucy, maybe, 'll know when she comes."

"Why ain't Lucy here, do you reckon?"

"She'll be here to set up," a neighbor volunteered. "She told me as I come on that she had been obliged to wash today; but she 'lowed to git here tonight."

"Late, I expect," said another, "for she'll have to carry that heavy baby. And she's been a-settin' up, her and Fan, ever since—it happened."

A low voice sounded from the doorway, and at least eight earbobs swung as one.

"Come to dinner," Fan Walton bade them quietly, "and please bring out four chairs."

From early candlelighting the house was full. And then, led on by those first comers, the whole gathering began covertly to watch Fan. Whatever she did was commented on. Sometimes when she passed there were whispered conversations; again an uneasy silence fell. Strange glances followed her through the doors, and when she was gone the subdued conversation began to fly back and forth. At last she caught the words, "He never would trust a bank, but—"

The significance of that phrase did not burn its way through her heavy thoughts until after she had quit the dimly lighted rooms and gained the quiet of the dark kitchen porch. Then, her noble strength deserting her suddenly, she dropped on the bench beside the crocks and churn; her cheeks burned in the darkness, and her mouth straightened to a hard line of suffering.

On the front porch Byron, half asleep after days of work and nights of watching, was stretched out with someone's saddle for a pillow, when he became aware of a point of light too low for a star, and sat up.

"Some of 'em pokin' about tryin' to find out something 'at's none o' their business," he decided, and roused himself with an effort. Visions of a lantern overturned in the hay hurried his feet across the lot. But it was no curious stranger; it was Fan, with her arms round Truelove's neck, crying as though her heart would break.

"Fan," he whispered, coming up, "don't—don't grieve so. . . . He was sure one good man; but he died about as he'd have chosen to,—all alive and hearty, and hard at work. He didn't suffer but a few days. He'd much rather have gone this way than—behind the bars. He took his chance—"

She put out a work-hardened hand without speaking, and he led her to the piled hay in the midst of the wide shadowy spaces.

"What did you come out for?" he asked, seating himself below her. "I fed everything. You ought to git some sleep."

"I wanted to get shut of all those folks," she answered, dabbing at her eyes with her apron. "Not you, Byron—you know they all talk so much. Oh, they're so—dirty! They shall not have Truelove, and the old man's team that he had so long, and the Durham heifer he raised: I'll kill the poor pets first!"

He nodded broodingly. "Fan—I don't want to push myself, but—you know what you told me oncet. If you still feel so—as soon as you can get consent o' your mind to let things loose here, why, turn 'em over to these folks. I want you to come to me. My house is a poor place—a poor home for a girl like you; but oncet you give me the right I'll make 'em careful what they say."

She shivered, and dropped her face into the cup of her palms.

"You're a dear boy, Byron. I could leave any time; but I—I don't know yet what I'm going to do. I want these folks out of the house, and I feel as if *he* does too . . ."

Byron was slow in replying. At last he said, "Well—I'll be around, Fan, any time you need me."

In the house the night wore on; the lamp burned strangely in the thick, drowsy air. The watchers seemed gradually to lose their individual characteristics, appearing neither young nor old,—like a row of images, presences vaguely unfriendly to each other and to the dead, they sat silent and grave, their shadows motionless on the wall. And still most of the men remained without, sitting on the steps, murmuring to each other in the desultory fashion of mountaineers; for death and birth are matters on which only women can bear to look.

"Mamma," whispered the young girl fresh from the Select Academy, "did you notice how short that Miss Walton's dress is made?"

The justice's lady nodded ponderously. "I wouldn't call it immodest exactly, but it don't, today, show a proper respect."

"What I want to know," intoned Marzela, solemnly, "is what she's a-*doin'* in this house all the time, day and night."

"You know she wouldn't let none of us feed the stock, nor do about in the house. It looks as if—"

"It does!"

" . . . She might know we'd think strange of hit."

"Don't you?" The speaker addressed Lucy directly.

The dead man's only sister had just come in. She was a small, worn, faded woman in blue calico, nursing her baby in a corner. Lifting her red-rimmed eyes, she answered from a kind of remoteness, as if rapt in sorrow: "Don't I what?"

"Don't you think strange of this Fan Walton bein' here?"

"No, I don't," she replied with more spirit. "I'd certainly think stranger if he'd a-lived here all these years without nobody."

"Well," said Marzela, "We 'lowed you might maybe know something about her."

"I know she took care of him like a own sister. I couldn't a-done better if I'd a-been here all the time."

"Well, but hit don't look right—a young thing like her. I'm surprised at you, Lucy, upholdin' such a—arrangemint."

"I'm surprised to hear all o' you'ns, that couldn't come about whilst brother Harmon was down and hurted to see how he was conductin' his house, come in now and take it all out on a defenseless gal!" cried Lucy. Then, remembering the presence of death, she rose hurriedly and carried her drowsy child out of the room.

The two in the barn looked up as the big doors swung a little apart, and Lucy glided like a mouse into the shadows which the lantern's rays only made more gloomy.

"I laid my baby on your bed, Fan, and come to see why you wasn't in it," she said in her gentle monotone.

"I can't sleep," protested Fan; but she accepted gratefully the homespun shawl her friend had brought, and wrapped it round herself and Lucy as they both rested on the hay. "We better go get them folks something to eat."

"I set it on the table afore I come out. You go to bed," said Lucy.

"I can't. . . . I can't think what I ought to do. I'll tell you and Byron how it really is . . ."

But a disturbance in the stalls had called the boy away. He found the stable overcrowded, and as he led the stamping intruders out, but few of Fan's words reached his ear—scraps of which he could make nothing:

". . . And I thought I should like it better here,—all quiet, with a whole house and farm to myself. I like to get out in the patch with a hoe—I like to make bread and wash clothes. So I wrote to him, and he said he'd be so glad to have me with him again. . . ."

When he passed a second time Lucy's arms were round the girl, and Lucy's voice was saying: "He was the best brother I ever had. If he hadn't helped me I don't know what we—"

From the house came the long strains of "Away Over in the Promised Land." He distinguished the preacher's "lead" and Clifford's bass, and Grandma' Bivins' quavering "high tribble."

"I can leave it all to them—I can make my way," Fan was reiterating. "But he wouldn't have wished that."

"Then tell them, honey; tell all the folks," counseled Lucy.

"He didn't want it known here, because he always meant to wind up his business and take me away. But he put the day off too long."

"Well, if I was you I'd stay right here," said Lucy. "I always thought there was something—and I know in reason they would of too, if they wasn't already eat up with suspicions. You'll be obliged to let it be known."

Byron approached the pair under the tentlike shawl.

"I've got three or four o' them strangers roped in the sheds," he told them. "I think they'll be quiet now." He sat at the women's feet, drooping over the lantern.

"Byron," said Lucy, "Fan's just told me something that makes a difference all 'round—"

"Hush," he bade her softly. "She's might' near asleep."

And so resting, they remained silent through the night.

At last the gray dawn glimmered against the smoky lantern; the watch was over. Lucy and Fan awoke, and went back to the kitchen to get breakfast.

Afterward a little procession filed across the fields, Grandma Bivins warning each member not to break the line lest he be next to die; and Harmon Ridge was laid in the good earth's embrace under soughing cedars of his own planting.

Immediately upon the closing of the grave, a clatter of harness-chains and much whoa-ing round the stable announced the general departure. But after each neighbor had spoken his farewell with a murmured phrase of gracious feeling for the family, Lucy looked out of a window and made mild eyes of surprise.

"Why, there's Clifford and Absalom and all their folks still waitin' round. They've corkussed and plotted and talked out there for I don't know how long."

"I thought they was gone long ago," said Byron. "Why, they're all a-comin' back to the house!"

Fan re-set the chairs in the strangely vacant-looking best room with a sinking heart that asked no questions. If it must come now, she would face it.

"Miss Walton," began the justice, clearing his throat, "we got a matter to bring up that we think needs namin'. If you—as you know all the house, and brother Harmon's ways, probably better than anybody else—if you can find—find—that is—unearth the money he left, you know—why, we'd be prepared to offer you a liberal amount of it—a share, in short."

The girl addressed lowered her eyes for very shame of his confusion. What a roundabout way he had taken to accuse her! She answered, "I don't believe he had any such amount as you all think."

She looked up. The silence was startling.

The next words were a veiled threat; they came from Absalom. "But we'd like to know what you—a young woman alone in the world, and without a home—propose to do? We cain't leave you here. And there's certain facts, if—if a heap o' people was to tell about 'em, might not sound well—might not be the best start for a young gal that's got her living to make, in fact!"

"In that case"—Fan lifted her head proudly, and faced the room-full—"I expect I had better stay right here."

"Why—!" If they had held their breath, they caught it now, hard. "You don't imagine you can hold this farm against the man's own blood and kin, do ye?" Clifford had not intended to go so far today; but neither had he looked to encounter such confident opposition.

"And Harmon not cold in his grave!" gasped Marzela.

"Don't anger her," whispered Susan pacifically behind her black veil. "I do believe she knows where the money's at."

"Can't you explain yourself—tell us what claim you've got on the estate, anyway?" probed the questioner, his eyes troubled with an uncertainty that was growing in his mind. "It ain't possible that—air you—a relative?"

Fan sprang forward with flushed cheeks and flashing eyes, throwing out her open palms. "God's my judge!" she cried in a clear ringing voice. "Can't you all see?"

And in her strong features, her firm neck and square-set shoulders so like those on which they had looked their last an hour ago through the glass of a coffin, they read the answer.

Byron was not the only one present whose heart leapt at her stand. At bay before them all, so young, brave, sweet, she stood, telling in a few words the story of her upbringing in the other valley. The blue of her eyes became brighter as she talked; she shook her head a little, and her rough reddish-brown hair came loose and swept down over her forehead in an unruly wave.

They did not ask to see the papers of evidence; not one but was glad to conceal discomfiture and mortal offense as inconspicuously and hastily as might be, on the road home.

"Well, I'm glad for ye, honey," was Lucy's parting word. "I'm a pore hard-run widder woman, but I'd rather have a niece like you than a share in what brother Harmon left. Now, run over to my house as often as you can, for you'll be lonesome."

"Don't say that, Lucy." Fan took the toil-worn hand and held it. "You come back tomorrow. As you say, I'll be lonesome; and I know *he*'d rather you'd be with me than anybody else. So you and the children bring this chap—" she stroked the baby's tow-colored head—"and move in with me, and help take care of the place and things. We'll keep 'em just as they was left—" A shade of her grief filled her eyes, and she turned away.

Byron was outside, drawing a bucket of water for the sorrel. Seeing Fan at the window, he came and folded his arms on the still.

"Well," he said, "I reckon you won't need me any more." The depth of his voice, the entreaty in his eyes, made her think twice of the words, though he tried to speak them lightly. "Not any more—ever."

She laid her hand on his head. "Why, Byron," she answered, "I'll need you more than ever now."

eleven

At the Top of Sourwood

From *Lippincott's Monthly Magazine* 89 (March 1912): 393–402

"At the Top of Sourwood" features a storekeeper, Noah Chadwick, whose marriageable daughter is pursued by both of his young male helpers. Rosabel clearly has a preference, but as is typically the case in mountain culture of this era, the father's word is the final one. When he refuses to approve the match, the young people take matters into their own hands. The plot is complicated by a theft of the proprietor's capital, but the would-be bridegroom saves the day. As Miles so often does in her fictional settings, she describes the actual general store on Walden's Ridge, which sat at the top of the "W road" that runs down the mountain to Chattanooga. In her journal and other writings, namely "Thistle Bloom" in this collection, she portrays the open-air dance pavilion that sat beside the store and the festive activities that occasionally took place there. This story was reprinted in the August 1915 issue of *Lippincott's Monthly Magazine.* Whether Miles received additional money for the second run is unknown, but doubtful.

The log house that was the Chadwick homestead as well as the general store sat perched like a cliff-eagle's nest on a jutting shelf of rock just where the old corduroy road went down a break in the mountain wall. By those who dwelt above its level, no less than by the five or six inhabitants of the sweep of mountainside that fell away sheer from its back windows, it was called the Top; and few were the articles required by their daily living that it did not carry in stock. The summer population whose residences gleamed white along the "brow" heights bought provisions for the season here; girls native to the coves and ridges came hither in search of print and ribbons for weddings and frolics, and young bucks in quest of the girls, as also of knives and ammunition, gathered on its cluttered stoop to exchange tales of prowess; grandmothers from remote cabins here bartered eggs and hominy for quilting thread and knitting needles; the housewife obtained here her salt and spoons, her spider and hearth-oven, and an occasional "chaney" dish to be cherished all the way home like a captive bird; men bought leather for half-soles in autumn, axe-helves in winter, and hoes in spring. The steadiest of staples was tobacco, which sold the year round to both sexes and all ages. Next in importance came powder and lead; coffee followed a close third; after them the salt pork and corn meal that were the mainstay of existences too thriftless to support a shoat or a patch of corn.

As the business throve and old Noah Chadwick found his hands overfull, he insured himself good service by taking on, instead of a single clerk, two youngsters of the same surname, Cairo and Cephas Plank. These boys were supposed to be cousins, although, in fact, no native of that intermarried district could say exactly what kin he was to any of the others.

"Sort o' half-Brindle to Buck, as your mam used to say about my yoke o' steers," old Noah remarked to his daughter Rosabel. "And so nigh the same age that whenever Cephas dies of old age Cairo can burn his hat. But they ain't no more alike 'n a sourwood and a black-jack. Cephas don't kill the timber a-bein' pretty, though he's some peart and soople when he's dressed up; but that there long-legged Cairo—he's ugly as home-made sin." He wanted Rosabel to say so, too; but she merely arranged the budding comeliness of her features to an expression of preternatural composure. "And works around here with his head up like a steer in a cornfield, as if he owned the store!"

From the first day of employment the boys had thrown their weight into the collar like a gallant team; but Chadwick's satisfaction in his advantage was moderated by some uncertainty as to his daughter's possible interest in either of the helpers. As a precautionary measure, he took to ridiculing both lads in her hearing. It ought to be easy, he thought, to show her that there were better and more prosperous men awaiting her notice. His hope was that she might incite them to continue the rivalry by favoring neither beyond his fellow, maintaining an even balance of smiles and friendly words from day to day.

On a morning when the sweet keen breath of the first frost was in the air, and the gold and azure of September was inclining toward the rich October purple and scarlet, Cairo was sent to the valley for a load of freight from the way-station. As the wagon came rumbling and clanging forth from the lot, Rosabel threw on her sunbonnet and ran out on the porch, calling to the driver for a ride as far as her uncle's house at the foot of the mountain.

He bent down and drew her to the high seat beside him; and Cephas, sorting late potatoes by the window, watched them ride away through the dreaming shadows that lay across the corduroy road.

When in the afternoon they returned, Rosabel's hat wreathed in flame-colored vines and her lap full of tart wild grapes and sugary persimmons, he became sullenly furious.

"Ol' man'll be apt to fire you, Cairo, 'f he ketches you takin' Rosie with ye round the country," he warned his yokemate.

"That's all right!" Cairo's voice was half friendly, half derisive. His steel-gray eyes held a genial light, but his chin was like the point of a flat-iron, and there was something square and grim, possibly from a far-away Cherokee ancestor, about his wide mouth. "You can stay and court the old man whilst we're out, and maybe beat my time a'ter all."

Cephas glowered across the crates they were unloading and found nothing to say. As for the girl, she had run into the house the moment she alighted, and sought her own room. She had something to tell her father—something that required all her resolution.

The next day Cairo was not surprised at being summoned to the back room, where the kerosene and sorghum barrels, the tubs of lard and sides of pork, the bags of feed and salt, lay in dim rows along a windowless wall. He entered with quickened pulses; but the old fellow only adjusted his spectacles and motioned his clerk, salesman, driver, and factotum to a seat on a bag of cotton-seed meal.

"Cairo," he began, "you've worked around this store a right smart while, off and on."

"Yes, sir; goin' on two year."

"And I've been a-payin' you regular, over 'n' above your board."

"I ain't never complained about that," said the young man, wondering whither this oblique approach might be tending.

"Now, then," challenged Chadwick, "I want the truth out o' you—how much have you got saved up in that time?"

Cairo's eyes narrowed, and he thrust his hands deeper in his pockets. "How much do you expect a man to save out o' three dollars a week?"

"I ain't sayin'. Though I made out to save on less, when I was a youngster. I'm wantin' to know how much you got, and where hit's at."

"Why, hit ain't a great deal, but hit's in a good safe place," Cairo countered, grinning.

"You've e'en-about butted your horns off, if ye did but know it!" Noah admonished him sharply. "I'm axin' because Rosie told me last night—something I'd as leave not a-heard for a good while yet. Anyhow, I aim to know something about the fellow that gits her."

"Don't ye know enough about me yit?"

"Not till I'm satisfied whether you're able to take keer o' my gal. I *do* know there's ne'er a foot of ground your'n, nor a stick o' timber. There's room in my house for the man that's good enough for my Rosebud; but you, Cairo, you're a-makin' too pore a start." He was silent a moment, and then repeated a mountain proverb: "'There's more marries than keeps cold meat.'"

"Well, Mr. Chadwick," replied Cairo, sobered, "I don't aim to give ye a short answer, but looks to me that's my business. *I* never inquared round what you was worth nor what you was liable to give her."

Noah drew himself up. "You didn't hafto ax what everybody knows."

To this Cairo seemed to have nothing to say. He opened his knife and began whittling—a tacit admission that the argument might reasonably be prolonged. The dim and dusty room, lighted only by two thin rays of afternoon sunshine through the chink of the heavy oaken door-hinges, was still—so still that they could hear the high squeak and chatter of a bat incensed at the wasps that circled over the drip of the vinegar barrel.

Noah's eyebrows began to work up and down on his forehead. "You dadlimbed cymblin'-head!" he burst out at length. "Got the imperence to marry my gal and set round waitin' for the old man to leave ye well off, have ye? You'll see in a minute where ye drapped your candy! Not a cent have you got only what you was lookin' to git from me; now, ain't that so?"

"I've got a right to say I won't answer! You've knowed me, Mr. Chadwick, ever sence I was as big as your fist. That ought to be enough."

"Well, hit is enough!" retorted Noah, now completely antagonized. "And you can leave my store if I ketch ye talkin' to Rosebud a'ter this."

"All right. I aim to wed her, though—and then if you give me and her ary thing, I'll be jist as good as you air, and give hit back to ye." Cairo shut his knife, and, getting to his feet, turned away.

"She'll never have my consent to wed ye!"

"She may do without it," was Cairo's parting shot, as he quietly left the room.

A few days later Rosabel's mother, a meek, hard-working woman who did as her husband bade her on all occasions, approached the assistant thus cast into disfavor while he was preparing to take his place in the store after breakfast, and began hesitatingly: "Cairo, I hate to tell ye, but pap, he 'lows I cain't feed ye no more." She wrapped her worn hands in her gingham apron and stood regarding him almost sadly.

"Cain't? What for? I know I hide white beans and biscuit as if my laigs was holler, but Cephas eats me a match every meal—or did until right lately," responded the young man, laughing.

"I—I reckon pap's afeared you and Rosebud's a-makin' it up to run away," she explained, trying to smile in response to his jovial bearing.

"He better watch closeter than what he's been a-doin'," chuckled Cairo. "Well, that's all right, Mis' Chadwick. I'll go and talk to him a'ter a while. Maybe he'll decide to keep me around."

In the slack of the afternoon he came out on the high back porch overlooking the valley, where in the shadow of the house two buckets of spring water sat on a puncheon shelf, and a pair of gourds swung gently in the breeze, since neither Noah nor his wife liked to drink from a dipper. The old man was standing before a second shelf that upheld a tin basin, a towel, and an eight-inch square of "bubbly" mirror, laboriously removing from his countenance a week's growth of gray stubble. He prided himself on shaving regularly once a week, "whether his face needed hit or not." He was contorting his features into more extraordinary grimaces than a school-boy behind his teacher's back, and took no notice of Cairo's advent except by grumbling to the mirror, "Dad-limb this old razor! If I cain't hone it into better shape again' next time, I'll hafto give up and grow a beard."

"You aim for me to leave, Mr. Chadwick?" asked Cairo, closing the door softly behind him.

"Hafto board somers else!" was the gruff reply.

Cairo, being disposed to grant the naturalness of his employer's resentment, would not make too much of this. "You mean you don't want me to work here no more?" he pursued.

"I ain't anxious either way." In truth, Noah could ill afford to lose his most wideawake assistant, but was in no humor to say so.

"Then," the young man continued, under his voice, "I've got a thing to tell you afore I leave."

"More out o' your sass-box!"

"No, no; hit's somethin' you ought to hear, and nobody else."

"Dad-limb this here razor! Hit's dull as a frow! No, I've heared enough about ye and out of ye, you high headed Two-by-Four!"

"This here's different; hit's about—"

"I've done told ye I don't want no words with ye."

"About the store—"

"You've made me cut myself three-four times a'ready. If you stand there a-jowerin', you'll have me scored, ready to be hewed. May do for Planks, but I'll be limb-juggled if I—"

"Well, I'm a-leavin'; but there's a word to say. Hit's about the store; and I miss my guess if hit don't find ye where you're at home," Cairo maintained with significant firmness.

"I'll run my store without any ad-vice. There! *Cut again!*" Chadwick turned, brandishing the offending razor. "Now, you git!"

Cairo flushed darkly as he turned away. "Well—if you was to happen to want me for anything next week, I'll be down at sis' Marthy's," he remarked as he went forth.

No sooner was the storekeeper alone than he began to regret his "tetchiness." This was not what he had intended. He wondered, and wondered again, what the boy could have meant to tell him. Some impertinence about his daughter, perhaps. Let him go!

"Shoo! Thinks he's a whole dime's worth o'nickels. With the town folks gone down for the winter, and trade gittin' below profit mark, me and Cephas can certainly mind the store without him. He'll be ready enough to come back again' the summer trade commences," Noah declared to his chin-lathered reflection.

Yet he could hardly eat his supper. He preserved a dignified and stubborn silence, as befitted the proprietor of the only store in that quarter of the country; but night fell with the clouds riding swift and low, across the sky, and found Noah in an unapproachable temper, Rosabel in tears, Cephas unaccountably absent, and the mother going heavily and silently about the evening tasks of the household.

An hour after dark Cairo stood on the platform of the little valley way-station, just out of reach of a cold drizzle that was beginning to fall. He examined, without appearing to do so, each member of the group that here awaited the coming of the south-bound train. Two loafers and a drummer, besides an old lady whose daughter kept reassuring her as to the safety of travelling by rail, he let go by with hardly a glance; a country preacher carrying a hand-bag, and after him a mountaineer with a jug, he regarded most closely as they passed under the dim and smoky wall-lamp; and at last his attention became fixed on a kerchief-muffled individual who stepped unostentatiously on to the extreme end of the platform a few moments before train-time. There was nothing remarkable about this newcomer, although the home-woven basket of oak splints, bulging with clothing and tightly roped, might in other regions have occasioned some amusement.

Cairo sauntered to and fro, softly whistling "Texas Rangers" between his teeth, and finally came to a stop directly behind the other and looked him over from head to foot, staring longest at the fringe of hair that remained visible above the coat-collar turned up to meet a low hat-brim.

The traveller, feeling the scrutiny, glanced furtively around, started at sight of Chadwick's employee, and moved nervously away from the dim light that struggled through the door and the window.

Cairo greeted him without receiving a reply, and added: "You're uncommon skeered of the toothache. Look like you had a bad cold and was afeared to ketch another on top of hit." As the other still made no answer, "You didn't 'low you could fool me, did you?" he continued, following a step. "Why, Cephas, I'd know your hide in the tan-yard."

The discovered Cephas, finding retreat no longer possible, faced the situation with a stuttered "W-what you—what you want, then?"

"Jist whatever you got in that basket."

"My—my clo'es?" Cephas glared, and involuntarily tightened his grasp on the stout receptacle.

Cairo laughed a little. "The money's in there, sure 'nough, then! I won't be hard on ye," he persisted. "I'll let ye have thirty dollars o' my own—enough to land ye safe in Florida, or Texas, or wherever ye was aimin' to go."

"You—you jist better let me alone, now—"

"Make up your mind quick," urged Cairo in the old half-bantering tone. "I seed the sheriff in the saloon as I come on by there. 'F he was to ketch ye with all that on ye, hit'd be all-night-Isom."

The train, after a long preliminary rumble rising to a roar, dashed out of the tunnel. The whistle screamed aloud; the two notes of its cry, falling one into the other, were caught up by the crags of Sourwood, echoed and reëchoed till the night was filled with its floating, flying tremolo, blown with the rain through the dark—a sound unwonted and disquieting to a country boy with senses already guiltily perturbed. Cephas stood confused and reeling.

Cairo advanced, holding forward three ten-dollar bills. And half still seeking a possible alternative, Cephas accepted them and gave up the basket. Then, realizing his mistake too late, he broke into wild and incoherent cursing.

"All abo-oard!" sang the conductor. As the fugitive obeyed the suggestion, he saw Cairo diving rapidly through the contents of the basket, making sure of his capture. Cephas sank into a seat and did not look up when the train began to roll slowly forward, until some one knocked on the open window, and there was his late comrade running alongside.

"Here! take your clo'es," cried the same half-friendly, half-mocking voice. "You'll need them shirts afore you git another job." And the runaway snatched the basket-handle just before the gathering momentum of the train swept home and friends out of his ken forever.

Next morning on the store at the Top consternation fell like a blasting wind. It was found that Cephas, their dependence, had not slept in his room, and, further, that the key of the strong-box which held the store's and Chadwick's available capital was missing. The same little boy whose untimely purchase of snuff and boss-ball thread for his mother's quilting precipitated the discovery was despatched in haste to Cephas's aunt, who recalled that the missing man had borrowed a basket of her the previous noon. She quitted her house immediately with a square of homespun thrown over her head, and in an incredibly short space of time, considering the distance between neighbors, rumor was abroad and active.

It was clearing colder after the night's rain; the broken clouds, as they sailed over, gleamed against a brilliant sky; the air was like wine. Leaves from the painted forest went swirling out across the valley, borne on the wind almost to the flying clouds. On such a morning every one must needs be astir on one pretext or another, and a crowd soon gathered at the Top, each man babbling of a theory and a plan of procedure that conflicted with all the others. The road was blocked with ox and mule teams and "tar-grinder" wagons, some laden with "spun-truck," fruit, and logs on the way to the valley, others coming up with lumber, "roughness" from lowland fields, and manufactured articles from Macklimore's shops; for not a soul was able to drive past the scene of so notable a robbery.

Hours were spent in discussion and argument before the blacksmith broke the lock of the box and the worst was known. Noah Chadwick was one of those old-fashioned people who distrust banks. He had long contemplated hiding his hoard as had his father before him, under some boulder in the breaks of the creek; but he had put the day off too long. Now, stunned by the knowledge that he was robbed, the old man simply cowered, shrunk into a heap on a cracker-box, his face drawn, his arms shaking, and allowed his neighbors as they assembled to offer consolation or encouragement unheeded. He would not be roused even by suggestions for borrowing the county bloodhounds or sending for the neighborhood wizard, who divined secret waters and treasures by means of a wand or a cup and ring.

"I'm a' old man and a little man," he shrieked once in a high, febrile voice of impotent rage, "but I can kill the sneakin' hound that stole my money!" and he felt the emptiness of the threat even as it was uttered.

His wife walked to and fro, whimpering, "Oh, I wisht Rosabel was at home. She'd know what to say to her pap if anybody could." She was not thinking of his loss or her own, although she had toiled as heavily as her husband for the slow accumulation of the lost two thousands. "Oh, Rose might understand how to ease his mind! I do wisht she was here!"

"Where's she at?" inquired a sympathizing woman whose hands were still pink from washing breakfast dishes.

"She went to stay all day with her uncle's folks. Oh, I wisht—"

"Some of you'ns ketch out my ol' Soapstick and go a'ter her," proposed the other. And a lad was ready with a neighbor's buckboard to go in search of Chadwick's daughter, when a shout went up from the small-boy contingent watching by the roadside, and she and Cairo came in sight, driving up the corduroy road in a cart hired from Macklimore.

Questions were called excitedly down the steep approach as the pair ascended; but Cairo merely laughed, and waved his hand. On reaching the store, he leaped to the ground, passed the file of waiting teams, and hurried in without a word.

"Cairo," the blacksmith hailed him as he entered, "do you know—know anything about this here calamity?"

"What time did you leave the store yesterday?" asked another.

He replied to the latter: "Right after I was fired."

"Fired, was ye? How much money did you take out?"

"Five dollars that was comin' to me," answered Cairo.

"Yes, I let him have that," corroborated Mrs. Chadwick, "and he went right off, too. Oh, Cairo, he'p me and pap to find out—" Her face crinkled distressfully.

"I will; don't worry," he bade her, a reassuring seriousness and warmth coming into his tones.

"You didn't have no more here your own self?" pursued the smith.

"Naw; I had thirty dollars in a safer place." He lounged against the elbow-polished counter. "I jist 'lowed this store might wake up some morning and find its cash gone."

"What fur?"

"Well, I been with Cephas Plank long enough to know in reason what he'd be apt to do whenever Rosebud turned him down."

At these sensational words, the circle swayed and jostled, while a tremendous chattering and whispering went up from the outer group of shawled and aproned women.

"Shoo!" The smith was first to recover himself. "You ain't got nothing to go on—that's jist your guess."

"That was all at first; but I noticed him git some things together yestidy that he wouldn't 'a' needed without he was goin' away; and I judged, too, that he'd whirl in and do some devilment whenever I wasn't here to sort o' keep a eye on him."

"Why in time couldn't ye 'a' said something about it, seein' ye knowed so much?"

"I did try to," explained Cairo equably, "and Mr. Chadwick wouldn't listen to me. He got so mad, I looked for him to throw me over the bluff."

He had missed the psychological moment for this laughing disclosure. The circle narrowed perceptibly; the men growled in their bearded throats, not half liking his light-heartedness.

"Maybe you know more 'n you've told."

"Maybe I do."

"Was it Cephas, then, sure 'nough?"

"Sure 'nough, hit was."

"Know where he's gone, do ye?"

"He's half-way to the Indi'n Nation by now."

Chadwick groaned, and got to his feet. "You holped him git away!" he groaned. "You ought to be hung in his place! You knowed all the time, and you let him git away with every cent I got! I'll see what the law—"

"Oh, no; he didn't git away with a cent o' your'n," pronounced Cairo deliberately. "Hit's all right out yender in the buggy with my wife."

"In the buggy—with your wife!"

"You didn't think we was goin' to stand around waitin' for your say, after you'd done told us we wouldn't git hit? We was married at her uncle's house this morning."

The little bride was already tiptoeing on the threshold, and now ran forward as the folk made way. "Don't feel so bad, pappy," she pleaded, reaching toward him a carefully tied packet. "Take 'n' count the money—look, hit's all here. Don't be mad at us; don't, pappy, will ye?"

Chadwick looked into her sweet, flushed face for a moment before he took the packet from her outstretched hand. "No, I won't be mad, honey," he said at last, slowly. "And—and don't you and him be mad at me. A man ort not to hold to all the contentious things he says, and—Cairo, ef the money's here—and hit is—why you and her'll have enough out of hit to start ye to housekeepin'. You will, won't ye?—something for Rose? I always aimed, whenever she got married—"

"I'm proud to," said his son-in-law heartily.

On each dour and stolid mountaineer face approval struggled forth like the sun through clouds. Every watcher drew breath as the package was opened and found to contain the money and every least security that Cephas had deemed negotiable. Rosabel and her mother were crying and laughing in each other's arms.

"Well, hit's my treat, boys." Noah came to himself as he closed his strong-box on its wonted contents. "And I ain't got a thing but cider, so I cain't ax y'uns what you'll have."

He turned to the counter. "Some of you boys make on a fire. Cairo, you he'p me about these here glasses and cups; and say, Cairo, wait a' hour or so and I'll ride back down to Macklimore with ye, and he'p ye git your things. I cain't do no business to-day. Let's all turn in and give this here couple a ch'ivari."

twelve

Enchanter's Nightshade

From *The Craftsman* 22 (July 1912): 387–97

"Enchanter's Nightshade" is a story of male sibling rivalry over two young women—demure Fedelma, already married to older brother Ransom, and vivacious Callista, clearly attracted to younger brother Atlas. But in a sparsely populated mountain community, a young person may have eyes for someone else's mate during the typically short courtship period. Such is the case with these four. Jealousy escalates into a fight between the two brothers, and only through the women's intervention is serious violence prevented. The "enchanter's nightshade" of the title is a plant associated in mythology with the magic of the enchantress Circe. The luminous plant, along with a bit of mountain whiskey, seems to have cast an evil spell on the young people, but their natural goodness ultimately prevails. Miles's desire for a happy ending and a moral lesson is evident in the denouement of the story.

At a merrymaking in Caney's Cove two brothers were dancing. They were both in the early twenties, blond, well formed and agile. They had been known as "them good-lookin' Reedy boys" before they were grown, and although demure Fedelma had married the elder a year ago, the maidens pressing their best plumage softly together in the doorway whispered to each other, "Ain't he straight!" as Ransom took the floor, even while all their arts were directed toward attracting the still eligible Atlas. Ransom was a smaller and finer edition of his younger brother; he had clearer features, bluer eyes, and fair hair curling close to the scalp where Atlas' mop was sandy.

Ransom's partner of the moment was, as it happened, the very girl whom Atlas had brought to the gathering—Callie Drane, a girl large for her age, whose vivid coloring and thick waving hair bespoke abundant vitality. With a grace like that of a wild creature she bounded to meet the young fellow in the middle of the ring; her eyes and her teeth gleamed as she gave him her hand, unconscious of the strength of its clasp. Catching the air from the banjos, she began to sing as she danced.

"The ficety thing," murmured some of the women. But others took up the melody, a native composition, and carried it all together:

"Some days seem dark and dreary, As though it was likely to rain;
Some clouds may float to center,
My love has gone off on the train.

"Oh it's hard to be bound in prison,
It's hard to be bound in jail!
To see iron bars around you,
And no one to go your bail!"

Callie moved to and fro lightly, her head high, her mouth well open, her face full of light, the song rippling from her throat as limpid and fresh as a streamlet from a mountain spring.

Her very antithesis was Fedelma, sitting mute and motionless by the wall. The bride of a year was not dancing this set, preferring, out of sheer pride in his appearance, to keep her soft dark gaze on her young husband. They were late in arriving because she had stopped to sew a patch inside the collar of his best shirt. Despite the meek grace of her neck and smooth brown head, she heard and rather resented the whispers; and at Callista's too eager advance she half-rose with a smothered exclamation. A little later she stood up, turning her head from side to side uneasily.

To a would-be partner she replied confusedly, "No—I—jist 'lowed to get me a drink; it's hot in here," and slipped out under the tranquil stars.

She had kept a beautiful secret to tell Ransom tonight; but something, some careless word of his, had postponed the telling until they should find themselves alone on the homeward road, and now—"I won't tell him a-tall!" she whispered fiercely, threading her aimless way through the undergrowth. "I jist won't! That big tomboy Callie—she came right into his eyes with that look o' hers, and he let her in—he let her in! . . . . They act as if they knowed something I don't." Her throat ached with rising sobs. "They used to go together, didn't they? No telling but they think of each other still!"

Her feet found themselves in the spring path. Wishing only to be alone until this unwonted flood of feeling could spend itself, she went slowly down the hill and seated herself on the puncheon bench, placed there for the support of washtubs. Before her, in the white moonlight, stood Bivins' springhouse, its walls of heavy logs and stones crossed by a delicate vine whose leaves and clustered berries showed translucent. Having once noticed, she could not take her eyes from the exquisite thing. The moon was mounting into the sky; she heard the whispered counsel of the leaves like a warning, and the night's heavy moisture spilling from leaf to leaf. A faint pattering footfall rustled in the thicket. She felt so afraid of the lonely woods that she ceased crying, and leaned forward as if to rise; but she sat on, looking at the pretty slender vine, wishing she had not come here or to Bivins' dance, yet perversely assuring herself that, if Ransom were really bent on reviving an old affair, nothing else could matter to him or to her.

A heavy, tramping step and a splash roused her from the mood into which she had fallen. She rose now and stood, a white slim shape in the cavern of shadow beneath the big tupelo that overarched Mam Bivins' washplace.

The newcomer was Atlas. "Hello! what you doin' here, Delma?" he asked, surprised. As she made no answer, he entered the springhouse, dipped his bucket and began fumbling along the walls. "Do they keep ary gourd here, that you known of?" he inquired, reappearing in the moon-drenched doorway.

"I don't know," she answered mournfully, speaking with an effort over the lump in her throat.

Replying to the tone instead of the words, he came toward her. In the moonlight she saw his honest face touched with concern, its big brows wrinkling together. "Is the' anything the matter? Does Ransom know you're here all by yourself?"

In the darkness she found his soft Southern bass inexpressibly comforting.

"I—jist wanted a drink." And out of pure pique she added, "He don't hafto know every step I take, does he?"

He answered with a little laugh that meant nothing except the blessed readiness of youth for laughter. "Let's git us a drink, if we can find a gourd."

She caught the quick spurt of a lighted match, an ejaculation as its snapped-off head hissed in the water. To the mountain girl there was a fascinating masculine recklessness in this dashing waste of matches.

He struck another, and looking up over its glow in the cup of his hollowed palms, found her face crowned with its wreath of jade and coral unexpectedly close to his own in the doorway, and smiled.

Fedelma drew back. "Well, there ain't a thing here to drink out of except that big wooden bucket," she exclaimed petulantly.

"Would ye take my hat?" he proffered, scooping a drink in its felt brim.

She drank and thanked him, but did not at once set off toward the house. Something in the deferential gesture with which he waited on her, some vibration in his voice, filled her with a sudden overwhelming curiosity as to how he would make love. She wondered, with a thrill of terror at her own daring, what were the deepest and tenderest notes of his voice, what the falling, hovering motions of his broad hands. One man's wooing she knew by heart; could there be another as sweet?—But was that, perhaps, Ransom's feeling about Callie? The racking anger came welling up again; and before she was aware it rose to words.

"Atlas, what makes you go with Callie Drane?"

He laughed again, a rich, pleasant chuckle. "Don't you like her?"

"Oh—she thinks too much of herself, I b'lieve! Whatever makes you—?" She checked herself, realizing that her speech was open to misinterpretation.

"Why—because I couldn't git you, I reckon." It was an absurd compliment, awkwardly turned; but finding Ransom's wife so unlike her usual shy and gentle self had gone to his head a little.

"Oh, shuh! You and me—" She really hardly knew what to say, "You and me ain't never went together enough to—to—to make you talk like that."

"Why—" He made a gesture of protest. "You remember the Three Springs picnic, don't ye?"

Of course she did, but she had never been sure till now that it was worth remembering. Had he meant it, then—all the play of that merry time? Her pulses quickened; she stood silent, lovely and alluring in the dusk of the perfumed woods. The red berries in her hair seemed to burn like a desire.

They moved forward together, and Atlas, knocking accidentally against a sapling, brought down a shower of starry drops from the branches all over her.

She gave a little shriek, and then laughed, dancing ahead under the moving shadows of the foliage, bent upon reprisal. Tiny drops like diamond dust glittered on the stray curls over her forehead, and on the leaves and berries of her wreath, twinkling with the tremor of her laughter.

Atlas stopped, his hands closing into fists. They stood facing each other, eyes answering eyes with something roused and dangerous. He recovered himself by an effort and drew back a step.

"You goin' back to the house?" he suggested, taking up the bucket of water.

She trembled, balanced, hesitated—then compromised, "Not yit a while." How far she had drifted from this morning's austere joy in her secret, after the nights of terror and doubt!

Atlas set down the pail. "Then shall I stay too?" He came and bent over her. "Do ye want me—to—stay with you—Delma?"

She did not look up, as she made room for him beside her on Mam Bivins' bench:—"only don't ye forget, Atlas Reedy, that I'm a married woman!"

"I won't if you don't," he laughed, fanning her with the hat she had drank from. Something in her fragility and helplessness moved him in a different way from Callie's robust buoyance. He could not deny that he liked doing little things for Delma.

From the house up the hill the music of banjos came pulsing out upon the ancient night, powerful with associations to those two—a music indigenous to the soil as the scarlet-berried vine.

"I have a great ship on the ocean,
All lined with silver and gold;
And before my true lover shall suffer,
My ship shall be anchored and sold.

"If I had the wings of an eagle,
Or either the wings of a dove,
I'd fly over mountain and rivers,
And rest in the arms of my love."

Of a sudden her face crinkled miserably. "I reckon Ransom's done forgot it already."

"How's that, Fedelma?"

"Didn't you see, Atlas?" Insensibly a note of sincerer feeling crept into her voice. She looked straight at him without self-consciousness. "Ransom and Callie?"

The hat quivered, and stopped, clutched hard. "See . . . . what? You tell me!"

"Nothing only—she looked at him, I thought. When they danced."

"Oh, she did, did she!" Atlas got to his feet. "I been afeared of it," he groaned. "Rans' was the first that ever went with Callie. . . . . They say a gal never forgets." He strode forward and caught up the bucket without looking round. "Let's us go back!" His voice went strangely harsh on the words. "By jacks, I've whupped Rans' afore, and I can again if he gits to lookin' too hard at my gal. Condamn that curly head of his!"

She had no choice but to follow, flung into a gulf of doubt and anger by his ready acceptance of her suspicions as valid. She would hurry to see what Ransom was doing now—oh, she must! What had she been thinking of, to leave him to his own devices for so long?

But it was Ransom who showed himself at the turn of the path, and demanding: "Been down to the spring, Atlas? Have you seed Fedelma anywhere? Oh, there she comes—"

Her heart at first expanded with relief; but she distinctly saw his start as he realized that she had accompanied Atlas. He stood before her, blocking the path, and did not speak for a moment. Atlas disappeared with the bucket of water; the dropping dew, the crickets and the katydids, possessed the stillness. They heard the banjos at the house, and the thudding feet of the dancers.

"Had you forgot you belong to me?" he asked at last. He stopped with his mouth open, and she smelt the product of Bivins' still.

"Rans'! Why, Ransom! had you forgot you wasn't goin' to touch whiskey tonight?" she countered. "Let's us go home right now, Rans'. Let's do!"

"Not till I've licked that—" Ransom's synonym for "cur" was polysyllabic but forceful—"for stealin' you out. And I'll see you afterward." He turned on his heel and moved away, a feeling of sullen resentment against her in his heart, suddenly estranged and isolated. He felt powerless to fight against the hideous doubts that took his mind by storm.

But his wife, following, clung to him, her arm round his shoulders. "Rans', he didn't. He didn't. You wouldn't think so if you wasn't drinkin'. Wait, honey—wait a minute—let me tell you! Atlas come down to git some water for the folks; I'd done been there for some little time. . . . . Don't you go to the house, Rans'. Take me home." She began to cry, stumbling along beside him. "I want to go home, Ransom! Hit's the best. I got something to tell you. You—you'll take another drink or two up there, and then first thing you know you'ns 'll all git in a jower and a jangle, and you or him, one'll be hurt."

"Sure will," he retorted grimly, moving doggedly forward. They came out into the open road, flooded with light.

"But I want to tell you something! Listen—"

He flung off her hands. "If hit's what I think," he said, in a tense undertone, "you better never tell it." His light-weight figure was drawn erect; his eyes glinted like steel.

"You and them for it, then!" cried Fedelma, stopping short with a gesture of despair. Her secret! Had he guessed it, then—and was this the way he meant to take it? She made no attempt to follow him farther; she forgot Atlas and Callie entirely; her deepest feelings were wounded now. "His baby, his own little—Oh, dear Lord, what shall I do! I'm a good notion to go back to Marion County and stay with mammy!"

She wandered, sobbing and wiping her eyes on her sleeves, along the road home.

Ransom, hurrying to Bivins' house, looked through the window at the lighted room. The rhythmic swing of the music urged the pounding of the blood in his temples. He saw Atlas join the dance again, saw a little flurry among the girls, and heard without noticing Callie's laugh. The little children, who had been allowed to sit up late, now began to nod over in the corners; the usual contingent of bad little boys arrived and, growing obstreperous, had to be hustled out of the way. The fun waxed furious; the figures wheeled and swung and eddied; coats were flung off, hand-clapping and stamping increased, laughter was continuous. At every shout he glowered more darkly through the narrow pane.

"I'll take one more drink, and then I'll call him out," he muttered to one who stood near him in the yard.

"Who?" asked Homer Bivins.

"Huh? Why, Atlas,—dam' his impident looks."

"What's he done, Rans'? I wouldn't, Ransom. Better not call him out, Ransom," said several bystanders quickly. For Ransom and Atlas had fought ever since they were boys on the slightest provocation or none at all; their only peace lay in keeping apart, although there seemed no ill feeling between them other than the ancestral rivalry between males of the same blood.

Old Bivins came from the jug hidden in the althea bushes, all solicitude for the success of his daughters' merrymaking.

"Looky here, Ransom," he began in a conciliatory tone, plucking the young man's sleeve. "Some day when we'ns ain't got no frolic afoot we'll make a ring, somers out, and see fair play whilst you and him settles it for good, and finds out which is the best man."

"No, by Jacks, I'll have him afore I go home tonight," cried the little man, exasperated at the quivering of Bivins' long beard. What business was it of anyone's? "I feel like I could whup him right now; I b'lieve I can."

"You go fetch his woman," suggested Homer aside to another. "Maybe she can do something with him. Lord, what a temper Rans' Reedy's got! I'll go warn his brother."

But Fedelma could not be found; she was already whimpering to herself, far in the moonlight; and Atlas presently came to Callie with a very serious countenance.

"Callista, girl, I've got obleeged to quit and go, I reckon. Do you want me to take you home now, or—but I declar' I hate to leave ye to ary other boy! Go now, will ye—with me?"

"What time is it?" she parleyed, reluctant. "I'm havin' such a good old time! Has something happened?"

"No—not yit."

"Then what you leavin' for?"

"Well—Rans' has took one or two drinks too many, and he's lookin' for me. You know, Callie, how he always was."

Her eyes opened. "You ain't afeared of him, air ye?"

"What would I be afeared of him for? I don't want to fight him; ther ain't no sense in hit when we ain't got nothing to fight about, and him and me has both swore we never would again."

The girl considered, her face still flushed, her eyes gleaming; and then, even while her foot still beat time to "Citico," she gave in. "Wait, then, till I say good-bye to Sally Bivins, and I'll git my shawl."

The music swelled to their ears in an appealing crescendo and diminuendo as they made an unobtrusive exit. "I don't much believe Delma was right about him and her," he was thinking. "If I 'lowed he was, though, Rans' wouldn't hafto look far afore he found me."

They gained the road with a reassuring backward glance to where Homer, with diplomacy slightly mistaken, was plying Ransom with more liquor.

"I like to walk with you this way," he murmured as they swung into step. He drew her hand within his arm and kept it there, pressing and pressing it, the unlighted lantern swinging at his side.

"Why," said the girl, perceiving a glimmering shape moving before them down the road, "somebody's went on ahead of us."

"Hit's a gal," he supplemented her observation. "All by herself. Why, I'll swar!"

"Don't do it," she laughed.

"I won't. I just said 'I will swar.' But I b'lieve on my soul that's Fedelma. What's the matter, Dell?" he called.

The forlorn figure waited for them to come up, and they saw that she was crying.

"Did Rans' make ye go home? Did he scold ye? Air you waitin' for him?" asked Callie, all in a breath.

"We left," explained the boy, "because he seemed to want to jump onto me. I 'lowed it would be best to keep out of his way?"

Delma nodded, but could find no words.

They were now all four at cross-purposes; and their hearts were all beating a little too fast.

"Well, walk on with us," said Atlas at last. "We'll sight you home; won't we, Callie?"

But as Fedelma joined the pair, Callie swung apart. "Why! you ain't aimin' to leave Ransom come home all by hisself, the way he is?"

"O' course; he'll be all right," answered Atlas. "Or, if he ain't, some o' them boys 'll see to him."

"How d'you know they will? He may go wanderin' about and break his fool neck."

"He wouldn't let me," protested Atlas; but he glanced back along the road uneasily.

"Dell!" The appeal was from one woman to another on behalf of an erring boy. "Ain't you goin' to wait for your man?"

"No, I ain't," declared Delma, speaking for the first time. "After the way he talked to me back yon, he can go on and break his neck for all o' me—b-hoo-hoo!"

"Then I will!" cried the girl, stopping.

"You won't neither!" snapped Fedelma.

"Why, Callie!" Atlas stopped, facing her. A jealous wrath surged up in him and burst bounds. "By Jacks, if there *is* anything between you and your old sweetheart, hit's time I knowed it, Callie! I want the straight of hit; I can't stand this—"

"Don't you name such to me!" She sprang back and squared away valiantly, like a man, with heaving breast. "Why—why then, the straight of hit is, I wouldn't leave a dawg to blunder around in these here woods, and him full o' Bivins' pizen! You'ns go on, I'll wait." She knew perfectly that this was ridiculous. "Or else we all wait, right here."

"Won't hafto wait long," muttered Atlas, hearing swift unsteady footsteps. A second later Ransom, whom Homer's wit and hospitality had not availed to detain long, burst upon them, wildly swinging a lantern covered with blazing oil, and cursing.

"Look out, you'll set fire—Put that light *down*, you firebug!" shouted Atlas, leaping; and then it happened. Whack, whack, whack; crash went the two lanterns; a yellow oily flame shot up from the sand; the two girls, in momentary terror of an explosion that distracted even their terror of the conflict, saw in the bright light the brothers at each other's throats, struggling, kicking, reeling to and fro. Into the shine and out of it they drove, now trampling the sand, now crashing through the bushes, till Atlas tripped on a root and was down.

"He's got a knife!" screamed Delma, catching the glint of a blade.

"Oh, my God, he'll kill him!" cried Callie at the same moment.

Together by a great effort the women dragged Ransom back by the arms. Never had Callie's splendid strength and courage served her so well as while she held the furious little man and shrieked, "Run, Atlas! for the Lord's sake, run!"

A second later she caught up Atlas' hat from the ground and set off after him.

Ransom, the knife still in his hand, stood blinking foolishly at the last flicker of the spilt oil. He drew a long breath, like a gasp.

"Let me have the knife, Rans," pleaded Delma. "Give it here. There, there, honey! it's all over; you won't need ary weepon." She approached timidly, feeling for his hand.

"Naw!" he said, and with a jerk sent the open blade whirling into the thicket. "Shucks! I never tried to knife anybody afore. . . . What's it all about, anyhow?" He seemed to have sobered all at once. "Shucks!" he repeated, looking down at the trampled road and broken lanterns. "Oh, shucks! Atlas. Oh, At!" There was no answer. "Done gone on, has he?"

"Let's us go, too," urged his wife.

He laid his hands on her shoulders and turned her to face him; then, putting both arms closely round her, he looked intently into her eyes.

"Tell me, Fedelma—was there anything to fight about? What was you down to the spring for?"

She responded gladly to his touch, as always. "Not anything. There wasn't no harm in that, was there?"

"What was he sayin' to you?"

"Not much of anything. . . . I—jist wondered how he *would* talk if—"

"Fedelma!"

She tore the wreath from her hair and sent it flying after his knife. It caught on a twig and hung, swaying a little, all transparent against the luminous background, each delicate leaf-rib clear as if formed of coral and crystal and jade. It seemed not to be of earth, but the last visible fragment of a dream-world, called up by a magician and on the point of vanishing.

"I don't know what made me so silly—especially seein' that I'll haf to face death my ownself in a while,—for you and yourn," she added, so low that he did not quite hear. "Ransom, it wasn't—real. Nothing is real but you for me. You've made my life for me, every day for a year now,—and, look!" She fumbled at his collar and turned it down to show the patch she had sewed there. Her neat strong stitches caught the light as clearly as the delicate interlaced veins of the wreath. "That's mine—you're mine! Don't you see we've growed together—we belong to one another. Nothing can change that. Nothing else is real. Only I wisht—I wisht I never had gone with any boy but you."

He pressed his lips to her face, feeling it cool and fresh as a fruit just freshly plucked. "Let's be good people, and not quarrel. I reckon we better go home and stay there."

"Air you hurt?" She passed her fingers over the curls she had so resolutely clipped the day before.

"Just a bump. Atlas give me one good lick if he never gits in another."

"And listen, Ransom," she continued breathlessly, nestling to him, "I'll tell ye now. . . ."

Callie fled along the road, her breath coming and going audibly, her dress flitting mothlike under the gliding shadows. "Atlas!" she called softly. "Oh, Atlas!"

In a moment he answered from a darker core of shadows under an oak, his deep voice vibrating like a soft gong.

"Here's your hat," she panted, coming close to him. "Oh, Atlas, air you hurt?"

"Not me. 'Magine he is. I fetched him one with the lantern, just afore I went down, that ought to a-stunded him if it hadn't a-glanced."

"Serve him right. Oh, Atlas, I always heared you was a beautiful fighter, but I never thought so well of you as when you jist wouldn't fight till you had obliged to."

"Then you do?" He put out his arm, still quivering with the strain of conflict, and she came within it. All the warm, splendid womanhood of her seventeen rough-and-tumble years thrilled to his kiss. "So you think much o' me, Callie?"

"More'n the world and all. Oh, I do!" Their untried hearts beat and plunged against each other.

"Sure there's nobody—none o' your old sweethearts, f'r instance—that you might come to think more of, sometime?"

"I never had—oh! If you mean Ransom,—why, I was a little bit o' gal then, and he's—he's married!"

"You—I thought you looked at him tonight—"

"How?"

"As if he wasn't, maybe."

"Why, you old jealous-hearted—You old fool!" Her voice broke with tenderness on the final word.

As Callie and Atlas went by Ransom's house a few days later, they stopped at the gate and called to Fedelma.

The young wife was rocking on her front porch, stringing beans. She rose, and came down to the fence, putting back a wispy lock and smiling. A new gravity and sweetness had come into her eyes since the night of the dance in the cove, and she, and Ransom singing in the field below, alone in all the world knew why.

"Come on in," she bade the pair.

"Can't," stated Callie. "We jist wanted to tell you that me and Atlas—that we was—" She flushed, looked down, and seemed unable to go on.

But the young man put his hand firmly over hers where it lay on the top rail. "We're a-goin' to be married a-Sunday, Delma, and we want you and Ransom to be there. Then we'll have a housewarmin' soon as I can git a shack ready, and you can tell him that's one dance where there won't be any liquor circulated."

Fedelma regarded them with a grave smile.

"We'll be glad to come and see ye married," she answered. "But if hit's all the same to you-uns, I reckon we won't be at the infare. If a body can't keep their heads at a frolic no better than we do—" the prettiest imaginable color crept up into her cheeks, and she did not look at Atlas—"I think they better not go. I never have jined ary church, but I ain't shore I b'lieve in dancin'."

thirteen

Thistle Bloom

From *The Lookout* 10 (Part I, October 26, 1912; Part 2, November 2, 1912), n.p.

A transition sentence or paragraph appears to have been omitted between the two parts of this story. I have supplied a few words in brackets in Part II to provide transition for the reader.

The tumultuous father-daughter relationship in "Thistle Bloom" somewhat parallels the one in "At the Top of Sourwood." In both stories there is an only daughter who enjoys people, parties, and pretty things. And in both stories there is a love interest to which the father objects. An added complication in "Thistle Bloom" is that the mother has died suddenly, leaving the father in sole charge of a budding woman he is ill prepared to parent. His harsh, judgmental oversight of her spurs Oran Shively, himself a brooding, critical young man, to declare his honorable intentions toward Seretha Massengale sooner than he might have. One has to wonder if Miles was once again drawing from her own experience as an only daughter whose father disapproved of her choice of a mate. Whatever the case, she allows herself the luxury of a digression about the dancing style of the mountaineer. Clearly, dancing among her mountain neighbors is a topic of great interest to the author, for she frequently weaves it into her stories.

I.

The old shed had not been used for a long time, but in this perfect September weather its broken roof and half-chinked logs afforded sufficient shelter. Before its door the earth-shaped apples glowed like fairy lanterns among the Limbertwig boughs, their winy scent mingling with that of ripening muscadines from the woods behind. In this hide-out Oran Shively was doing for himself, even cooking the supplies brought him daily by his brother or sister Libby; and they felt relieved, as they saw him sitting glum and sore from a recent hurt, that he was not at hand to spoil Seretha's visit.

Now and then, across the sunny loneliness of the orchard, he heard the new voice in laughter or song, and was glad, too, that he had absented himself from the house. He had heard of Seretha Massengale as a girl who accounted everything worthless except as it yielded her pleasure.

As he abode the time of her stay and his sprained foot's disability, he put over the hours whittling on the pieces of an oaken box, planning his care of the farm for next year, reviewing his chances of getting his stock through the winter, and playing with the four kittens. Today as the shadows lengthened, he hobbled on his rude crutch across the floor and seated himself on the doorsill. A thistle, rank and glossy amid the wirey autumnal growth, stood by the door in the sun. He reached out his knife to cut it before it could seed, but paused as a sulphur-winged butterfly floated out from the shadow and hung trembling like a flame, having unerringly discovered for itself the one bit of empurpled softness and sweetness among all those forbidding spines and prickles. He left the harsh thing to grow awhile—its visitant might return. Oran was not tired of going his own lonely, hardheaded way, but was fain to grasp eagerly at every gleam that fell across it.

The black kits leapt and tumbled over each other round his coarse shoes. Suddenly they sprang forward with a chorus of mews as their mother returned from hunting; and then he heard someone calling: "Kitty? Kitty-kitty-kitty-puss? Where you gone to, Kitty Blue?"

The stately Maltese only switched her tail and purred as Oran stroked her, but the kittens, with tails erect, went trotting towards the call along the faint path tangled with asters and overreached with bending goldenrod.

"Oh, oh, you cute things!—but not one as pretty as your mammy. Kitty Blue, I didn't know you was keepin' such a secret from me!"

Oran listened, frowning deeply behind his screen of yellow plumes. There was a light swift footfall, the swirl and flicker of a ruffled skirt among the green, and a girl stepped into view close by him, the four fluffballs cuddled in her arms. An easy bend of neck and graceful set of head; wavy masses of dark-brown hair; clear deep eyes—why, it was the visitor!

Whether he liked it or not, here she stood, her eyes bright with surprise. In the next moment the restless kittens slipped to the ground and scampered toward their mother. She met them halfway with the soft trilling coo that a cat makes only for her babies, and all together walked sedately to the hem of Seretha's dress. The girl stooped to stroke the arching cat. "She's a beauty, ain't she?" was her first remark. She put back a stray curl and smiled in face of Oran's frown. "I never could see where she went to, till just now, when I was after some of these here blooms." She came a step nearer, having already decided that she liked him—liked his clear though rugged features, his length and strength, his brown face with its sombre eyes. "You're Oran, Libby's brother, ain't you? When'd you git home?"

He replied to but one of her queries.

"Yes, I'm Oran."

The cat climbed to his shoulder and purred round his head, then capriciously leaped down and returned to the girl, who, seating herself on the weedy tangle, took the favorite into her gingham lap.

"Did you ever in your life see such a tangle of kits!" she laughed, revealing a dimple and a glimpse of delicate, even teeth. "Do they sure 'nough fight?"

For answer Oran picked up a bit of string baited with an acorn, and swung it over the kittens, who rushed after it tumbling and growling. As their fun grew furious he tossed the string over an apple-weighted bough, to dangle just within claw-reach.

"They're a-boxin' one another somersets!" She shook back the curl as she laughed up at him again.

Oran's face had lightened; but as one of the lithe, furry little bodies bore too ruthlessly on a weaker brother, he scowled again and snatched up his rude crutch to part them. The girl's face, too, grew grave as she looked on.

"You're lame! Does Libby know that? I'm so sorry!"

"Hit's a'gittin' well now," he replied ungracefully.

"Why don't you come to the house?"

"'Cause I'd ruther stay here alone." Seretha got up gracefully. "And she stays with you? She's the nicest old pet I ever saw. Ain't you comin' to the house none?"

"No."

"Then she won't stay with me a-tall. I'll jist come to see her, now I know where she lives. And I'll tell Libby I seed you," she smiled retreating along the path.

"Don't ye tell ary another one," he called after her.

Seretha was still puzzling over the encounter when she reached the house with her arms full of goldenrod. "I reckon your brother Oran's foot must a-hurted him bad," she said to Libby.

"How'd you hear about Oran's foot?" cried Libby, her good plain face changing with consternation. Was her brother ordained to break every earth-born butterfly on the iron wheel of his intolerance?

Seretha explained. "He looked so cross and soberlike, I 'lowed he must be hurtin'. Whyn't he stay here, Libby?"

"He's cranky, honey. Jist leave him alone." The motherly maiden turned her smooth dark head to smile at her adored guest. "I wish't you hadn't a-seed him; he didn't want you to find out he was ther—'feared hit would spile your good time whilst you're with us." she added, trying to soften the rudeness.

"Hit won't do that. He's got a right to his ruthers," replied Seretha, wonderingly. "I ain't a-keepin' him there, I reckon. Maybe, like my old dog, he wants to be left alone when he's hurted. I always think that's because he's cross then, and he's afeared he may bite if he's about where he' bothered."

Libby let it go at that. She could not help smiling at the aptness of Seretha's conclusion, although her private belief was that Oran liked to bite. She had seen him grow from a strange, silent, almost surly boyhood into a manhood soured by disapproval of trivial insincerities. He was industrious and saving, a young man still, though an older bachelor than is usual among the mountain people, for who would marry such a churl? Least of all could his own family bear with him.

The next day Old Blue was missing oftener than usual from the shop. It seemed to Oran, brooding in the doorway, that she was absent most of the time. The second morning she was gone when he waked, and at noon, when he had decided that something must have happened to his pet, Seretha came trippling along the path with the blue cat in her arms.

"She's bad company to leave you all alone by yourself, ain't she?" was her greeting. "I told her to scat back to her babies, but she let on not to hear, and hung around as if she wanted me to bring her; so I come."

The man shook off his abstraction by degrees. "She's all right. She goes out huntin', often," he replied slowly. He was thinking that the purple rays in the sun-illumined iris of Seretha's eyes were like those of the wayside asters.

"Have you ever named the kittens?"

"This," said Oran gravely, tapping a black velvet head, "is Matthew; this here's Mark; this 'n's Luke–'n'–John; and I ain't found ary name for the blue-eyed one, she's the prettiest."

"Maybe I'll think of a name. Is your foot-a-hurtin' much?"

"No."

"I must be goin'," she told him. "We are all a-goin' chestenuttin'.

"I 'xpect we'll find wild grapes and persimmons, too."

"They ain't ripe yit," protested Oran, in the unwonted process of groping for a last word.

The next day, just after his hermit meal, Seretha came.

"What you makin'?" she asked, seating herself on the grass.

"Box."

"What for?"

"Somethin' to do."

"Why, hit's goin' to be nice enough for a keepsake box!"

Oran carved away in silence.

But with deliberate kindly intent, to enliven his solitude, she lingered, talking of good times past and hoped for—of rides and play-parties and church yard basket-dinners, of fortune-tellers and young folk's "singin's," and all the simple feasts, frolic and fun of the mountains.

That afternoon the rude relief-pattern on the oak slab took on more elaborate curves as he worked and all unknowing dreamed. Sometimes his hands fell idle and he sat motionless, plumbing the purple distance with thoughtful eyes.

She appeared in the morning while the fairy napkins of cobweb in the grass were still gemmed with dew.

Oran was thinking of something. "Libby and Taylor aimed to have a play-party whilst you was here, and I wouldn't let 'em." He made the confession shamefacedly.

She put the confession tactfully aside.

"We wouldn't a-wanted one whilst you're laid up with that foot."

"Hit ain't too late now. We can let 'em all know—"

She shook her head, looking away from him. "No—I was aimin' to tell you I got to go home."

"What—right away?"

"Mother's ailin' and wants me. Jim Reedy brought the word this morning. Taylor's ketchin' out the mules now, to take me over."

They found themselves stranded, as it were, unable to talk after this announcement.

"I hope you'll git all right soon—Oran—Goodbye."

"Goodbye," answered Oran dully.

A month later, returned from his postponed hunting, he learned that Seretha's mother was dead, and that her father, embittered with grief and shaken with drink, was making her life a burden because she did not know [how] to keep house. Libby had been over to help her, but Massengale had almost asked her to leave the place and he would not let Seretha out of his sight.

"He's got the right idy," declared Oran. "She'd ought to been made long ago."

"Hit was her mother's doin' that she was brung up like she was. Her bein' the only child to live, Mis' Massengale spiled her, and the' old man never seemed to notice till his wife was gone," sighed Libby.

"Well, she'll learn now," was Oran's last word.

But he was glad to see her face again, that winter, at the Lowrys' dancing party. Lowrys' always had the best music and a good crowd, because the sawmill boys would be there. Libby and Taylor were looking after the farm and stock, and Oran was at the mill; so the party required him to call the figures, for dancing was his one dissipation.

"You didn't expect to see me, did you?" Seretha asked, as he and a partner stood near her while the set was forming. "I come with Susy." She did not say how she had dared fate in so doing. "You love to dance, don't you? How's Kit Blue and the kittens?" She put the troublesome curl aside with the gesture he remembered.

"All right." His eyes softened as they rested on her. "I've done named that kitten Aster." He turned to take his place in the "square" circle.

Seretha watched him as he danced, his perpetual frown lightened by the glitter of his eyes, but no softness reappeared. It was not the company he enjoyed, but the rhythmic movement. He called in a clear level voice, with only an occasional lift in the one. Between dances he stood by the fiddler and his banjo seconds, urging them on, suggesting the wildest melodies they knew. He was there to dance; he asked nothing of his partners but that they dance also, for the part's sake, with no pauses for dalliance on the long shadowy porches or in the moon-drenched yard.

All the fibres of his being were pleasurably loosened and quivering with the music. He danced mountaineer fashion, all over, with solemn intense enjoyment, swinging his elbows and shoulders no less than his feet. It was not the languid, bending, sloping dance of the negro, nor the leaping and skipping of northern races, but a loose-jointed, swinging, tossing, bounding movement distinctive as the music to which it kept time. The figures wheeled and swung and eddied; coats flung off, feet stamped heavily. Seretha, sitting motionless with two or three church-going girls by the wall, watched the fun grow wilder as the evening advanced, and shivered at thought of the cold hearth unswept at home. Clapping and stamping increased; the whirl grew more rapid as feet caught the swing; periodical backsliders forgot all exhortation, and joined the rout, laughing. And faster and faster rang the banjo; the merriment ended at last with a shout as one, outwearied, laid his hand across the strings.

A great oaken basket heaped with russets, winesaps, and Limbertwigs was brought in and munched in the firelight; then came farewells, and the melting away of the gathering by twos and threes into the frost-edged night. Oran approached Seretha and asked to walk with her.

"I'm just goin' to Susy's tonight. That's on your way, ain't it?" she replied.

"Git your things," he bade her.

"Oh, Seretha," called Susy Reedy as they left the porch, "you-all ain't goin' to your place?" She came closer, and added hurriedly, "you be sure and stop at our house; your dad would settle you, like he said."

"I was aimin' to stay with you till morning, Susy," was the answer.

"Why—don't your dad know you come?" asked Oran after a quarter of mile of silence.

"If he did, I wouldn't be here. I left him a note to say I was goin' to Susy's and I'd be back in the morning."

"You hadn't ort to do that way!"

She winced from his tone. "If I ast him I wouldn't never git out. I think long o' the time; and seems like I must git away oncet in a while."

"Git your work done and then go."

"That's what he says; but I don't know how."

"Learn."

"Ain't I tried and tried and *tried*—and it's no use! I cain't neber get things the way mother used to have 'em. She always said I was good help; but I had lots of days besides, to be goin' and to have fun.

"I think so long o' the time! I don't want to dance; but she always liked me to be with people and to have a good time, and I know if I could ast her about it she'd say go."

Oran found no more to say, as they walked the rest of the distance to Susy Reedy's home. And there stood Massengale before the gate.

"Come home!" he commanded, taking Seretha's arm in a grasp that made her catch her breath sharply.

At that, Oran shivered. And though he knew that he could not interfere, and saw that the old man was sober, he followed the pair to the edge of the Massengale place.

At the house door the father paused. "Git to bed," he ordered, almost throwing Seretha through the doorway.

Then he closed the door and put his back to it. "You out there—git! Don't you ever set foot on my land again. Hear me!" His voice was a discordant squeak of fretfulness on the mountain night. "I given you five minutes to be out o' sight and gone afore I shoot."

II.

[Oran left as bidden,] but the more he thought it over, the more he felt compelled to have an understanding with Massengale. When asked to go to meeting [next morning], he told his young host that he would rather go on to the mill and be getting some rest against the week's work. But he did not speak of his intention to pass Massengale's place on his way.

The house was closed and silent as he viewed it from the fence, not even a curl of smoke ascending, though there were chairs on its porch as in summer; and he recalled the saying that her father took Seretha to church. It was a colorless, quiet little home, regarding him wistfully through two small windows, from its brown clearing outspread in the pale sunshine and the gray transparent woods carpeted with brown leaves. The tap of an ax led him down the barn-lot lane. But it was not Massengale he came upon; it was Seretha, cutting brush into stove lengths.

"What you doin' here?" she stammered, her face pale with consternation at sight of him.

"Where's your dad?" he asked in return.

"Gone to preachin'."

"I'll wait."

"Don't do it, Oran," she urged. "He ain't spoke a work nor eat a bite since last night. Didn't even tell me to git ready and go to preachin'. Like enough he faults you for my doin', and he may make you trouble."

"I'll wait," he said again. And taking the axe, he cut the wood while she stacked.

"Oran," she kept pleading, "I do wisht you'd go—hit won't do no good for you to stay. Dad'll ketch you—and besides, there's work in the house I got obleeged to git done afore he comes."

"Come on in, then. I'll help ye." said Oran. And help he did. Used to doing for himself in camp and for his home folks from childhood, he knew just how. Together they washed and scalded, swept and straightened, and soon had the house in order.

"I wisht I could turn the work off that way all by myself," sighed the girl, looking round on the tidy kitchen.

"Learn," repeated Oran unsympathetically; but he was sure he would like to help her always.

"You must take a hand-bit with you now and go, Oran. Dad'll be a-comin' back and see you. You'll haf to go, Oran—" and the start of tears in her eyes persuaded him that the encounter had better take place on the road.

"Show me the way to the Gap and I'll go, then," he assented.

"Let's stop at the big rock and see if he's a-comin'," she temporized as they crossed the clearing.

All round the stark head of the cliff was a sighing cloud of dark pine boughs, whose purr undertoned the shriller music of a rivulet spilling over some hidden ledge. The lonely steeps were drenched in the pure light of the sky; below they discerned the cabins and little farms, cradled ever so softly by dreamy hills and ridges feathery with treetops. Faint and small and far, sounds rose to the winter-hushed summit—a pinpoint cockcrow, the lowing of cattle, herd bells in varying tones. The vast expanse lay still and dim as a vision, bathed in the gentle afternoon. To the left the Blue Springs road straggled through the woods; but there was no sign of Massengale on its tawny ribbon, and no sound of his coming reached them where they sat on the high point. Oran lingered while Seretha talked of how she missed her mother all the time.

"I know," he replied in a tone she had never heard him use. His hand came softly down over hers where it lay on the rock between them. "If you git in trouble, send me word, and me and Libby'll help you."

"Dad, he won't let ye," she reminded him.

"You let us know and we-ll sure try. * * * We ain't got no mother neither."

"I wisht," she murmured, tracing a pattern in the tinted rock-moss with a pink finger-point, "that Libby could stay with me a spell and lesson me some. But he won't hear to hit; says I won't never learn with somebody to do for me."

An azure shadow crept slowly from the side. At the same time innumerable small replicas of it started from the crest of every hill, the apex of each haystack, and the ridgepole of every cabin in the valley.

"Come on to the Gap?" he requested, getting up.

"Hit's below here, a ways to the right. I'll stay and watch you down to the trail. See them steps like, on this side the rock; them a steep path—that's the way."

"Don't forgit—if you need help." He slid over the sloping surface.

"I won't. Tell Libby I wisht she could come." She tucked her feet under her as she leaned over the edge looking down at him.

"Next week's Christmas. I've got the box done. Can I bring it to you?"

His voice became, of a sudden, rich with feeling.

Seretha was surprised and thrilled. "But—I ain't got a thing to give you for Christmas," she softly hesitated, "so I—I reckon you'd best not."

"Maybe you'll find something by then. Anyways, I want you to see my box. I'll put Aster in hit for a keepsake. Say, can I bring it?"

His dark eyes were on her; the deepened voice so softly urging her, compelled the breathless answer.

"All right. Goodbye."

"Goodbye till next week, Seretha," he returned, moving on along the path. But he looked back once more, to see her gazing after him with such a new expression on her face that he wheeled about and paused.

Instantly she hid like a partridge, by simply drawing back from the edge.

"Seretha! * * Seretha!"

"What!" she answered from back on the rock.

"Can I come back up there—now? Seretha—say, can I come? Can I?—If you don't say, I'm a-comin'."

"Don't Oran—don't you now," she protested softly, still in hiding. "If you do I'll run to the house."

"Look over then and say goodbye—just oncet more, Seretha!" he begged winningly, waiting to see again the sweet revelation in her face.

But the answer shocked him. White and pinched with terror, she peered at him of a sudden, her trembling lips whispering tensely. "*Dad!* Git on! git *on!*—he's a comin', Oran—he's here!" And he heard a scramble and a rush, as she fled across the rock and into the woods.

Oran came up the cliff in great leaps to a sight which filled him with fury. Seretha had tripped and fallen, and her father stood over her stripping a green withe and calling heaven to witness that he would no longer spare the rod and spoil the child.

The young man flung himself upon Massengale, seized the hickory, and raised it high, meaning to use it with all his raging strength. But Seretha staggered between them, shielding her father. Through her alarm she was conscious of a desire to steal away to the unforgotten quiet doorstep in quest of the Oran she knew—the patient carver, the friend of creatures soft and small.

But he put her violently aside, and flung the hickory far into the thicket, and stood facing the old man who was standing all atremble.

"By the Lord, Massengale, you'd ort to be hung! * * * Come on to the house," he exclaimed, and taking Seretha's hand, he led the way to the front porch.

The father shuffled after without a word; and fell into a chair; he appeared to have aged in the past few moments. Oran put the girl into the big rocker, where she remained limply quiet, only turning her head aside against the back cushion while tears coursed down her cheeks.

Oran's fists were clenched; but he rammed them into his pockets, and walked up and down before the porch till his hot blood had time to cool.

"Mr. Massengale, I come here," he began at last, "to tell you that you hadn't no call to dare me off your place last night. As you was away, I waited for you to come back. Seretha ast me not to, and then I aimed to meet on the road and tell you my say. I know you was hard on Seretha, and I don't doubt you had reason, but I did think you was man enough to be a decent father to her. What you done jist now was the way to treat a dawg, not a woman."

"Oran—" pleaded the girl, leaning forward. "Oran, Dad was mad. He ain't never done me so afore, though I've needed whuppin' many's the time." She turned, clasping her hands. "Oh, Dad! Dad, what made you do it now? Why'n't ye take 'n whup me when I was a-growin' and make me grow right, so sech as this wouldn't a-come to us? Oh, mother—mother!" Then, at its sharpest, her voice broke; she flung herself forward, hiding her face on her knees, and sobbed unrestrained.

"Don't, Seretha; don't ye, gal," begged her father, getting stiffly to his feet and coming over to lay his trembling hand on her hair. "I reckon I be crazy sence—she's gone. Seems to me I been in a bad dream, a-missin' her all through everything, a-wantin' her till I was sick body and soul. And I—I got scairt you'd go wrong without her. Then at church to-day the preacher helt you up for a 'zample to all parents, for what come o' sparin' the rod; he was givin' it to 'em about these here play-parties and dances—and I went fair wild, thinkin' you might be everlastingly lost—you! Mother's gal she thought so much of, the gal she left me—the one—Seretha!"

Oran, standing rigid and grim on the step, turned away, for his eyelids stung.

"Oh, little gal! Tell me—tell me your ownself hit was a bad dream and ain't nary word true!" Massengale knelt with his arms round his daughter, looking intently into her wondering eyes.

"Dad," she demanded, "what did them folks say?"

"I jist overheard a word in the churchyard a'ter preachin' was out. They named my gal and—Oran here, and when I thought of how you said you was goin' to Reedy's for the night and that I found ye comin' from a party alone with him, I—sort o' thought there might be somethin' to hit."

"Is hit anyways true, gal? Air you the same as when your mother left? Seretha, tell me—oh, tell me!" His voice was awful in its intensity.

"Hit ain't true! No, Dad, no! No. I ain't a bad gal except about workin'. I—"

"Thank God for that—thank God!" And the slow shuddering sobs shook the man as he laid his head on his daughter's knees.

"Tell *me!* Who was hit anyhow—" Oran began. But she motioned him to be silent.

The girl laid her hand on his arm. "Don't Oran. Hit's all my doin'. I'd ought to be whupped, and talked about too; I been too careless, a-wantin' [to] be happy all the time."

He looked down into her sweet pale face, set like a moon in her cloudy hair, and a great yearning swept through him.

"You'd ought to be happy, Seretha. And if you'll let me I'll ask no better than to try to make ye so. Say the word—give me the right, and if anybody turns their tongue to your name I'll make 'em wish't they hadn't." He laid his hand over hers on his arm.

A delicate flush overspread her pallor, and [she] put back the curls and smiled with tremulous lips.

"Seretha—gal—" The father put out his hand.

"Come—with me." Oran drew away.

"Seretha—you ain't goin' to leave me this way," Massengale implored, reaching toward her as he watched Oran crossing the yard.

"Hit's all right, Dad. I'll never blame you for what's been." She raised her arms, and her light sleeves fell back from them as she put them round his neck. "I'm jist goin' to marry Oran."

fourteen

A Dream of the Dust

From *The Lookout* 10 (December 28, 1912), n.p.

In the original publication the last paragraph has garbled sentences that I have rearranged in what I believe is the order intended by the author.

Different in both content and style from Miles's other stories, "A Dream of the Dust" depicts the great love a husband and son have for the wife and mother who has left them far too soon. In her lifetime she had the soul of an artist who saw beautiful pictures in her mind; she tried to re-create them without benefit of lessons on the cheap paper that came her way. On a rare visit to an art gallery in town, she spotted a majestic marble sculpture of the Madonna; she declared that image was what she always tried to paint. After her death, the husband and son devise a way to honor her and show her their love. Having now come into money from a mine on their property, they buy the Madonna statue from the artist and erect it on the mountain in front of her cave-tomb. Over the years the marble Madonna on the mountain has become a legend, though few know the real story of this magnificent piece of art. Perhaps as she wrote, Emma Bell Miles had her own artistic vision in mind, as well as her own hardships as a mountain wife and mother—and possibly even her own illness, which was to take her life at age thirty-nine.

No one knows how the marble Madonna came to be in the Gap except some few mountaineers. She was touched only by the winds of heaven; her feet even are scarcely wet in the low-browed rock-house, on days when the woof of the forest is pierced by needles of rain. No one asks about the matter today; the mountain folk are not of an investigative turn of mind, and the mining settlement is busy with its own rapid growth; or perhaps the jewel in its setting is so near holiness that none dare venture, either curiously or rudely, or in too familiar admiration.

But rugged iron-gray hunters come upon the white wonder standing in the cliff, vivid against its dark niche, a blooming of phantasmal beauty alien to this wild land; cattlemen passing the Gap—men who know nothing of sculpture beyond the rude squaring of sand-stone for a hearth, a landmark, or a grave—ride out of their way to look upon it; women on bare brown feet, coming down to dig ginseng, pause to turn their heavy eyes toward the stranger queen of sorrow; and little sisters wonder with quaint unchildlike gravity of mountain babes concerning this doll that is not a doll. And old mothers whose part it is to keep alive tradition and folklore talk of her over dying coals at night telling how Abel Kilgore and his son set the statue in the rock in memory of the light of their loneliness that went out here.

Year after year, through wet Southern snows that drift upon her garment in tufts, when the marble is not more white and still and glittering than the woods below; through softer snows of bloom, when flaky masses of rain-weighted laurel let loose their hold and shatter down the rock; through the drowsy quiet of autumn noons when only cowbells and the falling mast are heard in the uplands—year after year she has looked out unchanged, serenely gazing, like the gray bluff itself, across the Gap and down the valley where the distance is blue as the heart of a gem.

Here is her story.

The difference between country and town is not so marked at twilight before the streets are strung with cores of sharp electric radiance—washed out as it were in gray seas of the blending evening. Abel Kilgore's wife, lingering at the door of the great art store felt this, and gained courage. Why, yon towering structure might be the rocky pillar on Wolf-pen Gap. The pictures in the plate-glass window before her, seen in this cloudy light, seemed no more awe-inspiring than the dreams that came to her as she spread clothes to dry on the flowering bushes of her yard or dipped water from a spring in which the sunset burned like a reflection of passing angels armed for God's vengeance. She drew a deep breath, and disregarding her garb of print and linsey shawl, pushed open the door and entered. Her little boy, clad in a coat of his father's, came in with her and walked beside her down the aisle. But Abel staid by the door, his weatherbeaten country clothing and labor-stooped shoulders seeming to belong to the gray outside, no more intrusive there than a wisp of its fog blown across the threshold. The woman accosted a salesman.

"I want to sell some pictures," she said. Her voice was sweet and hushed, like a nun's; her bearing so quiet the man addressed did not guess how her heart was thumping.

"We do not buy second-hand pictures," he replied.

"Why—them's all second hand," she insisted gently. "You-all didn't paint 'em—here in the store?" the oddity of the idea made him smile. At that moment the lights were turned on, and out of the gloom on every side started glowing visions of ideal, beautiful beyond her dreams. "O," she sighed over a forest dark as the rock-rimmed ones she knew, and "Oh!" with a sharp intake of breath, to a Good Shepherd.

"You mean—" the salesman said tentatively, seeing that she had forgotten him.

Her gaze had wandered past the attractions of the front and was seeking a glimmer of white in a curtained alcove.

The boy plucked her sleeve. "Show 'em to him, mammy," he reminded her.

Without bringing back her eyes from the white wonder that evidently held her whole being in thrall, she mechanically took a roll of paper from her arm and laid them on the counter, saying in the spirit of one granting a favor, "You can look 'em over."

Because he saw no other course open the man opened the paper and revealed a series of sketchy paintings. The little mountain woman with her crude ideas of art—she must have acquired a few in some country school—had chosen to draw one figure only, a woman clothed in white standing now on the brow of a grim cliff, now in a copse of wild apple bloom, again by the cardinal-flowers and orchids on a marsh. The background was varied, but the figure—ill drawn, worse colored, done on paper meant for street and kitchen uses—was always the center of interest. Possibly in the attempted contrasts of dark pines and snowy garment there was a hint of merit that might have come to something with the proper training and environment. He rolled these up and returned them to her with a shake of the head and a kindly excuse: "Sorry, but we do not—we are not in need of anything like this at present."

The boy received them in his knobby little brown hand, his face showing keen disappointment; but the mother noticed neither him nor the refusal of her wares.

"Kin a body go back there and—and look?" she asked hungrily.

The salesman awakened to the fact that this was an occurrence not usual to the day's work. It was a dull hour, and he permitted himself to take interest.

"Certainly," he consented, and led the way to the department of statuary, touching to life electric bulbs as he came to them. The boy beckoned his father, and the man slouched after.

The woman caught her breath. All about her were figures of beauty ethereal as those fashioned by white waves of storm. Here was a dancing girl poised like a flower; there the gladiator, muscular, intent; yonder little loves, chubby and sweet, or frost-fine ladies in curls and jewels, or praying angels cold to others' prayers; statues Greek or Sylvan, or Catholic and saintly, and historical ideals of figures veiled in the mist of time. The salesman noted that the boy and man looked only at the woman. If she coughed they sighed; at her smile their faces brightened. Nothing to them was all this world of strange loveliness like moonlight wrought into story, except as she was pleased.

She came to a stand before one figure, the one that had first caught her attention. They saw her bosom heave, and the tears come into her eyes.

The statue was of an unusual type that might well have represented Faith or Memory. The features had not the immobile breadth and grandeur of the classic type; there was a tenderness in their modelling that removed this Virgin from the circle of goddesses. Like the great Venus, however, was the slightly bending, meditative attitude; and the straight simple garment, with its looping band above the hips, could not have been other than the peplos of ancient days. From the pearled smoothness of the shoulders it fell in a cataract of fine swift wrinkles over the grand limbs—over the woman-frame, type of all fragility and tenderness, down it flowed, shattering into a crumpled foamy chaos round the perfect feet. In the pose of the head, with its simple arrangement of hair, was an indescribable winning gentleness. One hand was raised, the palm turned inward toward the rounded breast; the other caught and lightly drew the drapery to one side.

The thin, homely, toil-degraded woman gazed and gazed, till her very soul seemed to feed itself through her eyes. But at her side the mountaineer grew more and more uneasy, and finally spoke hesitatingly.

"Mammy—we'll be all night on the way ef we don't start. Hadn't you better come now?"

Silently she let herself be influenced. As she reached the store door she turned for a last look at the Mother of Sorrows.

"That there," she said, "is what I'm always tryin' to paint. I ain't never seen her before—only in little pictures."

The salesman was moved. He had been here long, and he, too, loved the Madonna. To discover a similar admiration in the heart of this mountain waif was inexpressively touching to him. He busied himself behind the counter a moment and returned with a Perry print of the statue. "I should be glad to give this to you," he said simply.

The woman thanked him with real dignity and grace, and selecting one of her drawings from the roll in the boy's hand, offered it in return with a courtesy sincere as his own. He took it, bowing. When he looked up again she was bowed over from coughing, and the other two were supporting her; but she held the Madonna print against her heart.

They went from the store and up the quiet street—for it was one of the city's still hours, an indrawn breath in the midst of its busy round. At the sheds Kilgore got out his wagon, softly cushioned with hay, and helped his wife to lie down in comfort. The boy sat on the seat with his father. They drove slowly out among the smaller buildings, across a meaner suburb that twilight filled with its own enthralling charm, and so to the open country.

The night grew darker, till their road was almost invisible. They rode silently except for a low-spoken word to the team, for they thought "Mammy" slept. Over the mountain was a lighter space, which became more definite till the last slope was outlined by a golden halo. Then the road plunged into utter darkness between high wooded banks, climbing by a tedious ascent to emerge, suddenly, beyond the last long ridge of the foothills, into brilliant moonlight. The harness glittered; long shadows steamed westward through field and forest; distances became luminous. And there in the soughing pines, only a little way from their wagon, hung the moon.

"Them trees might be cut out of black velvet and pasted on silver paper," said the woman at last. "Look, Carson!" The boy climbed back and curled up in the hay beside her.

“I wish’t I could a-made pictures that would sell, Carson,” she went on. “Pears like I ain’t no use at all. I ain’t strong enough to work and I can’t make no money.”

“But pap’s got that mine,” the boy reminded her. “Jist wait till hit’s makin’ money, and you can take it easy.”

“I can’t wait,” she told them. “I’ve seen beautiful things in my mind all my life, but this here—” she referred to the Madonna print—“is as nigh as ever I come to havin’ anything like hit for my own. I wisht I could have done something beautiful to stay up in the mountain and show you’ns, show the neighbors too, what I thought about, what I felt in my soul. Hit seems like the mountain would a-been a better place ef what I think of could be set up to look at and see—like—like I feel hit! But—I can’t do nothing—and I can’t wait.”

Carson kissed her. They rode on in silence, Kilgore humped over.

The moon rose higher and higher in the quiet splendor of the night, the lines urging the team a little where the grade was easy. They had nearly reached the Gap when the woman asked, “Are we mighty near home? I want a drink. I want to get home.”

“Air you worse, Mammy?” asked Kilgore.

“No,” she reassured him. She lay looking at the picture. The moonlight pointed each blade of hay in her bed until all around her seemed to shiver and glimmer in pale flames.

“Hit’s so beautiful,” she said faintly. “Git along as fast as you can, pappy.”

After her death, the cabin at Wolf Pen Gap was deserted for years, used only for a night’s shelter by wanderers. One day Abel and Carson came up the mountain to pick berries. All around their old home stood the fragrant forest, dark with summer, in the golden silence of afternoon. Over its clearing, where during the mother’s lifetime had been a patch of potatoes and garden-truck, lay now a jungle of matted briers, all bowed, some lying flat, weighted down winy fruit, shining darkly like clusters of faceted rubies and garnets amid the green. The house itself listed to one side like a wrongly ballasted ship; the door sagged on its hinges and swung at the wind’s will to and fro. Three or four old apple-trees leaning to the shadowy eaves bore faithfully, the last of the untended orchard.

Carson, now a stripling half grown, walked to the front of the house and set down his heaped up berry bucket. He looked at the sunshafts that fell aslant between the glittering leaves, and deciding that it was too late to attempt another pailful before building a supper-fire, seated himself on the smooth doorstone where his mother had nursed him.

"How soon you aimin' to quit, pap?" he called to some one invisible among the tangle, and was answered "Pretty soon now, Buddy."

He curled himself down for the wait, looking out between the trees with dreamy eyes. His mother's presence had seemed to come and go all through the long silent day; the place was peopled with perfumes and memories. The sweet low sounds of summer—gurgle of water in a run, notes from warbler and wood-pewee, and a soft purring monotone of deep melancholy fell athwart his face; he sank lower, and pillowed his head against his arm. "Mammy, mammy!" he murmured.

"Asleep, son?" inquired the man's voice by and by, and he sat up to find Kilgore beside him.

"Nuck," he answered. "I was jist a-studying'."

The elder man did not ask what he was "studying" about; perhaps he had no need to do so. He placed his burden of berries carefully beside the first bucket, and seated himself also on the stone.

"I can't hardly abide to come back to this place," he said. "We must put the house in shape afore we go tomorrow anyway. Look at hit!"

He pushed open the door with a great brown hand. The sun was low now, and a broad ray, passing beneath the oak and apple boughs, lit the dusk within. In that dim coolness briers and vines went groping, blanched ghost-white and seeking the ruddying sunbeams. Part of the floor had been torn up by hunters; there was a litter of camping over the rest. The fireplace was wide and deep and high; its jambs were smooth with many knives that had been sharpened there, and with the clinging of Carson's baby fingers; but the hearth in whose red heart she had seen so many pictures to tell about was chocked with a heap of trash, old rags, and ashes.

"Hit must not be left this way. I'd dream about hit," said Kilgore. "Seems like every time I come back here—She wants something—She wanted enough things all her life; and I couldn't—" He broke off, and turned from that blighted interior to stare into the shadows of the woods.

His old fields at the foot of the mountain, which once could scarcely be given away, were now priceless because of the mine.

"I been a good fighter for a pore man," said he. "I stuck to 'em like a cuckle-burr, and got my dues at last. This money'll put you through school, son, and fix us as good a home as we know how to live in. We'll do well. But—hit won't never buy your mammy a silver spoon nor a chaney cup; nary a lace collar, nor a organ, nor a lamp and lookin'-glass nor white window-curtains. Dead now, and can't hear no music nor see none o' the pictures she thought so much of and craved so. Nary thing could I get for her. I never will be satisfied in my own mind whether she even knowed that she died in her pretty new home, like she'd wanted to."

In the spring hollow the dew began to slip from leaf to leaf, and keenly cool as something drawn up dripping from the bottom of the spring. The man's voice, as it came and lapsed, blended perfectly with the thrush's evening song. [Through all] rang the hum of double-winged night-beetles in and out of the oaks overhead.

"All I could do was to promise that I'd bury her in the one place she was set on. She talked so much about it. Time and again, days when I might' near swultered, she'd 'low that the heat didn't make her suffer whilst she kep' her mind on that cold cave and spring; and thar would she be buried."

The sun sank as he talked out his heart, and from behind the massed foliage of the forest a plangent tide of roses and golden light came washingly from eastward to break against the silent coast of twilight-land. Abel stood up, lifting a face convulsed with grief to the fading light.

"Mammy, mammy!" he cried, as the boy had cried, but with an intense immediate longing and bitter pain to which youth is stranger. "Oh, if I could only give ye what you craved for one hour."

The lad glanced up with a compassionate look, and turned his eyes to the woods as one who has seen that which he dares hardly look upon. There was a long silence. Neither had a thought of the evening meal of bread and berries they had intended to prepare; and the moonless night closed round them ere either spoke again. At last the boy offered his mite: "I know one thing ye could buy her, pap—even now." He made the suggestion timidly, for his mind played with an idea of fantastic strangeness. "Do you ricollect that there white starch-statue, that marble figger she seed in Knoxville, and that she 'lowed was the sightliest thing she ever laid eyes on?"

"She talked a heap about it," replied the man. "She sure liked that figger."

"I've seed the like on tombstones, ain't you?" pursued the boy. "Don't you reckon she'd c-cared—she'd like hit if you was to git her that?"

"I could—and set hit up right thar in the rock where she is," said Abel, evidently struck by this proposition. "I do wisht—I wonder if hit would mean anything to her now! . . . She did so love pretty things—pictures and sech that she never had . . . I vow! I'll do hit. Set it right in the rock."

"I meant that," said Carson. "I've heared them things costes a power o' money; account of there bein jist a few that ever learns to make 'em, I reckon. But ye take my sheer, all what ye was aimin' to put by for me. I can make my own way," said the boy.

"Oh, I don't reckon there's any necessity for that. She wouldn't want me to; she thought a heap of you, Carson—more than you've got any idy of. You're the only one she left me, out of seven; and she'd fur ruther I give ye a good chancet, if hit comes to choose, than to have a sightly gravestone. But I know in reason there's a plenty to do both, and if it takes all we got, we can still make a livin' off the land here and down yonder. Let's you and me go—where was hit, anyhow, that we seed that marble figger?"

"Hit was in a store of some kind. There was more stone figgers. I'd know the place again."

The stars throbbed out in the violet sky, and flamed and quivered like big drops of liquid fire ready to fall. From the trees swung out the quiver and lash, quiver and lash, quiver and lash of a whippoorwill's thong-like note, so near that they caught the clucking, gasping after-breath of his passion of song.

"I reckon everybody in these parts 'd call me a fool if they knowed what I paid for hit," said Abel, sitting contentedly amid the confusion of a widower's house, worse confused just now by the litter of the statue's unpacking. He and Carson had just lifted it out of the box, very gently, holding their breath as though the Madonna were a young maid sleeping whom they feared to awaken.

"But there ain't nothing like it in these mountains—never has been I don't reckon," said the boy. "I never seed anything so pretty in my life." He shook his head slowly, "I never seed nothing at all like her."

"No more did I. I don't doubt she's wuth all I paid," said Abel.

He need not; for the sculptor, hearing from Abel's own mouth the story of longing and regret that could not be otherwise assuaged, had given the work of his hands for half what he refused from a wealthy connoisseur some months before. "He parted with hit like as if hit had been one of his children," said Abel wonderingly. "Must be powerful hard to make them things."

In the bare, cobwebbed room the marble shone like a spirit, the whiter by reason of the dingy walls.

Carson caught his breath a little. "Will hit be safe, set out thar in the woods, pap?"

"Safe—why, yes. Who'd steal a tombstone? But you know the way the rockhouse lays, with the grave in the fur opening, we can easy fill up the passage behind, and then hit'll be all sealed up in a room to itself, where nobody can reach to. And hit can be seen as well as ever from the ground below."

It was done as Abel had said. In the threshold of the "rockhouse" they placed a block of stone, carefully squared and fitted to the cloven floor; and on this pedestal—in appearance diminished and made fairylike by the surrounding massiveness, although it is at least half life size—they set the Madonna.

High in the Gap the marble grows grayer every year. Yellow stains and threaded fungi have discolored the carven draperies, and across the feet set so daintily firm a red rust of dripping chalybeate water has spread. Moondawn perhaps restores the Madonna by its magic, arraying her in her pristine whiteness; but even under merciless sunbeams there is yet upon her the deathless seal of the master-touch—and like a living aura, a desire and an ideal befitting the mystery and sweetness of a womanhood half divine.

fifteen

Love o' Man

CAROLINE WOOD MORRISON
AND EMMA BELL MILES

From *Lippincott's Monthly Magazine* 93 (March 1914): 354–61

The only coauthored story in the collection, "Love o' Man" treats a subject area that Emma Bell Miles has not previously explored. Today we might apply to the central event a contemporary term that neither Miles nor her coauthor Caroline Wood Morrison would have known: magical realism. Terms of explanation more common in their time would have been "the sight," "second sight," or even "witchcraft," coupled with superstition or belief in supernatural beings. Terminology notwithstanding, Morrison and Miles introduce a "sylvaine" into a mundane boy-girl relationship. The consequences are immediate and heartbreaking for one of the party. Though the situation is ultimately resolved without tragedy to Isodene and Peter, the young woman's extrasensory perception is squelched and her submission to societal expectations complete.

The slopes of the majestic knob that shut the high-hung valley where Isodene and Peter lived were astir with tiny lives innumerable; the tide of spring washed over everything in deep waves of beauty and life. The very fields seemed unreal in the haze of spring bush-burning; the dead branches tossed like gray foam against a smoke-faded horizon. Here and there a single tree grew dark against the sky as it thickened with countless little leaves, and its shadow, falling, outlined contours of boulder and ravine.

Dimly on the face of the brown fields, a youth appeared with a mule and a plow, advancing, turning, and retreating along the dew-darkened rows.

On the lonely road that meandered between two farms a girl walked slowly, swinging at her side a stout basket woven of white-oak splints. Here, among the fence-row weeds and brambles, fine green films of spring were stealing over all that was stiff or colorless. In the same way the girl's presence, homely though it was, and tiny in space and time, seemed to nullify for a moment the stark and desolate facts of a sordid, lonely existence. For in her homespun garments blossomed some old pagan fancy; her shawl was saffron-dyed, her dress was the mellow old-gold hue of peach-leaves, and her neckerchief, which she had bought at the store, a deep, opulent yellow.

The plowboy halted his mule at her approach. "Howdy, Isodene! Where you goin'?" he greeted her with the heavy courtesy of a good-natured man dulled with toil.

For answer, she showed him the basket that contained her father's midday meal. "There's too much for one, Peter," she commented, looking straight at him with blue eyes that held always behind them a cloud of dreaminess, of other-worldliness. "Have a piece of pie."

"Ef it won't disfurnish your pap," he answered, accepting the proffered refreshment.

She leaned on the top rail and silently watched him eat, sitting on the plow.

"Seems like I can hear a noise under the ground," he remarked, looking curiously at the earth beneath his bare feet.

She also bent downward and appeared to brood or to listen in a sweet melancholy.

"Like water a-runnin', or like somebody talkin' and movin' around," he continued, gesticulating vaguely with the half-eaten section of pie.

"I know what it is," she said, after a pause. "It's the Sylvaines!"

Peter scratched his head under his wide straw hat. "You mean one o' them ha'nts you're always a-seein'?"

"No—no ha'nts nor boogars." Folding both arms on the weather-blackened rail, she fixed her lack-lustre, indwelling eyes upon him. "The Sylvaines are—well, roots: the roots of plants and trees," she told him earnestly. "They have shapes somethin' like people. Ain't you heard tell of mandrakes and potatoes with faces? They move round and creep, soft and slow, in the earth when it's warm with the sun. This time o' year the sap runs in streams—they're all awake and reachin' deep in the ground. They have their own rules and laws; they can see; they can move back and forth; they can talk! I know! I know a heap they say—or that they think, anyhow."

"You know a heap!" he gibed good-humoredly.

"Yes, I do," she assured him. "My mother is Scotch-Irish. She's a seventh daughter of a seventh daughter, just like me. She can visit with fairy folk in the evenin'. I used to wake up and listen at her when I was a little chap. But Father 'lowed it might be resky in some way, and he made her stop. And I used to listen at the Sylvaines with her, but I don't any more now. Brother Lominack said for us not to—that it might be dangerous."

Peter laughed sheepishly and slapped the lines on the back of the drowsing mule, as though to move on.

"Let your plow stand still a minute, and I'll tell you what they're a-sayin' right now, if you don't believe I can," she challenged.

"Let's see you—ef you ain't a-feared," he answered, half daring, half hesitating.

She crossed the fence and flung herself on the newly turned earth, her ear close to the warm, dark loam.

"They must be havin' a meetin'," she murmured in a tone that caught Peter's interest and touched his imagination. "They're all talkin' at once. I can't understand when they mutter away so fast. . . . Oh, I can tell you! It's a new plant they're fixin' to set out right here. A young one—a Sylvaine has to hold it until the flower opens. They're makin' out to tell her somethin' particular—oh, somethin' wonderful! This is the seventh seed of a seventh bloom, and so it's got a blessing on it—"

"Huh!" grunted the listener, incredulous. How could there be a blessing on mere natural objects—on anything outside the church?

"I can hear them now," the interpreter continued, "sayin' that if two mortals, two that love each other, try to pick the flower at the same time, the Sylvaine will come to life and be like us"—she seemed far away—"so long as she can hold to the flower, so long as she can keep it in her hands. It will give her a chanst, they say, to find a soul of her own; but it'll have to be before the flower fades. . . . They're all talkin' again," she lamented plaintively. "I can't catch a word." She rose to her feet and shook the clinging fragments of soil from the dull gold of her gown as she seemed to shake herself free from a spell.

"I don't believe a word of—of that!" Peter cried passionately. "Yes—ef I was your brother Lominack, I'd see to you! I sure would!"

"Ffttt! He don't know nothin' about me—and you won't tell," she replied, but the blue eyes widened uneasily.

"Have you ever said anything about—this here—to anybody but me?" the boy asked.

"No; and I ain't liable to name it to you again, nuther," she retorted.

"I'm tellin' ye for your own good. Where do you expect to go to, holdin' with such?" His voice was harsh. "I wisht you hadn't been born with a veil like they say you was. Ha'nts don't do nobody no good. The Bible names them, and says not to have nothin' to do with 'em. They'll wither your time. But it don't name no Sylvaines, nor them fairies nuther. I don't believe in no such—a-tall!" His voice rose almost to a shout.

Half ashamed and half angry, she turned away to cross the fence and regain the road. Awkwardly, Peter reached a helping hand; yet when she touched him he snatched it suddenly away.

The boy was half afraid of the girl.

She gave no sign, but caught up her basket and walked steadily on. He stood grasping plow and lines, watching until the warm-hued figure was far away in the shortened shadows and quivering air of noon.

It was always this way with Peter. She had forgiven him many a rudeness in the past; but this she resented smoulderingly. For days thereafter, until the spring plowing and planting were finished, she went and came silently on her lonely road between the fields. And though, later, she made friends with him, she would never discuss the sylvan mystery of which she had once spoken so boldly, putting aside his tentative questions.

"It brings bad luck to name them things, just like you said. It made us quarrel that time."

Singularly, he felt no triumph in this admission. "I named Sylvaines to my mother," he said sheeplishly. "She 'lows they're gypsies. I've heared they live in the open and cooks outdoors. Pappy traded horses with 'em oncet."

Isodene maintained obstinate silence.

They were standing on the spot where the end of Peter's furrows brought him near to Isodene's path, and she swung the pail with the daily luncheon for the husband and father of a seventh daughter of a seventh daughter.

"Pappy says," continues Peter, "there's a bunch of 'em camped now down the river a piece. Folks that's been missin' their chickens lays it onto them."

Isodene's lips parted; but before she was ready to speak a stormwind drew across the knob in enormous, shivering sighs. The woods, the blades of sprouting corn, moved, fluttered, and whispered together. Eerie shadows leaped forth as from hidden lairs, and flung their formless duskiness across the fields. Thunder rolled, deep and ominous, in the clouded west. In their flight for shelter, neither Peter nor the more observant Isodene saw that a brilliant scarlet flower had opened at their feet.

Again next day they failed to see it. Isodene had trudged faithfully in draggling weeds to carry her father's dinner. Both countrymen were afield in spite of threatening weather, for the summer was wet, and they utilized every moment of sunshine.

There had been a quilting in the settlement, and Isodene was accusing Peter:

"You walked right through the room without speakin' to me. You never even looked at me."

"I looked," said Peter meaningly, and turned red. "I seed your pink dress. It—it was powerful pretty."

His unaccustomed tone and manner made her eyes droop. She twisted the corner of her apron, dropped it, reached vaguely for its support, and looked about for a new subject of conversation.

"Oh!" she cried, perceiving the blossom and coming closer to it. "How pretty—like something alive!" The flower on its tall, slender stem, wafted by some vagrant breeze—or impulse, was it?—leaned toward her. Peter reached for her hand as it slipped below the scarlet cup. Both, startled, stepped back and half turned away. The dank mist, rolling up from the creek, enveloped them closely. Conscious, embarrassed, they stood perfectly still for its passing.

When the wind lifted the fog, the sun shone clear on a group of *three* where but two had been.

In place of the blooming plant an elfin shape clothed in tints of browns and grays swayed slenderly; dark hair curled over slim shoulders and around a dark-eyed, pointed, wonderful little face; all brown and gray save red, red lips and the scarlet flower clasped tight—a flower whose petals shivered with vitality, of a color rich as blood of youth and bright as flame of desire.

"It's the Sylvaine! It's the Sylvaine! Let's run away quick before we-uns is bewitched."

Peter did not hear. He had forgotten Isodene. He saw only the beautiful, bewildered stranger, who, meeting his admiring eyes, smiled timidly and moved towards him.

The boy held out both hands. His shyness even was overborne by the rush of new emotions, whirled away and lost like a dry leaf in the flame of the hearth as the boy, under the influence of beauty and mystery, became a man.

"Don't be afeard," he said in tones new to Peter's tongue. "Come home with me—to Mammy's house."

The other murmured words in a strange language, looking at him with her great eyes. She seemed not to see the shrinking Isodene. Peter pointed to the smoke rising from his father's house, and she let him take her hand and guide her toward the gray roof.

Isodene, alone and forgotten, ran after them a little way, but they did not glance back and would not heed her appeal. Pride came to her aid. She would not follow, though she could not force herself to go home. The bitterest drop in her cup was that she herself had evoked this apparition!

From afar now, she saw Peter with the exquisite stranger, pointing to various objects, already trying to find some method of communication, to teach the new-comer his rough, earth language.

Doubts as to Peter's safety mingled with Isodene's anger at his desertion. That night she stole by his window, where the red firelight streamed forth, a square shaft, into the thick mist and flying rain. She was spared the sight of Peter's rapt, adoring eyes; the narrow pane showed the stranger only, framed the lovely form and spirituelle face, like some painting. She was dancing. Without music, without other rhythm than the swift, resonant patting of Peter's hands, she was dancing as Isodene and Peter had never seen any one dance before—dancing all over, alive with poetic grace to the tips of her fingers, to the swift, soft pressure of feet no larger than might set firm on a man's heart. Not the loose-jointed swinging, tossing, bounding, of the mountaineers, but a bending, melting, swaying movement that went weaving to and fro on the homely braided rug, her dark eyes flashing, the flower of her mouth parting to disclose heart of pearl.

Isodene, out in the rain that was falling again, shivered and turned away with a sob. The loneliness of unshared gayety struck into her heart. Peter's voice held her:

"I don't want nothin' better than to pet you and wait on you!"

The Sylvaine laughed aloud. Peter dragged forward a chair, and she threw herself down, panting, quivering, a-glow, in a pretty abandon.

"You shall always be waited upon," said the young mountaineer, with unexpected eloquence. "I'll spend my life bein' your slave. And when Pappy and Mammy come back from town there won't be nothin' too much for you to ask. They'll be proud to do hit!"

Isodene pressed closer to the window under the streaming eaves. She must watch lest the Sylvaine do him occult injury. And now she saw him bring fresh milk, newly baked oval pones, services and wild berries drowned in cream.

As she ate, the Sylvaine's eyes blessed his ministry. Always her left hand clung to the flower.

"Oh, but you're fine!" jubilated the boy. "There never was anything like you in this world till to-day. Smile, you pretty child! I never will make you cry. I won't have no aim but to make you happy. It don't make no differ now whether it rains or shines. Ef you smile, I'm jist plumb content!"

That his words were not comprehensible by her appeared not to trouble him. Only once was his mood shadowed. Bringing a vase for the flower, he met with a shaken head and frown of refusal. But he had so completely forgotten Isodene that even her story of the Sylvaines and the magic red bloom was obliterated from his mind. He felt only that he had erred in one effort to please, and tried another, bringing a drinking-cup.

Isodene, outside, in misery, thought that the girl, unaccustomed to light and love, drinking from the cup he held to her lips, letting her hand rest in this big, fine lover's, must feel like a spirit newly received in heaven. Surely one so happy could work no harm to the mortal that loved her.

"I ain't needed, not even to take keer of him," Isodene told her heavy heart.

The two rapt beings in the firelit room heard soft, swift sounds, a pattering as of heavier drops—it was Isodene's feet fleeing from the window, out into the wet fields, the drenched night, the lonely road. Her eyes, aching with unfallen tears, saw at last into the little cabin where her mother held hard-bitten lips to deny the "visions" that came to her wild, Celtic blood in midsummer nights like this.

The next day Isodene, hidden in a fence corner behind a tangle of undergrowth, saw him come, leading his horse, whereon perched a small brown and gray figure holding against its breast a brilliant flower.

Very tenderly and carefully Peter lifted the little Sylvaine off at the field's edge.

The music of bird and insect thrilled all the opal summer air. A gurgle of clear water sang in the dell. Peter bent his head above the stranger's happy, eager face.

"I love you," he murmured, "I love you!" and leaned yet nearer to illustrate his meaning with a caress. The soft dark eyes widened, then suddenly changed to a look of alarm.

There was a sharp cry of jealous pain; Isodene flung herself across the low rail fence and snatched the "red flower of life."

The lips that Peter would have kissed vanished! The slim young form in its dull grays and browns, the little pointed face with the big eyes, disappeared like a wraith of the mist out of which she had come. Where her bright young life and loveliness had delighted the earth, there drifted now but a passing cloud of golden motes that were slowly drawn up in the long afternoon sunshine.

Peter and Isodene faced each other, alone. Dazed and perplexed, they waited each for the other to speak. At first there was a space between them—where the Sylvaine had stood. The breeze blew Isodene's full skirt forward and bridged it.

On Peter's yokel countenance a great wonder erased his first expression of horror and grief.

"I—I t-told you it was bad luck to name the Sylvaines!" panted Isodene, her apron to her eyes.

His mind adjusted itself. He had been in love—beauty had set his thick pulses to fluid ecstasy. That beauty he suddenly suspected of being insubstantial, not natural. But another woman was here in place of her whose lips he had been about to press! Strange! Still, there was the mitigating fact that the other woman was Isodene, whom he would have liked to kiss long ago, had he not been afraid. Since her eyes were hid in her apron, he lost the old timidity. His big arm went naturally around her sob-racked form.

"We-uns has been bewitched, Isodene Deever," he said in tones not free from fright.

By accident his broad sole trod on the flower Isodene had let fall.

The vision had faded—the red, sweet flower was perished—the man's foot was set on its perfumed ruin!

From a fence-row clump of bushes that shook, a face, pale with the sudden fright of Isodene's onslaught—a pointed little face with pathetic eyes—peered forth on the reunited pair. A moment it glimmered there—a moment long enough to stamp and fix upon it the cruelty of love's lesson—and then was withdrawn. A low sob came to their ears; in the drone of June meadows soft, pattering footfalls mingled with the hedgerow voices and whir of filmy wings.

"What was that?" cried Isodene, leaping to Peter's arms in terror. "I heared somethin'—somethin' run!"

"'T ain't nothin'," he assured, his manhood conquering superstition as he felt the weaker woman-girl clinging to his brawny neck.

"We ain't agoin' to be bewitched no more from nothin' from the underworld. As long as we live together, Isodene, don't never say no more the word that done hit!"

As long as we live together! And but an hour ago she had been forgotten! But Isodene saw in a confused way that such is the love of man—and, such as it was, her nature cried out for its possession. Perhaps it was never to be hers in its entirety—perhaps she could never utter the same appeal to his fancy as the vision lost. Perhaps all women would hereafter seem to him large or dull or heavy. But she clung to Peter, murmuring over and over the sweet assurances of her faithfulness and her love.

"Them gypsies is gone," said Pappy Bell, returning with his spouse from an excursion into civilization. "They 'lowed in the valley that one of the youngest gals—she peddled 'pressed flowers' they called 'em—was lost up yere on the mountain and come back nigh about dead. They air queer folk, a-wanderin' an' a-wanderin' to and fro. 'Pears like they jist simply ain't human. An' the jargon these talked! Some of 'em didn't know a word o' real langwidge like we-uns speaks. 'Pears like they ain't scasely human!"

"Don't you listen to no such, Isodene," warned Peter, catching the last words only, and dragging his promised wife out of ear-shot, "I don't want you to have no dealin's with any such truck as Pappy's speakin' of."

Isodene lifted to his, humble, wistful eyes. "I won't, Peter," she promised. "As long as we live together I won't never no more talk erbout nothin' strange or—underground"—she whispered the word—"or that ain't like other folks. We'll jist be content with what we can get our hands on—us women-folk has to anyhow—and not try to know nothin' else. I'll do jist what you tell me, Peter," she said; and he gave her a kiss and the promise:

"I'll make ye a good man, Isodene, an' allus aim to see atter you the best I know how. You're the onliest woman in the world for me!"

And the little red flower lay dying, and the summer drifted a few leaves—not having many to spare in the season's busy heat—above its lonely bed. Its episode had been a fairy tale that is told.

sixteen

The White Marauder

From *The Mother's Magazine* 13 (August 1917): 727–29, 798; illustrated by R. F. Tandler

"The White Marauder" was the last piece of fiction published in Miles's lifetime. When the story appeared in *The Mother's Magazine* in August 1917, Miles was hospitalized in Pine Breeze Sanitarium, slowly dying of tuberculosis. In her personal journal entries for August, she makes no reference to the publication, perhaps not even aware of it. Evident in the story are Miles's discerning ear for the dialect of her mountain characters and a sense of humor even in the midst of chaos created by the white mare's ravaging of Letty Kindred's garden. The major conflict of the story is between the young wife Letty and the owner of the mare, old Captain Charley Bushares. Poverty and hunger surface again, as in "Three Roads and a River," but with much less serious consequences. The relationship between the wife and her husband is a recurring theme.

Waked in the night by a sound of trampling hoofs, Letty Kindred sat up and the creak of the bedcords under her movement aroused 'Bithie, her husband's twelve-year-old sister who slept beside her. They were not in the least afraid, although they were alone in the little cabin and only a wooden latch, rude and flimsy, held the door between them and the world. But when the trampling was followed by a swish as of ripping silk, they were aroused.

"Hit's that ol' rogue of Cap'n Charley's in the corn agin. You git the broom, 'Bithie honey, and I'll take the poker."

Out they dashed into the early April night, and gave chase to a white mare, gaunt and ghostly under the stars. Impudently the creature flung up her heels, and trotted twice around the clearing, snorting defiance; then, being hard pressed, she sailed lightly over the fence and disappeared into the woods.

"Now that's the fou'th night she's broke in sence we planted. And last summer you ricollect she never stopped till she'd eat up mighty nigh the whole patch. Lawsy-massy, I jist wisht you'd look here how I've tore my skyirt!"

"Yes, and I e'en-about ruint my feet, when I took out a'ter her th'oo them briers along the fence," complained 'Bithie.

"My feet's a-bleedin' too; but I don't keer for that," said Letty. "My feet'll git well and mend theirselves, but my dress won't. Nor the corn won't neither, ef she's tore hit up much bad. I aim to light into Cap'n Charley about this, right soon in the morning."

"I like to busted her ol' jaws with a rock, anyways," crowed the younger girl. "Let's go make a light and see what she's et this time."

Too anxious to wait for daybreak, they kindled a sliver of pitch-pine by some coals that were buried in ashes on the hearth, and inspected the damage. The young corn indeed was considerably torn and trampled; a whole row of beans was gone entirely; worst of all, the tender mustard was ruined.

"I wouldn't a-hated nothin' so bad as losin' that there mustard," lamented the wife, who was but a few years older than her companion. "Hit had leaves over a inch long, mighty near big enough to eat. And I'm so hongry for green I declar' I'd go and pull me some brier leaves and weeds ef I wasn't afeard they'd pizen me. Jist a handful o' green and drap o' vinegar would piece out our cornbread and pork into full rations; but we ain't had nary mess, nor any gyarden-sass only 'taters, sence away last fall." She was thoroughly angry as they trudged, shivering in the chill dew, back to the cabin where they warmed their feet on the hearth. "Now, ef Mansell had only fixed that fince afore he went off to work in the valley! He had plenty of time durin' the winter. Or ef he'd a-notified Cap'n Charley to put up his critter!"

"Cap'n Charley's had a plenty of notice from other folks to put her up," said 'Bithie shrewdly. "She's a ol' rogue. He knows good an' well she can jump ary fince in the county."

"Well, I aim to take it out of him and Mansell, too; come down on 'em like a hen on a June-bug, I will. You see ef I cook a bite, now, when Manse comes a-Sunday! Not till that there fince is mended."

"On a Sunday?"

"On a Sunday! The better the day, the better the deed. Ah—ho—hum! I ain't goin' back to bed for this little piece of a night. You can." And 'Bithie did, while the young wife sat beside the hearth alone, considering what she should say to the Captain.

"I hate to raise a fuss with him; Aunt Minar Bushares was good to me when I was sick. And she's a own sister to him, though nobody'd think it. But thar's all our truck spiled!"

By the earliest light she prepared breakfast—corn cakes baked on the coals, coffee and a wee rasher apiece of the salt fat which is the regulation meat of the mountaineer. Then they ate, hurriedly washed the two plates, made haste to redd up the house, and set forth—florescently sunbonnetted though the sun was not yet risen—for Captain Charley Bushares'.

A morning mist hung over the budding woods, shaken with all the sounds of April—frog trills and bird song, and the hum of honey-lovers' wings. But the two girls did not notice these things. They walked with nods and gestures and quaint posturings, making threats against the Captain and his mare as their warlike mood dictated.

The old soldier's habitation was not a hollow tree, though a glance at his beady eyes twinkling from out a thicket of furry gray might have led to that supposition; he lived with camplike simplicity and neatness in a cabin by the Gap road. Almost from his door the mountain side fell away in a magnificent sweep of unbroken forest. Behind the house was the spring, where they found the old fellow filling a bucket.

The ceremonious greeting, with its usual "Toler'bles," and the customary invitation to stay to breakfast, were far off the key Letty intended to strike, but for the life of her she could not see how to omit either. No, they had just been, she said; and no, they couldn't stay long enough to set, even on the puncheon bench by the spring-house. She hesitated in great embarrassment and finally plunged, trembling a little.

"Your mare she went 'n' got into our corn again last night, Cap'n Charley. I do think on my soul you ought to do what's right about it. Hit's—now—hit's jist more'n I aim to put up with, her a-roguin' this way every summer."

The grizzled Captain eyed her a moment, then set down his bucket and dropped into something like a fighting crouch. As if by instinct he made straight for the weak point in her battle front. "Now, here-here, Miz' Kindred, let me remind you, the woods is free in this part o' the State. Has your corn got ary fince around it?"

Letty thought best to evade this point. "You know how last year she come in and eat up the whole patch—"

"Oh, Miz' Kindred; not the whole patch—no-no-no! And for what she did eat I paid you with my 'pologies—now didn't I so?" He began to prance about in a semicircle. "That's what I done, wasn't it, Miz' Kindred?"

Letty was a little disconcerted by the formal "Mrs.," and more than a little anxious to keep the conversation off the condition of the fence. At the same time, she wasn't going to be diverted from her claim.

"You paid us a dollar, Cap'n. But I never come over here a'ter no dollar this morning. Hit ain't right and hit ain't fair, the way you let that mare run over folks' places, and I want you to stop hit and pay for what she's done. I jist wisht you'd come over to my house and look at our gyarden."

"I don't see how I'd stop her without you'ns built a fince. I cain't keep her in the stall all the time." He came to a stand, with the air of being ready to listen. "Now, I ain't a onreasonable man, Miz' Kindred. What do you hold the rights of the matter to be?"

She was not clear on this point either. Oh, if she could have consulted Mansell! But now she had come she must say her say, and coerce this old man and his mare, alone. If only he wouldn't crouch and stare like a wild creature about to spring! She put up one hand to her burning cheek uncertainly.

"Two dollars, tell him," whispered 'Bithie, plucking at her sister-in-law's sleeve. "Let's take hit and go."

"Two—two dollars," stammered Letty.

Captain Charley jumped as though on the release of springs, his stubby forefinger emphasizing every word: "Two dollars! Two dollars! Why, Miz' Kindred, you surprise me. I don't believe there's a truck patch on Sourwood Mountain wuth, as hit stands to-day, two dollars for everything in hit; I don't for a fact."

“You owe me two dollars for that mare’s damagin’,” insisted Letty, but feebly.

The agitated finger came closer. “I do not owe you a cent, madam, not a cent. I’ll give you two dollars ef you air in need of hit; but I won’t be held up for no sech amount—”

He recoiled a step as if from the attack of a “flog” hen defending a brood, and the overset water-bucket rolled down the hill unheeded.

“You won’t neither give me—You won’t do no sich a thing, you great big ole—” she hesitated and used no word at all. “You talk about givin’ me ary cent only my dues—why—” Her little fists were clenched, her eyes flashing; she stamped her foot.

“Oh, well, I’ll take that back—I’ll take hit back ef you say to.” Instinctively he made shooing motions with both hands.

“You better!”

She found that she couldn’t, to save her, think of another word. Nor could he. But neither disputant was standing still. To the sole onlooker it seemed they were dancing round and round each other like a pair of belligerent bantams; and so absorbed was ’Bithie in the spectacle that all her ten fingers stood out in ten different directions.

The old soldier was the first to recover the thread of argument—probably because he and his mare had already figured in several court-rooms.

“Now, here-here, Miz’ Kindred. As I’m a livin’ sinner, madam, I didn’t know nothing about this—didn’t know you’ns had a gyarden even. And I may say I don’t like to be jumped onto onexpected this way, let alone threatened.”

“I ain’t aimin’ to threaten ye,” said Letty more mildly. “But ef I was you I would be keerful how I talked and went on.”

“Ef you, or either your husband,” he began judicially, “had a-come to me in the first place, and told me the mare was breakin’ in; and ef then I had reefused and neglected to keep her up; and ef then your fince was showed to be in fair good order and condition at the time she jumped hit—why then, Miz’ Kindred, you might have reason to fault me with your troubles, and you might recover damages accordin’. That’s the Law. That’s how the Law reads. But you come and jump on a gray-headed ol’ soldier disabled sence the Wah, for somethin’ he knows ab-so-lute-ly nothin’ atallabout—I tell ye, madam, and you’ll find hit so, there ain’t a court in Tennessee that’ll sustain ye.”

"Ef I had a Bloody Sixth record endurin' the war, the less there was said about hit the better I'd be suited," retorted Letty in the heat of the moment. She had not meant to pour such vials of contempt upon her antagonist; for the Bloody Sixth had been a disreputable bushwhacking company, never proved to have taken part in a single genuine engagement, although the Government, after some litigation, had given its surviving pensioners the benefit of the doubt. Locally, the whisper of "Bloody Sixth" was accounted the bitterest of taunts.

"That ain't the p'int; that ain't got nothing to do with hit," argued the Captain unabashed. "I ax you, Miz' Kindred, why didn't you come to me the first time you seen the mare in your field; or else why didn't you ketch her and put her up, as the law requires?"

His calm refusal to be crushed by her heavy ammunition daunted Letty, who was sure his war record ought to be at least as sore a spot as Mansell's fence. She felt her courage flagging, and knew that she was going to cry. "Aw, I ain't got no time to run around; and you know I cain't come within bridle-reach of that mare's heels."

"Then where's Mansell?" he pursued.

"Why, he's a-workin' in the valley."

"Workin' for my brother, too, ain't he? Now look here. My brother's give Mansell a job that's kep' him all winter; and ef you was to count up all that my folks have done for you and him, at one time and another, hit would 'mount to more'n a dozen truck-patches—ain't that so? What do you think Minar Bushares'll say when she hears how you've talked to her pore ol' brother?"

He had missed the psychological moment for this. Letty had retired some paces, but now whirled and flung off her bonnet. "That's every word true," she exclaimed. "Your folks air good folks, Cap'n. I ain't got a better friend on earth than Aunt Minar; and ef you tell her what I've said to you this morning, I want you to be shore and put in what-all you've said to me, too. 'Cause ef you don't, I will. They've done for me time and again, your folks have; but ef ever you've done ary thing for anybody but your own self, Cap'n Charley, I never did hear of hit. And what's more, I don't believe you've got a brother nor yit a sister that would keep stock that bothered the neighbors."

The Captain tossed his head as she got breath, and sneered: "Then I must be the only scoun'l they is in the family." But he felt the need of a more effective reply.

’Bithie, fearing that her side was getting the worst of the encounter, shrilled forth unexpectedly: “I thest aim to maul the ghost out of that ol’ nag anyhow, ef she jumps in to-night.”

He turned on her: “Air you the malicious little whiffet that raised sech a welt on my mare’s jaw? I seen she’d been hurt, when I fed her this morning. Now I let ye know, that’s more’n ye dare do, whatever she eats. You understand that! Jist you lay a hand on her again, that’s all!”

“Then you pay for what she’s eat and tore,” cried Letty. “My mustard—all pulled up and trompled. You never was hongry—you’ve got your pension—”

“I don’t owe you nary—”

“Tell that to Mansell a-Sunday; I bet you don’t shake your finger in *his* face!”

The old fellow looked at the offending member with compunction, really sorry to have forgotten his manners; but he seized the opening for a new line of attack.

“Mansell he comes home of a Sunday? Was he there last Sunday?”

“Yes; he brung some provisions.”

“Well, had the mare broke in afore that date? Did he know—”

“I told him, and so did ’Bithie, but—”

“Then—” the uncontrollable finger emphasized the point—“what’s the reason he didn’t come to me last Sunday?”

Letty, white and trembling, laid one hand over her racing heart as if to cover a wound. Whatever was said or left unsaid, she must not admit Mansell in the wrong!

“Because—because,” she stammered, “Manse is jist like everybody else round here—he thinks there ain’t no use comin’ to you for any rights or fairness between neighbors; and I see now he was edzackly right!”

It was but a Parthian arrow, and the last in her quiver. She turned, and holding ’Bithie’s hand, took the road along which they had come—defeated. The younger girl looked behind at the turn and saw the gray figure still prancing with extended forefinger and still vociferous.

“Letty, Letty, he’s a-callin’us.”

“Oh, I don’t want to talk to you!” Letty sent back wildly, and burst into tears. The two went home slowly, under drooping sunbonnets.

Once inside the quiet cabin, however, Letty seated herself on the edge of the bed and talked over the situation calmly enough. Her wrath against the Captain had well-nigh expended itself; she was half-laughing as she commented.

"Well, I've always mistrusted them fine manners of his'n, and now I'm glad to know what they're wuth."

But her resentment against Mansell's neglect went deeper, ached cruelly. He knew that she had worked hard planting and hoeing that handful of truck. What did he mean, leaving things in this shape? He might at least have kept up the fence; there was plenty of rail timber in the woods. Hadn't he spent half of last month picking the banjo?

'Bithie, casting about for comfort to offer, suggested that they go together to seek a mess of "wild sallat" or "sissles." The hardy rosettes of this humble member of the dandelion family would not replace the lost mustard, but would be a bite of green. An abandoned field near by was chosen as the likeliest hunting ground, and the two girls set forth once more, this time with a half-bushel basket woven of oak splints.

The lines of long-vanished fences yielded few "sissles" to their eager scrutiny, but there were also tender shell-shaped leaves of plantain, bunches of speckle-john and narrow-dock, Indian lettuce, bear-grass, and silvery tips of lamb's-quarter in the old field, among dry sedge and last year's leaves. They patiently culled every least sprout; but the final result scarcely covered the bottom of the basket. The season was so late at this altitude—and far below them spread the kindly valley, visibly and luxuriously green!

On reaching home they washed their precious hoard at the spring, and hung it over the fire in a pot with a tiny cube of pork for seasoning. Neither spoke of dinner, though the sun was past the noon-mark on the floor.

Their hunger grew with the passing of the hours. A catbird sang in the garden over his meal of cutworms; a drift of dogwood petals blew across the porch; a yellow "news-bee" hung round the door and buzzed off into the world again. There was nothing to do but wait, from time to time putting a handful of chips under the pot. As the shadows lengthened they mixed and baked a dodger in the hearth-oven. At sunset they turned the handful of greens into a dish.

"Don't that smell good!" exulted 'Bithie. She took a mouthful and looked up, puzzled. "Why—why, Letty this here sallat—hit's bitter!"

Letty, who was breaking the steaming pone on a plate, made haste to investigate the strange flavor. They looked at each other in consternation. The child had by mistake gathered some leaves of bitter dock!

Letty did not scold her; instead, she comforted when 'Bithie showed a disposition to cry. But she cried herself, after the young girl fell asleep and night had closed on the cabin. Oh, why couldn't Mansell provide better—give them just enough to eat!

Again a sound of trampling, thrashing feet brought her instantly upright, straining forward, hunger adding to her exasperation. She seized a billet of firewood and opened the door.

"I certainly will brain ol' Soapstick this time—Why! Manse! I wisht I may never! Ef you hadn't a-spoke I'd a-knocked your head off."

She took his basket that he might have one arm free to put round her, and they entered the cabin together.

"I was tired enough to have waited till morning," he admitted, throwing the bag of provisions off his shoulder. "But this mornin' we was clearin' around a ol' burnt shack, and I come on a patch o' poke. Everything's forwarder in the valley, and I 'lowed you and 'Bithie hadn't had ary mess o' poke yit. So I brung up a basket afore the leaves had time to wilt." He laughed.

"I started 'bout a hour by sun, and could a-made hit home for supper, but I come by ol' Cap'n Charley's and nothin' would do him but I must go in and eat with him. He given me a big bunch o' them early shallots o' hisn. Said he owed 'em to you'ns. I couldn't make hit out—he talked funny, like he'd been drinkin'—but here they air in the basket. They'll go good with pork and greens. What's the matter? You sick?"

Letty went limp all over as though fainting. "Hit ain't nothin'—nothin' at all, Manse. Only—I'm so glad you brung me somethin'. Our supper was all spiled. And I thought—I thought shore the ol' Cap'n was mad at me and maybe Aunt Minar Bushares would be, too, and then maybe you'd lose your job—and hit would be all my fault." And she told him all about it.

"Oh, well," was Mansell's conclusion, "hit ain't as big as all that comes to; but ef you was to werry yourself sick, now, that would be a whole dime's wuth o' nickels." He laughed again, with huge enjoyment of the Captain's manner. "I reckon he jist didn't want to turn loose two dollars."

Next morning the gray mare, edging round and round the clearing, a glimmering shape in the gold and green of the shadowless April woods, distinguished a new odor among those issuing from the cabin chimney. Mingled with sharp frying fat and richly browning meal was a savory tang of boiling pokeweed. And cocking an ear, she caught a sound of singing. Letty was recalling a ballad of her scarce-past girlhood:

"Oh, green grows the laurel and so does the rue,
So lost was I, Polly, at parting with you."

None of this interested old Soapstick much; but another sound, close at hand disturbed her so that she shook her head till her shaggy ears rattled impatiently against her bur-encrusted foretop. It was a noise of maul and wedge, of hammering and splitting. Mansell Kindred was risking the disapproval of the neighbors and the probable condemnation of the Recording Angel, defending and maintaining the welfare of his house and home by Sunday labor in main strength and awkwardness.

He was mending the fence.

seventeen

Turkey Luck

From *Youth's Companion* 95 (October 13, 1921): 568; illustrated by Sears Gallagher

Miles's last story, "Turkey Luck," was published posthumously, two years after her death. Most likely she had sold the story to *Youth's Companion* several years earlier. Reminiscent of her book *The Spirit of the Mountains,* this tale recounts many of the folkways of mountain people—from simple celebrations of Christmas to superstitions about the first visitor on New Year's Day. Old Dartus and Aunt Lucy, known for their never-empty coffeepot, show themselves to be congenial hosts, eager to hear the news and to share their provisions with those who stop in. While so many of Miles's stories rail against the dominance-versus-submission relationship that exists in most mountain marriages, this one reveals equality and true companionship between the elderly husband and wife. The unexpected ending follows the local colorist heart-of-gold formula that the author sometimes utilizes. Perhaps the warmth and positivism of this final story are Miles's own Christmas gift to the reader.

Old Dartus Rhea and his wife, whom everyone knew as Aunt Lucy, lived on the road that climbs out of Puncheon Camp Creek up to Moccasin Gap and crosses Sourwood Mountain. Their house was a convenient stopping place for the tanbark men and drovers who came up the mountain from the far valley on the way to Watauga. From the road a man could see the roof spread out like an old hen's wings among the apple trees, and the bee gums round it like little chickens; but if he wished for something to represent a rooster he must have strained his fancy to make one of the log barn, or of the great rock, from under which flowed the spring where Aunt Lucy kept her piggins of butter and crocks of cream.

From their back porch the Rheas could see all over three counties, and the view was equally wide from the middle entry, where the loom sat all summer. There also, from the time the peachblows cast a shadow and the coral honeysuckle budded out, Uncle Dartus used to sit, listening to his bees and the running spring branch and telling tales of the war. To look at him you would never have thought that he had been with General Miles in more than a dozen battles. And he never spoke an ill word of anyone.

Uncle Dartus and Aunt Lucy never felt lonesome, although the nearest neighbors lived in the coves and ridges far below. For it was known to the country round about that their coffeepot never went dry or got cold by day; and any stranger who lost his way between the last cabin above the gap and the first in Red Gully Cove was always directed to Uncle Dartus's.

"Come right in and wait for supper time," the old man would say. "Lucy she'll make up some good biscuits; and we'll go in the smokehouse and cut a ham." They always had honey and apples.

One fall it happened that they both felt unusually well and hearty. They had done fairly well for old folks that season, what with their truck patch and trading and a few pigs and sheep that ran over the ridges. A heavy mast of acorns and chestnuts fed the pigs fat, and all three cows brought heifer calves, and the chickens turned out well. Aunt Lucy thought that her luck with the chickens was because she had invited old Ann Goforth to stay with them on New Year's Day and had given her a poke of dried apples and eggs. Old Ann was part Indian and never was good company, but if she had not come early to sit by the fire that New Year's morning the first visitor of the day would have been Preacher Drane—and that according to local superstition would have caused all the settings of eggs to hatch out roosters, and might also have hindered Aunt Lucy in her soap making.

Aunt Lucy's luck held in other ways. She sold a six months' accumulation of spinning truck and received cash for it. She could no longer see to weave the old-fashioned coverlets and counterpanes, although she made all her dresses of linsey-woolsey and "checkerty-plaid" cotton, dyed with copperas, indigo and madder and peach-tree bark and walnut leaves; and her good honest blankets were warm and lasting. They came to the notice of some people from Watauga, who bought all she had made up.

Then Dartus's nephew, Timon Poe, brought his young wife, Cynthia, to visit them in the early summer, and while they stayed he and Dartus lined bees. They found three or four rich honey trees and added the wild colonies to the home stand. So what with one thing and another the old man and woman had reason to feel contented and comfortable.

When the frost came, ripening the muscadines and nuts and making persimmons sugary, they sat by the fire talking things over; but they did not let each other know that they were in high spirits, for they believed that it is bad luck to boast of good health and bad manners to boast of good living. Dartus, however, rubbed his hands together and said: "I'll be limb-juggled, Lucy honey, ef I ain't in-about minded to git us a turkey this Christmas."

Perhaps the turkey would have been more appropriate for Thanksgiving, but, although they had heard of such a holiday, they were not sure of its date and would not have known how to keep it.

Dartus talked on of the time when he was a little boy and his people sat by the fire Christmas Eve with whatever company had gathered and sang songs until after midnight. He had honestly believed, he said, that the elder bushes bloomed out in the snow at twelve o'clock and that the cattle all went down on their knees round the manger.

"I don't know but what they do too," he declared. "Because I've waked up on a bitter cold Christmas Eve and heard 'em a-lowing and a-mooing; and I've seed the elder buds all busted out and frostbit the next day. Oh, yes, a body always ought to try to keep Christmas!"

Then Aunt Lucy told how her father's family generally killed a deer and baked a great apple cake nearly two feet high, or else roasted a shote with sweet potatoes.

"Now, you and me, Dartus, we couldn't make out to eat a whole shote, without some of my folks was to come from Meigs County to help us," she said; "but I aim to bake us a little small cake."

“And maybe I can polish up Old Sister,” said Dartus, as he looked up at the long muzzle-loader that with its shot pouch and powder-horn had hung over the fireboard since they were married, “and I’ll kill us a wild turkey or a pheasant, or anyhow a mess of quail.”

The reason that they had fallen out of the habit of keeping Christmas was that they were both good church members and did not approve of the misrule that some people in the mountains set up from the new Christmas Day to the old, which falls twelve days later. They might have joined in the usual round of visiting, but it happened that all their near relations were away at one distance or another. Roistering with gunpowder and moonshine whiskey and cards was not what they wanted. But as the winter deepened over Moccasin Gap they felt more and more like celebrating in some way.

All the week before Christmas was dry, clear weather, crispy cold. Old Dartus was out with his rifle every day on the mountain side and in the breaks of Puncheon Camp Creek. But he was not, at his time of life, as quick with “Old Sister” as a frightened turkey hen can be with her legs and wings; and all he brought in was one opossum, tolerably fat, that had lived on stolen corn and chickens. He put the creature, grinning and snapping, into a coop; and the next day he hitched his mule to the spring wagon and set out for Watauga.

It was the Saturday before Christmas—the country people’s day for going to town. Every wagon that came down the gap rang loud and far on the frosty air, for the road was hard as iron. Aunt Lucy heard them and stood by the fence with a homespun square pinned over her head, saying, “We’re jist toler’ble. How’s your folks?” to everyone that passed. She was kin to nearly everyone in the far valley, and some stopped and talked a long time with her.

When Eph Latiner came by she was glad to have him stay and tell her all the news from Blue Springs and Carson’s Cove. His wagon was piled with holly and mistletoe and club moss and cat brier that he was carrying down to sell along the streets; but underneath the green he had a coopful of fat young turkeys that he was taking to market.

The way Uncle Dartus had spoken made Aunt Lucy believe that he was more than half joking about having turkey for Christmas dinner, and she thought that it would be an excellent idea to surprise him; so she bought a fat turkey from Eph with her own blanket money.

But when Dartus drove into the lot that evening, with provision of salt and water-ground meal and lamp oil and coffee and a little sugar, which was about all that they ever bought, he, too, had a turkey.

"Well, Lucy, we cert'n'y surprised one 'nother," he said. "It was more'n we really ought to 'a' spent, but never mind I believe the one Eph raised is a leetle the biggest. Fat, ain't they?"

Dartus locked the two birds in the henhouse together, and gave them all the corn that they could eat the next morning.

On Christmas Eve the weather turned colder, and a sharp wind blew down the valley. Everyone that passed was glad to stop and get warm by Dartus's fire and drink a cup of Aunt Lucy's coffee. Coldest of all travelers on the road was poor Timon, Dartus's nephew, tramping homeward with a sack of meager supplies on his shoulder.

"What you-uns goin' to do for Christmas, Timon?" inquired Aunt Lucy.

"Mighty little, Aunt Lucy," he answered, spreading his hands to the blaze. "Cynthy's poorly, and the baby, it favors a little picked bird. I ain't got to work at nothing all fall for havin' to take keer of them. I reckon me and her'll jist set and look at one 'nother for our Christmas."

She noticed then how thin his clothes were and how out of heart he looked; and she went into the kitchen and made haste to pack a bucket of honey to send to Cynthia. By the time it was ready she thought of something else and looked about for Dartus, to consult with him. But Dartus was not to be found at the moment, and Timon was in a hurry; so she ran out to the henhouse and, groping in the dusk, found a turkey. Tying its legs handily with a soft rag strip, she presented it to Timon.

She felt reluctant to tell her husband of what she had done on impulse—"me a-givin' away all that good turkey meat, and it so high! He'll be apt to read me the parables about it." She put off telling him until the last minute on Christmas morning; when he came in with a blank expression from a trip to the henhouse, she knew that she must make her confession.

When she had finished, Dartus said sheepishly, "I toted one of them birds across the holler yestidy evening to pore old Ann Goforth."

"You did!"

They looked at each other across the scalding water and carving knife that she had got ready.

"Well, thar goes our Christmas dinner," he said ruefully. But he crossed the kitchen and kissed Aunt Lucy's withered check. "Old honey girl, I wouldn't 'a' thought of you doin' that; I didn't 'low you thought that much of my kinfolks."

"So it's you and me, instid of Timon and Cynthy, that will have to set and look at one 'nother Christmas Day," she answered; but she said it happily.

“Well, ’y jings, Lucy, it wouldn’t be so bad ef we was to,” he reflected, noticing her mounting color and her smile. “But there’s the possum. I’ll go out and skin him whilst you fix a potful of sweet taters, and I reckon we won’t go exactly hungry.”

suggestions for further reading and research

Abrahams, Roger D. Foreword to *The Spirit of the Mountains,* by Emma Bell Miles, v–xii. Facsimile edition. Knoxville: University of Tennessee Press, 1975.

Brooks, Shannon. "Coming Home: Finding My Appalachian Mothers through Emma Bell Miles." *NSWA Journal* 11, no. 3 (1999): 157–71.

Brosi, George. "The Heart-Wrenching Life of Emma Bell Miles." *Appalachian Heritage* 33, no. 4 (2005): 11–21.

Brosi, George, ed., and Grace Toney Edwards, guest ed. *Appalachian Heritage* 33, no. 4 (2005).

Cox, Steven. Introduction to *Once I Too Had Wings: The Journals of Emma Bell Miles, 1908–1918,* edited by Steven Cox, xxv–xlvii. Athens: Ohio University Press, 2014.

———, ed. *Once I Too Had Wings: The Journals of Emma Bell Miles, 1908–1918.* Athens: Ohio University Press, 2014.

Edwards, Grace Toney. "Emma Bell Miles: Appalachian Author, Artist, and Interpreter of Folk Culture." PhD diss., University of Virginia, 1981.

———. "Emma Bell Miles: Appalachian Poet." *Now and Then* 2, nos. 1–2 (1985): 18–21.

———. "Emma Bell Miles: Feminist Crusader in Appalachia." In *Appalachia Inside Out,* vol. 2, *Culture and Custom,* edited by Robert J. Higgs, Ambrose N. Manning, and Jim Wayne Miller, 709–13. Knoxville: University of Tennessee Press, 1995.

———. "Emma Bell Miles: Pioneer Folklorist of Appalachia." In *The Many Faces of Appalachia,* edited by Sam Gray, 23–28. Boone, NC: Appalachian Consortium Press, 1985.

———. "Emma Bell Miles: The Spirit of a Crusader." *Appalachian Heritage* 15, no. 3 (1987): 5–9.

———. "One Hundred Years of Spirit from Emma Bell Miles." *Appalachian Heritage* 33, no. 4 (2005): 54–57.

Engelhardt, Elizabeth S. D. "Carving Spirit into Rock." Foreword to *Once I Too Had Wings: The Journals of Emma Bell Miles, 1908–1918*, edited by Steven Cox, xi–xvi. Athens: Ohio University Press, 2014.

———. *The Tangled Roots of Feminism, Environmentalism, and Appalachian Literature*. Athens: Ohio University Press, 2003.

Gaston, Kay Baker. *Emma Bell Miles.* Signal Mountain, TN: Walden's Ridge Historical Association, 1985.

———. "Emma Bell Miles and the Fountain Square Conversations." *Tennessee Historical Quarterly* 37 (Winter 1978): 416–29.

———. The Kay Baker Gaston Collection of Emma Bell Miles Materials. Special Collections, University of Tennessee at Chattanooga.

Miles, Emma Bell. *Chords from a Dulcimore.* Chattanooga: Self-published, 1912. Available in Jean Miles Catino Collection, Special Collections, University of Tennessee at Chattanooga.

———. "Fountain Square Conversations." *Chattanooga News*, April–July 1914. Available in Jean Miles Catino Collection, Special Collections, University of Tennessee at Chattanooga.

———. Journals. 1908–18. MS. Available in Jean Miles Catino Collection, Special Collections, University of Tennessee at Chattanooga.

———. Letters. 1907–17. MS. Chattanooga Public Library, Chattanooga, TN. Copies of the letters are also available in Special Collections, University of Tennessee at Chattanooga.

———. *Our Southern Birds.* Chattanooga: National Book Company, 1919. Reprint, Morristown, TN: Globe Book, 1922; and Signal Mountain, TN: Walden's Ridge Historical Association, 1983.

———. "Some Real American Music." *Harper's Monthly Magazine* 109, no. 649 (1904): 118–23.

———. *Strains from a Dulcimore.* Edited by Abby Crawford Milton. Atlanta: Ernest Hartsock, The Bozart Press, 1930. Reprint, Signal Mountain, TN: Mountain Press, 2001.

———. *The Spirit of the Mountains*. New York: James Pott & Company, 1905. Reprint, Knoxville: University of Tennessee Press, 1975.

Miller, Danny, Sandra Ballard, Roberta Herrin, Stephen D. Mooney, Susan Underwood, and Jack Wright. "Appalachian Literature." In *A Handbook to Appalachia: An Introduction to the Region,* edited by Grace Toney Edwards, JoAnn Aust Asbury, and Ricky L. Cox, 199–216. Knoxville: University of Tennessee Press, 2006.

Prajznerová, Kateřina. "Bioregional Biography: The Landscapes of the Lives of Emily Carr and Emma Bell Miles." In *Alternatives in Biography: Writing Lives in Diverse English-Language Contexts*, by Stephen Hardy, Martina Horáková, Michael Matthew Kaylor, and Kateřina Prajznerová, 231–300. Brno, Czech Republic: Masaryk University Press, 2011.

———. "Emma Bell Milesova." In *Literární biografie jako křižovatka žánrů,* by Michael Matthew Kaylor, Stephen Paul Hardy, Martina Horáková, and Kateřina Prajznerová, 169–76. Brno, Czech Republic: Masaryk University Press, 2011.

———. "Emma Bell Miles's Appalachia and Emily Carr's Cascadia: A Comparative Study in Literary Ecology." *49th Parallel* 20 (Winter 2006–7): 1–16.

Whisnant, David E. Introduction to *The Spirit of the Mountains,* by Emma Bell Miles, xv–xxxv. Knoxville: University of Tennessee Press, 1975.

www.ingramcontent.com/pod-product-compliance
Lightning Source LLC
Chambersburg PA
CBHW070009120726
47909CB00003B/851